Shadow's Kiss

T. M. Hart

Shadow Series : Book 1

"Beware that, when fighting monsters, you yourself do not become a monster . . . for when you gaze long into the abyss, the abyss gazes also into you."

~Friedrich Nietzsche, Beyond Good and Evil

PROLOGUE

I RAN. I STUMBLED.

It was the blackest time of night, and the rain was relentless. My clothes had been stripped of me. Thunder reverberated through the sky, and lightning cracked. Tresses of long dark hair lashed around my face.

I was not supposed to be alive, but somehow, I was. My mind was lost to me. The only certainty I knew was pain and fear. There was no earth and no sky, only a storm within a black void.

Suppressed sobs shook my body. I wanted to die, to simply give up. But I did not. And in that moment, at the darkest hour of my existence, when there was no possibility for me to ever be whole again, I was saved.

I collided into a tree. I would have fallen backwards from the impact, but the branches of the tree wrapped around my waist and kept me upright. I could not understand how it was possible, but I was too exhausted to care.

I tried to fight the void of nothing that lapped at my consciousness. I was too weak. I gathered the last of my strength and wailed at my failure. A bolt of lightning lit the sky. The last thing I heard was my name, and then for quite some time…there was nothing.

CHAPTER 1

THE RAIN WAS FIRST. I could hear it falling. Somewhere in the distance was the underscore of rumbling thunder.

I opened my eyes to dancing flames. It took a moment for my initial confusion to subside before I realized I was lying in front of a fire.

I was covered by a quilt on a small couch. The scents of honey, lemon and pine hung in the air of the wood cabin. It was dark aside from the burning fire in the stone hearth which cast deep shadows across the room. Two large bare windows ensconced the fireplace, and rain ran in rivulets down the thick panes of glass.

I could feel a warm peace in the cabin. It was a shelter from the storm outside. I felt comforted in those first moments of consciousness. But that feeling of comfort and peace, like all precious moments, was fleeting.

I looked around the cabin and realized I had never seen it before. I tried to remember how I had come to be on that couch in that cabin, but I couldn't. I tried to retrieve the last memory that I had, but nothing existed before that moment.

And then my body caught up with my consciousness. An icy pain tore through my abdomen, and I doubled over on my side wrapping my arms around my waist. I tried to suck in a breath, but each inhalation was agony. My shallow breathing caused me to cough onto the back of my hand. Despite the debilitating pain in my midsection, I froze, all my attention suddenly diverted to my hand. What looked like black sludge was splattered there.

I stopped breathing and strained to listen when I heard a man's voice. His words grew louder as he came closer. The person speaking was clearly infuriated, but he was keeping his words low. I got the impression that this was a private conversation, and I was not meant to overhear it.

"…tainted and ruined, she's got another thing coming to her. You tell her that I know of the *tanjear*, and I am coming for her. She is not untouchable. I know her pressure point and I am about to squeeze until she begs for mercy. And you can also tell her that I have *none*."

After a brief pause, his voice sounded again, closer and louder from somewhere in the shadows.

"You're awake." It was not an observation but an accusation.

I tried to sit up. Yet all I could do was moan in pain.

The man picked me up into a sitting position on the couch and wrapped his large hand around my throat, squeezing.

I looked up at him in shock. I was utterly confused. A rush of fear pumped through my veins temporarily paralyzing me.

11

He was towering over me. At least six and a half feet tall, his massive shoulders and chest were straining the fabric of the flannel button down he wore. The firelight cast flickering shadows over his face, but I could clearly see an aggressive snarl across his lips. He seethed menace and aggression. His tousled blond hair and the stubble across his jaw amplified the wild ruggedness of his look.

"Why are you here?" he growled.

My heart hammered beneath my ribs. I didn't know. I didn't know why I was in the cabin. I didn't know why I was in so much pain. I didn't know this man. And I had no memory of...*anything*.

I couldn't respond to him for lack of breath. My lips moved soundlessly. The man eased the pressure on my windpipe just enough that I could take a shallow breath.

"Don't...know," I wheezed. "Please...let go." My vision swam. I was about to pass out. My head lolled to the side and my eyelids drooped.

The man slapped me across the face. "You will not faint. You will answer me." He was snarling so viciously; his words were almost unintelligible.

Tears stung my eyes and I cried out.

He shook me by the neck. "Do not think for a moment that I will have pity on you. Did you really think this would work? That I wouldn't be able to sense what you are? You're vile abhorrent filth. You can't hide that. That bitch is having a good laugh about this, isn't she?"

The look of revulsion that accompanied his words left no doubt in my mind how disgusted he was by me.

"What? Did you think you would take me out in my own home?" He was roaring now, his features tight with rage.

"I'm sorry," I whimpered. "I'm so sorry. I'll leave. Please. Just let me go and I'll leave."

"There's no leaving for you. You end here and now. I'm sending you back to her in tiny little pieces." His eyes began to glow in the dark room. A brilliant gold seeped through his brown irises in a jagged ring.

I knew that he was about to harm me. Some instinctual response caused me to put my hand over his own where it held my neck. Before he was able to swipe it away, a warmth spread under my palm. The man's eyes widened in surprise and he jerked back from me. Cradling his hand, almost as if burned, he stumbled backwards into the flickering shadows.

It was as though the scene we were acting out suddenly paused. Neither of us moved or spoke, both trying to understand what was happening. The man remained absolutely still in the shadows as I froze in the firelight. The sounds of the storm outside, the crackling fire, and my ragged breaths were the only noise filling the silence.

I could sense the man was confused. Whatever had just happened between us, he had not been expecting.

I looked down at my hand in surprise. The warmth in my palm had seemed to provide a reprieve from the icy pain in my abdomen.

Without a word the man slipped away into the darkness of the cabin, and I was left alone on the couch in front of the fire.

I sat there with my thoughts churning in a foggy, uncertain haze. It was foolish not to try and find an immediate escape, but everything was happening so fast. I didn't know what to think, let alone what action to take. So, I sat there.

In addition to my inability to act, there was another factor that caused me to stay where I was. In some indescribable way, I could *sense* that the man no longer had an intention to hurt me—at least not at the moment.

It didn't matter anyway. He emerged from the shadows once again, stalking towards me.

The robe I was wearing had come loose and was gaping dangerously wide at the chest. I clutched the lapels together, trying to cover up.

"Drink this." He held out a mug, but I didn't react.

"Take it!" he shouted at me.

I held out my hand. It shook uncontrollably.

"Fuck!" As he let out the irritated curse, he ran his free hand through his hair in frustration. The movement made the large muscles in his arm and chest contract and strain against the fabric of his shirt. I couldn't help but think of the raw strength he possessed and how easily he could have snapped my neck.

"So now I have to hand feed you?" The disgust in his voice was cutting.

I remained silent, not knowing what to say or do.

He advanced until he was looming over me once again. I shrank as far into the couch back as I could, clutching the robe to my neck.

The man thrust the mug into my face without a word. He didn't have to tell me how disgusted he was to be serving me. The loathing and irritation were seeping from his every pore.

I hesitated for just a moment, and that was all it took to set him off.

"Drink!" he roared, cracking the handle of the mug.

Startled into action, I leaned forward and touched my lips to the mug while cupping it between both shaking hands. The drink was warm, not hot, so I gulped down as much as I could. However, given how coerced I was in that moment I don't think a scalding temperature would have stopped me.

My response placated him enough so that when I finished drinking, he pulled the mug back.

"Please just let me leave."

"That's not going to happen."

Since he didn't bellow at me or try to strangle me again, I pressed on. "What am I doing here?"

He gave me an assessing look before asking, "What's your name?" The way he asked the question made it seem like a test.

"I..." I looked around the room as if I could find the answer somewhere. But the flickering firelight did nothing but cloak the small space in uncertain shadows.

I was shell shocked. I had no idea how to answer his question. I looked up at him with a desolate mien.

"I don't know."

"Well you better figure it out, princess," he spat.

He held my eye for a moment. His were brown with bright gold flecks, and they were somber and serious. There was something else in his eyes. I didn't know what it was.

That inexplicable something drew me to him in two very different ways, neither of which I could understand. Part of me wanted to reach out and brush my fingers over his lips like a

15

lover's kiss. The rest of me wanted to ram my fist into his chest, rip out his heart and feel his warm blood gush down my arm.

Then without a word, he simply walked away into the darkness of the cabin.

CHAPTER 2

WHEN I WOKE FOR THE SECOND TIME, I at least had an idea of where I was. I could remember the cabin and the man and our earlier exchange. I was on the same couch in front of the fire where I had become groggy and passed out. I realized there had been something in the tea the man had given me to make me sleep.

Unfortunately, I still had no memories of what I had done before I came to the cabin or of who I was. It was dark outside the windows, and rain continued to pour down. I didn't know if I had been sleeping for a couple hours or an entire day.

It was difficult to sit up, but after struggling, I managed to right myself. I looked around for a way out. The fire in the hearth was the only source of light, and the surrounding cabin space was hidden in darkness and shadows.

I braced myself against the arm of the couch and tried to stand up, but I overestimated my strength. My legs were weak and didn't hold my weight. I collapsed into a side table bashing my head and knocking over a vase. The glass shattered to the floor and flowers and water pooled around me as I slumped in a helpless heap.

"What the hell do you think you're doing?"

When I glared at the man, something warm trickled into my eye. I reached up and touched my forehead. My fingers came away with blood on them and I realized I had cut myself in the fall.

"Get back on the couch," the man barked at me.

"I need to use the restroom."

I made an effort to put as much authority behind my words as possible. I didn't want to play into the submissive victim role he was trying to force on me.

I tried to stand up, but my legs gave out. Before I knew what had happened a boulder was digging into my stomach. The man had slung me over his shoulder and he was striding away from the small living room, taking me deeper into the shadows of the dark cabin.

A rush of fear spiked through my chest. I couldn't let him take me to another part of the house. At least in the small sitting room I had a chance of finding a way out. If he took me to a basement or a room without windows, I would have much less hope of escape. I knew I had to try and fight him.

I slammed my fists into his back, hoarsely screaming at him to put me down and trying to kick my legs into his torso. It didn't seem to bother him. Finally, I bit the back of his arm right before my butt hammered down onto a porcelain toilet lid.

He squatted in front of me and shoved his finger in my face. "That hurt."

"Good."

He grabbed my wrists in a bruising grip. "Do not make me angry."

"Don't make you angry? Don't make you angry?" I screeched. "I can't walk. I don't know who I am or what I'm doing here or what has happened to me. You have physically attacked me and have threatened my life when I am not trying to harm you in the slightest. And you don't want me to make you angry?" I yanked my wrists back and he let them go.

The sound of my heavy breathing filled the room. There was a single large pillar candle flickering on the sink counter. In the darkness of the tiny bathroom, the flecks of gold in the man's eyes seemed to glow. He let out a heavy breath and stood up. After running the faucet for a moment, he shoved a damp washcloth into my hand.

"Here."

I didn't know where I had been cut on my forehead and I wasn't facing a mirror. I reached up with my free hand and began to feel around for the gash.

"You're making a mess," he said as he smacked my hand away and grabbed the washcloth from me.

He was squatting in front of me again and began dabbing at my forehead. Because he was so rough, my head kept jerking back. He slid his free hand to the back of my neck in an attempt to hold my head still. Warmth bloomed across my skin where he touched me. The heat from his palm sent a shudder of pleasure rippling through me.

He slowed his ministrations and eased the pressure transitioning from aggressive blots to soft strokes.

I chanced a glance at him and those gold flecks in his hazel eyes were burning even brighter.

I closed my eyes. I told myself it was so I didn't have to look at the man, but in truth, it was to savor the relaxed sensation I was feeling. For some reason the man's touch was soothing. While he had given me every reason to fear him, he was incredibly gentle with his touch.

When I opened my eyes, he was mere inches in front of me. He smoothed a bandage over the gash on my forehead, but he didn't pull away. Instead he continued to gently rub his thumb back and forth in a lazy manner over the bandage.

Heat began to spread in my chest, replacing the icy cold that had been present since I initially awoke. A tingle ran down my spine when I realized it was because of him. For some reason, there was something between us. Some essential connection.

I could feel it as if an invisible string connected our two chests. I would have thought I was being delusional if it hadn't been so clear. So undeniable. I had the overwhelming urge to get closer to him. I craved more contact. What was even more incredible was because of the strange connection we had, I could *sense* that he felt it too.

His gaze was focused on the spot where his fingers caressed me. He seemed to be transfixed by the simple touch. With his features relaxed, I realized that he was…*handsome.*

He was overtly masculine and appeared to be in his early to mid-thirties. The blond stubble, his angular jaw, full lips, and deep-set eyes made him ruggedly attractive. And the jagged glowing golden ring through his brown irises was mesmerizing. His blond hair was perfectly tousled from running his hand through it, and it was pushed off his face to reveal every inch of his enticing features.

The glow of the candle light accentuated the smooth tanned skin visible at his open collar. His casual flannel button down and well worn, low slung jeans did nothing to hide his big body. The lines of the clothes simply highlighted his broad shoulders, muscled chest, sinewy arms and strong legs.

I hitched in a breath at the absurdity of fawning over his looks. He had viciously strangled me. He had threatened me and *hit* me. I called to mind how he had looked aggressively snarling at me and it broke the spell of the moment.

Before I knew what was happening, he picked me up with one arm, lifted the toilet lid with the other, and dropped me back down. "I'll be back in in a minute," was all he said before he walked out and shut the door.

It was embarrassing that he had to help me like that, but I didn't waste any time and took advantage of where he had placed me. It was easy enough to do since a robe was all I wore. However, that fact was unsettling. Why wasn't I wearing any clothes or undergarments?

After flushing the toilet, I struggled to hold myself up against the sink counter while I put down the toilet lid and then let my butt fall back onto it. It was a small victory and it may have been prudish of me, but I felt more dignified sitting on the closed lid.

I had seen movement in my peripheral vision when leaning against the counter, and I realized that there was a mirror running along the wall behind me. I leaned over towards the counter again and twisted around.

In the mirror was a woman I had never seen before. She appeared to be in her mid-twenties. Whereas the man was utterly masculine, she was utterly feminine. She had long dark hair, fair porcelain skin, plump pink lips, and large blue violet eyes. Her irises were lined with a conspicuous, unearthly violet ring that also seemed to glow in the candlelight. She was stunning, and not just in her beauty. There was something graceful and ethereal about her.

I reached my hand up to touch my cheek and the woman in the mirror mimicked me. Her hand was slender and elegant. There was a ring with an oversized gemstone on her left ring finger. I looked at my hand and the ring glittered and sparkled in the candlelight.

The ring was remarkable. What was most striking was its color. The stone was an intense black and yet it had an almost luminescent quality to it. It was in an antique looking square setting with glittering diamonds surrounding it.

I looked back at the woman in the mirror. I reached my hand up to touch my face and so did the woman in the mirror. When her fingertips brushed her cheek, black lines began to branch through her irises. They continued to web through until her irises were flooded with black. It was a horrific sight to behold.

Pain tore through me, and I doubled over clutching my stomach. I tried to scream, but ice constricted my lungs and suffocated me. The pain pulsed through my body threatening to render me unconscious. At that moment, the door burst open.

The man grabbed my chin and yanked my head up, searching my eyes. "I fucking knew it!"

He pulled my back into his chest, wrapping one muscled arm around my neck, and grabbed my shoulder with his free hand. He began hauling me out of the bathroom, and I stumbled along with him trying to hold my weight up but mostly being dragged by the man.

Before I knew it, we were outside. The rain was pounding all around us in a torrent. Thunder rumbled just above, and lightning arced in the black sky. A bitter wind brought gusts of cold air that pierced the flimsy material of my robe and stabbed at my skin like needles. I was soaking wet and freezing almost instantly.

The man shoved me down to the sodden earth by a large tree stump with logs piled next to it where I sprawled on my butt. He grasped an axe wedged into the stump and tore it free.

"How?" he yelled over the noise of the storm. "How could you falsify the bond?"

I pushed the soaking hair out of my face. "Please, I don't know what you're talking about!"

"I have been waiting my whole life for what is owed to me! And you think to toy with me?!"

I had no idea what he was rambling about. But I did know that he intended to kill me and there would be no stopping him this time. The decision he had come to was final.

And yet, I tried in vain to have my life spared. "Please don't do this. Please just let me go. I don't understand what's happening. I will leave here, and you will never see me again. Please."

"I have no mercy for you." He hefted the axe and I knew he would strike.

"Stop!" The woman's clear commanding voice rang through the night and even overpowered the clamor of the rain and thunder. She had appeared behind the man. In the darkness, she radiated a pure white light. She was a beacon in the midst of the storm.

Wearing a white ceremonial robe, her long blond hair was loose about her perfect face. But her absolute beauty was overshadowed by the wings of light outstretched behind her.

"You have no authority to harm her while she is still of this world. You assume too much, Elijah. If you forfeit her life, you do so with your own as well. The Council has ordered I take your head for the crime you are about to commit."

Elijah didn't tear his hate filled gaze from me when he responded. "She is a *nightwalker*. The House of Shadows has sent her here. She is not as she appears. She is a threat to us. Somehow, she was able to manifest the Vinculum. If she is able to do that, there is no telling the extent of deceit and machinations she is capable of. And if you try and stop me, Daphne, so help me I will be the only one left standing here tonight."

"Look again. It is *her*, Elijah. This is no fabrication of the Dark Court. The Vinculum was pure. The ripples from the energy connection were felt by The Council. There is hope for her still." In what seemed to be an afterthought, she added, "And for you."

Confusion contorted the man's—*Elijah's*—face as he stared at me. He wasn't the only one having a hard time understanding what was going on. I wanted to scream at both of them to shut up. I couldn't understand their convoluted conversation, and I did not want to be the focus of it.

It was all too much. How was I supposed to react, to keep my sanity through all this? I had no memories prior to awaking in Elijah's cabin. He tried to kill me then shared some weird connected moment with me before trying to kill me once again. And now what I could only imagine was an angel had arrived to demand Elijah spare my life because of something called the *Vinculum*.

I wasn't well. My mind, body, and soul had been ravaged. I couldn't say how or why, but there were things wrong with me. Sprawled in the soggy earth, with unrelenting rain pounding down and having just escaped the swing of an axe, I reached my breaking point. I fell back onto the sodden ground as a blessed blackness swept through my consciousness and I escaped the current inane reality that was apparently my life.

CHAPTER 3

ELIJAH JERKED ME INTO HIS ARMS and carried me inside the cabin. Though I was aware of what was happening, I was in some kind of groggy emotional torpor, no longer caring what he was going to do to me. The robe I wore was drenched and plastered to my body, as was my hair. I was cold to my bones. I shivered uncontrollably and my teeth wouldn't stop chattering.

He took me up a flight of stairs and deep into a part of the dark cabin where the steps from his bare feet echoed ever so slightly, and then firelight flared to life. When he set me down on my feet he kept his muscled arm around my waist, preventing me from collapsing onto the floor. Then he seemed to twist his body away from me.

I heard the spray of water and after a moment steam began to waft around us. I realized in some hazy part of my mind that we were in a shower. With my back against his chest, he began to undo the belt of my robe.

I feebly slapped at his hands without any true vehemence.

"You're covered in mud." His tone made it seem like it was *my* fault that I was filthy. "I can help you or I can leave you here and you can sleep in the shower tonight, wet and dirty."

I was so exhausted and emotionally drained that I just didn't have the strength to give a damn. I let my hands fall back down to my sides. At this point, he could do whatever he wanted. What did it really matter. He was a nasty bastard and I couldn't care less what he thought of me or my body.

There also was no chance of being forced into any physical intimacy with him. He had displayed such revulsion towards me that I had no fear of that.

He undid the belt of the soaked robe with a few flicks of his wrist. His hand traveled up to my shoulder, and his fingers brushed my collarbone as he inched them inside the neckline. If I hadn't been in such a state of delirium, I would have been surprised at how gentle he was with his touch.

He began to push the wet material down my arms. Goose bumps broke out over my skin at the slow descent of his hands. As he pushed the robe down, it peeled away from where it had been molded to my breasts. And then he slid the robe completely from my arms, pulling it out from between us and tossing it into the corner of the shower.

The spray of water began to patter across my chest as Elijah turned and positioned me under the shower head. I noticed a hard length brush against my lower back as he moved behind me and I was suddenly yanked back into reality.

He's aroused. The realization shattered the daze I was in. Although he still wore his drenched clothes, I could feel his erection beneath his jeans.

As my head began to clear, I also realized that I could actually feel his desire emanating from him like a blast of heat. His breathing was heavy too. The massive chest that my back was pressed against was billowing with hectic breaths.

That damned connection that I had felt with him earlier was burgeoning uncontrollably.

The absolute worst part of it all was that my body was responding. There was no stopping the answering rush of excitement. My breaths grew shallow causing my naked wet breasts to heave. I began to ache at my core and I couldn't stop from rubbing my thighs together.

Becoming aware of my body's response to Elijah made me look down and realize that I had no memory of my figure. I was seeing myself unclothed for the first time since waking at Elijah's cabin.

I had long shapely legs, a trim flare of hips that tapered into a flat tiny waist, a delicate rib cage, and full pert breasts. My smooth unblemished skin was fair with a rosy hue. Based on his reaction to me, I knew Elijah found my figure pleasing.

And in an instant, I had become acutely aware of Elijah. His breathing. His scent. His skin. The raw power of him as he supported my weight and held me against him. Everything about him was enticing.

What was most pressing was the demand I felt to soothe his aching need. There was a primal instinct that insisted I tend to him, and I briefly wondered if that was why he had earlier, and was at the moment, tending to me. Perhaps he felt the same insisting call.

I did not *want* to feel these things for him. But what I wanted, what was logical, didn't matter. It was not simply a battle between the head and the heart, it was so much more than that. So much more basic than that. It was as though Elijah held a piece of myself, maybe my very soul, and all his needs and wants were my own. To deny him anything would be to deny myself air.

I couldn't help but think back to the conversation he had had with the beautiful luminescent creature outside and I believed this bond I felt to him was the *Vinculum* they spoke of. The one he thought I had faked.

In that moment, I actually wished it had been falsified, although he would have killed me for it. I wished that I could control what I was feeling. He had been incredibly abusive towards me and almost ended my life and yet I could not stop the need sparking between us.

Elijah let out a ragged breath. In the angry way he had about him, he snapped, "Let's just get this over with," and dunked my head under the warm spray from the shower head.

I sputtered at the unexpected face full of water. Although my anger at him quelled the worst of my desire, it wasn't extinguished altogether. And because of the intrusive connection I was experiencing with him, I knew, in spite of his harsh demeanor, he was still aroused.

With one arm banded around my waist, he reached for a shampoo bottle sitting on a sleek ledge in the spacious shower. I looked out through the clear glass of the modern shower walls and saw that the bathroom was incredibly large and luxurious with its own oversized fireplace. As with the sitting room in the cabin, the fire was the only source of light in the bathroom.

After flipping the top of the shampoo bottle open, Elijah squirted about half of the contents onto the top of my head, before tossing the bottle down by our feet. He began grumbling as he roughly smeared the shampoo in a thick layer over only my crown.

"I don't like this any more than you do, buddy," I told him.

Elijah reached for a bar of soap and his erection pressed against my butt. I squirmed at the contact wanting to get away, but all I ended up doing was wiggling my ass against him.

"Stop that!"

"*You* stop!"

Elijah let out a ragged breath. "Just, just stay still. Alright?"

"Don't get all up on me and I will."

"I swear to the fucking Light, I will drop you on your ass and leave you here."

I was about to snap back at him, but I stopped myself. Weary exhaustion swept over me in a wave that weighed a thousand pounds. I was so tired. The kick of adrenaline I had experienced was tapped out, and I was crashing hard.

After a moment's pause, Elijah seemed to regain his composure. He began rubbing the bar of soap over my shoulder and down one arm. Then he switched his hold on me and did the same on the other side.

The steamy warmth of the shower and the massaging strokes of the soap made my eyes close. Elijah continued to pass the bar over my skin, avoiding my breasts and between my thighs. He only stroked over sections of my skin that he could easily reach.

32

A limitation for which I was grateful since it kept his erection from prodding my butt again.

Just as he had with the shampoo bottle, Elijah unceremoniously dropped the soap onto the shower basin without a care of where it landed.

Voice gruff, he said, "Lean your head forward and rinse your hair."

I did as he directed and kept my eyes closed as the shampoo rinsed clean from my hair. He hadn't massaged the shampoo into my scalp and he hadn't even washed any of its length, but I kept my critique to myself.

After I lifted my head up, Elijah reached to the side and shut the water off. I guessed I was not going to be treated to any conditioner, but that would fall towards the bottom of my list of complaints.

Somehow Elijah had procured a towel and he quickly wrapped it around my torso. Right as I was wondering if I could manage walking out of the shower on my own, he swept me up into his arms and I was pressed against his damp chest.

Out of reflex, I wrapped my arms around his neck. I tensed as soon as I brushed the ends of his golden hair, realizing it was an intimate touch. I braced myself for some abrasive response from Elijah, but he said nothing, continuing to take us through the dim cabin and into a dark room. A fireplace flared to life as he placed me onto a bed and drew a thick fluffy comforter over me.

There were so many questions to ask. So much I deserved to know. Things I needed to find out. And I was determined to get answers.

But it would have to be tomorrow, because I was caught in a rip current of sleep. My eyelids blinked shut. Once, twice, three times.

Between each flutter of my lashes, I saw the bedroom had one wall made entirely of glass from floor to ceiling. In the midst of the storm that raged on the other side of the glass, a bolt of lightning streaked from the sky illuminating a valley below the cabin property in a flash of brilliant light.

It was desolate and lonely out there, with not another soul for a far as the eye could see. All that stood for miles upon miles were lone trees, swaying and quaking from the onslaught of the storm…but remaining upright all the same.

CHAPTER 4

"GET UP."

Elijah was standing at the foot of the bed looking down at me. In the dim firelight, I could see his golden hair was still tousled, his jaw still covered in stubble, but he was dressed to go out. In addition to the worn jeans and freshly changed flannel button down, he wore a heavy coat and boots.

In his hands was more clothing. He tossed everything he was holding onto the bed.

"Get dressed. We're leaving."

I sat up and pulled the comforter to my chest. Wary.

"Where are we going?"

"To see someone. Don't ask questions. Just get dressed. Can you handle that, or do you need me to coddle you some more?"

Although the fire crackled in the room's hearth, outside the glass wall the storm continued, unabated, in the black night's sky.

I couldn't imagine trekking out into such dark violence, but I didn't say anything.

"Get dressed and meet me at the top of the stairs." He crossed to a bureau, opening one of the drawers and left it agape. "You can find more items in here."

Then he crossed to a walk-in closet (the size of a small bedroom from the looks of it) and disappeared for a moment before coming back into the room with a pair of women's boots in hand. He threw the boots onto the floor, in what I'm sure was purposefully a demeaning gesture, and walked out of the bedroom without a word.

Sitting there on the bed, I considered my options. I could refuse to cooperate and...*what*? Demand a phone call? I didn't know who I would call. Demand to be taken to the nearest town where I could seek out help? Pretend to cooperate and then make a break for it?

I didn't really think Elijah would be receptive to any requests. If I refused to get dressed, he would probably just throw me over his shoulder in the towel I had wrapped around my torso and carry me off against my will.

And glancing out the large glass wall in the bedroom, I couldn't imagine getting far outside on my own. It was dark and the storm raged viciously. I had been drenched and cold to my very bones, not to mention blinded by the rain, within moments of Elijah dragging me out of the cabin the night before.

I reached down to gather up the clothes heaped on the comforter. They were women's items and I wondered where they had come from. Elijah had also pulled those boots from the closet as if that was their permanent residence. So did he live here with a woman? And if so, where was she?

Among the clothing were cashmere socks, a pair of jeans, a soft cream sweater, and a heavy camel button-down coat. All were designer labels and each piece looked sleek and expensive. I awkwardly realized there were no undergarments included in the pile, which was a problem for me since I had slept with only a towel and comforter. The sweater I was supposed to wear was thin, and from the looks of it, was going to be snug. While I certainly did not want to wear another girl's underwear, I definitely needed a bra.

At least Elijah had left the room, for which I could not have been more grateful. The last thing I wanted was to dress in front of him. But still, I made sure the towel was wrapped securely around my chest before heaving myself out of the massive white bed.

My legs were incredibly weak and sore, and I wondered what on earth had happened to me, but I managed to painfully trudge over to the bureau by bracing myself against the perimeter of the wall and the various furniture in the room.

The drawer Elijah had left open was full of lacy bras and panties. Despite how uncomfortable it made me, I snatched a bra from the collection. The idea of borrowing panties was just too awkward, and I didn't bother with any.

As I shut the drawer, though, I noticed a small satin box in a decorative bowl on top of the dresser. There was no reason for me to pick the box up. And I can't say why I did, but I took it out of the bowl.

It was the type of jewelry box that holds the promise of luxury. It was already in my hand. I had no choice then but to open it.

I gasped. The diamond ring that sat nestled in the box was incredible. It was a large stone that was so perfectly cut and so unerringly clear, it brilliantly refracted the firelight. I couldn't help but wish I could see the stone in the sunlight. It would be a vision.

I gingerly lifted the ring out of it's setting in the box and turned it this way and that watching how it glittered. Although I was mesmerized by the single large diamond in the setting, a flash of elegantly engraved script caught my eye and I inspected the platinum band.

Always waiting, always you

The engraved words were meticulously scripted with a dramatic flourish, and my neck heated. I was suddenly embarrassed. I was intruding on something personal between two individuals.

The most obvious scenario was that Elijah had given the ring to the mystery woman who lived here. But I couldn't know for certain. Perhaps it was a family heirloom. Maybe this wasn't even Elijah's cabin. There was a long list of plausible explanations. The one thing I knew for certain was that it wasn't mine and I needed to quickly put it away.

Besides, I looked at my hand. I had my own incredibly stunning, other-worldly stone already. I needed to figure out the significance of it before I began analyzing another's. I put the ring back and returned to the pile of clothes.

I managed to get myself dressed quickly enough. It was unsettling, almost eerie really, how perfectly everything fit.

Apparently, I was the same size as Elijah's woman. Whoever she was, she had great taste.

I could see in the large bureau mirror that every piece accentuated and highlighted my figure in a pleasing but sophisticated way. My small round ass popped in the curve hugging jeans. And the snug sweater emphasized my tiny waist and full breasts. The boots had a label on the heel that read *Sorel*. They were all-weather with laces that climbed up my calves and tactical straps and buckles. I had to admit, they were pretty fantastic.

My chestnut hair had dried into loose waves. I quickly braided the face framing strands on each side and then intertwined them where they met at the back of my head, leaving the rest flowing down my shoulders and back.

Since I hadn't heard any grumbling from Elijah, I chanced a wobbly trip through the large archway into the connecting bathroom. Doing a scan, I realized that it was the bathroom from the previous night. The large glass enclosed shower was definitely the one in which Elijah had helped bathe me. The discarded shampoo bottle and bar of soap still lay on the shower floor. And in the corner my robe had been forgotten in a soggy heap.

My face flushed at the memory of what had happened—at the response I had had to Elijah. Just the memory of his chest against my back, of his large arms around me, and his blatant desire for me…

I shoved the thoughts aside. Clearly, he was just as much a pawn to the strange connection, the *Vinculum,* as I was. He had been nothing but rude and abrasive just now, his contempt for me made crystal clear. Repeatedly. I would fight the responses I had to him tooth and nail. His masculine, rugged handsomeness could take a hike. His good looks would not make me desire him in the slightest.

Feeling resolved, I picked up the wet discarded robe and hung it on a towel rack. Then I turned my back on the shower and spied an elegant vanity. Expensive cosmetics were laid out. I was already in another woman's bra, what would a few swipes of mascara be?

I left all the other items where they were. The mascara alone was plenty. The face staring back at me in the mirror had flawless ivory skin, naturally blushed cheeks, and pink pouty lips. Her eyes—*my eyes*—were large and thickly lashed. The bright blue irises and surrounding lavender ring...

I whipped my head away from the mirror. The vision I had witnessed last night (the black branching through my irises) flashed through my mind. I squeezed my eyes shut, trying to erase the sight. Trying to ease the panic rising from my chest. *What had happened to me?*

A *nightwalker*. That's what Elijah had said I was. It was a word and nothing more. It told me nothing.

"Move your ass!" Elijah shouted from outside the bedroom.

I let out a deep breath and made my way out to the landing where he waited, pain shooting through my stiff legs with each shuffling step. I didn't care for his treatment of me, but at least his bellowing snapped me away from the harrowing memory of the night before.

As I hobbled along, I realized that my internal injuries seemed to be healing. The intense icy pain I had felt in my abdomen when I first woke on Elijah's couch was a manageable ache. It had not flared up again.

Elijah didn't spare me a glance once I emerged; he just started down the wide wood stairs. I followed behind him, but each step proved difficult for my weak legs and I descended at a snail's pace. Elijah, such the gentleman, waited impatiently at the base of the staircase, staring in the opposite direction and grinding his teeth.

Once I reached the bottom stair, he started off, obviously expecting me to follow. The entire cabin was dim with only the light from the fire in the sitting room and some candles here and there to illuminate the way. Every so often flashes of lightning would lend an extra flicker of brilliance. The storm was relentless outside, with heavy winds sometimes rattling the windows as if charging to enter, and thunder rumbling a heavy underscore.

I tried to keep up with Elijah despite the pain shooting through my legs. He pulled a cell phone out from his pocket and made a call.

"We're on our way," he told the person on the other end. "No that won't be—" He let out a groan of frustration as his sentence was cut off, and I got the impression that the person on the other end had hung up on him.

He continued to walk along a narrow hallway to a door at the back of the house and opened it. There was an old wooden flight of stairs which led into what must have been the basement. Lit candles lined the stairway. Elijah began to descend in a hurried manner.

I tried to follow but as with the previous flight of stairs, I had no choice but to take each step slowly. Elijah stopped where he was, turned around, and walked back up to me.

"We don't have time for this," he groused as he picked me up and carried me down the stairs.

Being pressed against him, I felt that inexplicable pull towards him again. It was almost as if I were a magnet. The closer I got to him, the more attracted I was to him. And somehow, I had no idea how I knew it, but Elijah felt it too. I knew he was exercising extreme self-control. I could sense a need and longing in him, and it was directed at me.

However, the instant we got to the bottom of the stairs he practically threw me out of his arms. I stumbled a few steps backwards and fell flat on my ass. I glanced up at Elijah. He didn't look the least bit remorseful.

"You're a real jerk, you know that?"

"You need to toughen up," was all he said. He walked over to an enormous bookshelf with multiple sections that seemed to house tools and basic garage paraphernalia. He flipped open a section of ornamental molding and there was a keypad housed within.

After punching a code into the keypad, the massive bookshelf slid to the side on some unseen tracks. Behind it was a huge dirt tunnel that disappeared into darkness, and a shiny grey utility vehicle sat at the maw of the tunnel. The back of the car read *Land Rover Defender*. It looked rugged but also pricey.

I dusted off my bottom. "What the hell is this? Your top-secret garage?"

"Basically."

"Is this really necessary?"

He didn't answer me.

"Who are you?"

"Get in the car." He walked over to the driver side and got in.

"You have terrible manners. Do you know that?" I said as I clambered into the passenger seat. "You're a savage."

His lips thinned. "You have no idea, princess," he replied. "No idea."

Elijah started the car and I was surprised to hear it purr rather than growl. He tapped a remote on the visor and took off down the tunnel without hesitation. In the passenger mirror, I could see the bookshelf sliding back into place.

And leaving Elijah's home, I couldn't help but wonder... *Where was my own?*

CHAPTER 5

I HAD THOUGHT THAT THE TUNNEL would immediately begin to incline and we would travel up to the surface, but instead the dirt road remained level. The tunnel twisted and turned underground framed only by the shifting light of the headlamps.

"Are we going to be underground for the entire trip?" I asked.

"Yes."

I looked over at him. Elijah's rugged features were highlighted by the glow from the dashboard. "Is it safe to drive through here with such little light?"

He turned his face to glare at me, holding my eye for much too long.

"Okay. I'm sorry. Please, just watch the road."

He held my eye for a moment longer and turned back to the windshield.

"What happened last night?" My question was soft, testing the waters.

Elijah was quiet and I didn't think he was going to answer me.

"Look," he finally said, "we're going to see someone."

"That means nothing to me."

He ground his teeth. "You can talk to her."

"*Her?* Does she know me? Will she be able to answer my questions?"

"I have no idea what she'll do or say in regard to you."

"Does someone live with you?"

"No."

"Well whose clothes am I wearing?"

His face fell. It was only for a moment, and then he composed his features. Yet, I had noticed the falter. I felt a flicker of emotion from him, experiencing it for myself. Loss. He felt loss. No response followed, and I didn't think it would be a good idea to push the subject, so we fell into silence.

With the headlights from the Land Rover slicing into unending darkness, and the tight twists and turns of the tunnel, I began to feel car sick. I closed my eyes and leaned my head against the seat.

I have no idea how much time passed, but eventually the cabin of our SUV was flooded with bright light. I opened my eyes to see what was going on.

"Stay in the car." It was clearly a command and not a request. Elijah got out and leaned against the front bumper with his arms folded across his chest.

A rugged vehicle driving towards us stopped a few yards in front of Elijah. Both the driver's door and the passenger's door were thrust open simultaneously.

Two large men approached Elijah. They were dressed similarly in black fatigue pants and black t-shirts. Even the guns that were blatantly strapped to their chests were black in black holsters. In addition to the two guns each man carried in a shoulder holster, there was also something strapped to their biceps, and I was willing to guess that they were knives.

The driver had strong square features with wild blond hair. The massive muscle bulk he carried did not seem to hinder his fluidity of movement. He looked like he could be a Norse god.

The passenger had golden brown hair in a color that any woman would be envious of and boyishly handsome looks. Even saddled down with all the combative gear, he looked like a heartbreaker. Although he wasn't as broad as the driver, he was taller and perfectly sculpted with muscles.

It was clear from their expressions that they meant business. In spite of their intimidating frames, neither was quite as large as Elijah, though.

Elijah spoke first. Although his voice was muffled, I could still make out his conversation. "No one looks at her, speaks to her, or comes near her. Is that understood?" Elijah demanded.

The two men looked at me through the windshield of the car, and they both seemed to do a double take when they saw me.

Elijah was already turning back to the car, not waiting for any indication of response from the duo. The one with the golden-brown hair opened his mouth as if to say something and took a step towards my door with his gaze intent on me. However, the Norse god slapped him on the chest, stopping the heartbreaker in his tracks. The blond gave a sharp shake of his head in negation. It looked like his partner was about to argue, but then thought

48

better of it. They turned back to their car, but once inside, the heartbreaker's intense stare through the windshield unsettled me.

They turned their car around in the tight space of the tunnel and we followed after them. I was about to ask Elijah if I was really so much of a threat that he had to order these large armed men to stay away from me. But then I remembered his entire spiel to that woman the night before about how I was a threat sent by the House of Shadows. Which, like pretty much everything else, meant nothing to me. But apparently, it was a big deal to him.

Elijah took a sharp turn and then braked suddenly behind the leading vehicle. The two front doors of the other SUV opened and the men got out. Before I had a chance to say anything, Elijah was out of the Land Rover and crossing the nose. He yanked open my door and reached across me to unbuckle my seat belt.

"Out," he commanded.

When I didn't immediately follow orders, he encased my small waist with his large hands and lifted me from the car, as if I were a rag doll, setting me on my feet. Then he grabbed my upper arm and began dragging me down an off shoot of the tunnel.

A growl that sounded like it was from a wild animal caught my attention, and I looked over my shoulder. The heartbreaker was stalking towards us with a murderous look in his eyes, his gaze drilling into the back of Elijah's head. In his palm, he white knuckled an unsheathed blade, the tendons in his forearm popping against his skin.

"Don't do it," Elijah warned.

"Do what?" I was breathless from all the commotion.

49

"Give him any indication that you want to talk to him. You'll only be signing his death warrant. Might as well remove his head yourself. As much as I detest it, I am feeling very possessive of you right now. If that little pissant so much as puts a finger on you I am going to lose it."

Elijah was right. I had wanted to find out who the heartbreaker was. That look of recognition he'd given me had felt like a life raft in the middle of a stormy ocean.

"Who is he?"

"Nobody. Just a kid who needs to learn some respect."

I looked back over my shoulder as Elijah continued to march us through the tunnel. The blond friend launched in front of the heartbreaker, wrapping him in a bear hug and pinning his arms down at his side before slamming the heartbreaker's back into the dirt wall of the tunnel. There was nothing about either of them that indicated "kid." They were both two huge aggressive men from what I could see.

They stood together like that in their rough embrace for a moment before the blond friend said, "Let's get in the vehicles and take them back to the compound," in the same way one might talk to someone about to jump from a ledge fifty stories high.

I wasn't able to see any more of what happened between the two of them because Elijah and I took another turn down the tunnel. I could sense something both exhilarating and terrifying up ahead and my gaze whipped forward.

Down this portion of the tunnel, at the very end, was a bright light. I dug my heels into the dirt and stopped walking, holding my hand up and trying to shield my eyes. A part of me reveled in the intense beams of the light, wanting to bask in them and try to draw upon the intense energy. But another part of me shrieked in revulsion. In agony. The urge to get as far away as possible was undeniable.

I tried to take a step back, but Elijah's grasp held fast on my arm.

"Let go!" I demanded.

"The more you fight it, the more painful it will be," he countered.

"Fight what?" I moaned. "What the hell is this?" I wildly tried to twist from Elijah's hold, desperate to get away. Nausea roiled and I was afraid I would vomit.

"This is our way out, princess."

"No. No, we have to turn around!"

"This is a barrier meant to keep *nightwalkers* out."

I screamed out and fell to my knees. The small window of time when I could have turned around and ran away had closed. The nausea, the pain, the burning. It was all too much to bear.

"I'm going to have to take you through," Elijah continued, paying no heed to the agony I was in. "The more connected we are, the easier it will be." He yanked on my arm where he still held it in a bruising grip. "Stop being so dramatic. Get up."

"Get...bent," I gritted.

"I'd love to sit around and chat with you all day, but we've got shit to do. Now it's time to go." With that he swooped me up and threw me over his shoulder before charging off.

Even with my eyes squeezed shut and my hands covering them, I could sense the light we were approaching. I could tell that it was somehow a barrier, like a curtain separating our side of the tunnel from the other. I surprised myself when through all the pain, I let out an involuntary hiss.

Then I felt us break the barrier of light and the strongest sense of duality overtook me. There was a part of me that relished in the sparkling waterfall of light through which we passed. The light strengthened that part of me. The light also connected me to Elijah in some way that I couldn't comprehend. I was rejuvenated and refreshed. I was resurrected. A very ancient and primordial sense of power overtook me. I throbbed with inextinguishable strength.

The other part of me, however, was immersed in bitter agony at the touch of the light upon my skin. The other part of me was repulsed and disgusted by the curtain of light. I wanted to extinguish it into oblivion so that it had never been. The energy of the light burned my skin. It burned my insides, and I knew that it was going to kill me.

Before I could let out a scream of agony and ecstasy, we were through the curtain. Elijah dropped to his knees and I fell from his shoulder onto my ass in front of him. He was breathing fast and heavy. His massive chest billowed in and out, and his head dropped into my shoulder.

"Elijah?" The excruciating pain which I had felt dissipated once we had passed through the curtain of light. I was still nauseous, but it was bearable compared to what I had felt on the other side. I didn't experience the same debilitating pain.

Elijah, on the other hand, was clearly suffering. He tried to stand only to fall onto his hands and knees. His head hung between his shoulders.

"Elijah?" I kneeled next to him and placed my hand on his back. The last of his strength gave out. His arms buckled and he collapsed to the floor with his head in my lap. "Elijah, what's wrong?"

His response was staggered. "Just...need...a minute."

A light sheen of sweat covered his forehead. I didn't know what to do and I looked around at where he had brought us. Although we were still in the dirt tunnel, we were in front of a large stone archway housing two doors that must have been twenty feet high. The doors were also made from some kind of ivory stone with intricate patterns carved across the surface.

I momentarily contemplated turning back to find those two men, but the mere thought of passing through that veil of light made my stomach pitch.

I turned back to Elijah. His breathing was slowing and the strain in his face was easing. I tentatively held up my hand to stroke his hair. The need to comfort him was an unwelcome urge that I couldn't tamp down.

Before I had a chance to decide what I was going to do, there was a loud scraping sound behind me. I whipped my head around and saw that one of the stone doors... was opening.

CHAPTER 6

A DAZZLING VISION OF A MAN stepped out from behind the door. The man was exuding pure white light just as the woman in the storm had.

Although he looked solid enough to touch, his corporeal being was greatly overshadowed by the light which radiated from his core and beamed outward in all directions, illuminating him. And he too had incredible wings of light that flared behind him. The resulting effect was a majestic air of reverence.

"Eli, you fucking idiot." The man's voice was the most glorious song of deep bells.

Elijah raised his middle finger to the man briefly before letting his arm fall back down.

"And you," the man shifted his gaze to me, "you have been causing quite a stir, haven't you?"

Elijah tried to sound as aggressive as possible while breathing heavily and collapsed on the floor. "Do not look at her. Do not talk to her. Do not get close enough to touch her. And stop showing off."

"Please, Eli. Spare me your aggressive male posturing. It's a wasted effort. You know I can't connect with her. I've passed on, dumb shit." Even the profanities which passed through his lips were the most gorgeous music I had ever heard. "And you know I like to make an entrance."

The man...*angel?* Turned to me and it was as if he had turned off his internal light switch. The white radiance and those wings of light faded. However, the absence of light did not diminish his appearance in the slightest.

Holy hell, he was jaw droppingly hot. He was just as tall and muscled as Elijah but not as rugged. With his moussed blond hair and sharp blue eyes, he looked like he could be typecast for an all-American quarterback or an early 2000s Abercrombie & Fitch model. He also appeared more mid to late twenties in comparison to Elijah's thirtysomething.

He wore boots and jeans like Elijah, but I had a feeling he didn't take himself as seriously since his long sleeve tee had *DO IT LIKE A DEVIL* printed over a pair of horns. Although he was dressed casually, a large sword was strapped to his back.

"So, I hear you're not right in the head anymore, huh babydoll?" he asked me.

I realized I was gawking. "I'm sorry, what?"

He simply laughed in response.

"I mean it, G," Elijah growled.

The man smirked, clearly amused by the rise he was getting out of Elijah.

"Alright, look," he said, "our little lady here has been through hell, so why don't you pick your lazy ass up and help her inside."

The man winked at me and nodded his head towards the stone doors. He made a gesture for me to help Elijah stand up. I understood that in reality I would be the one helping Elijah inside and not the other way around.

I nodded and stood while attempting to help Elijah up as well. The man Elijah called G went to his other side and the two of us helped Elijah shuffle through the door.

We were in a circular foyer with a domed ceiling that soared high above. There was something that looked like a small star which floated, suspended in midair, in the center of the dome. The surrounding curved wall was filled with doors—some particularly ornate and adorned with brilliant gems, some which looked to be made of ancient rotted wood, and everything in between.

G directed us towards a whitewashed door and placed his hand on it. A glow of light pulsed from his palm for a brief moment and then the door swung open. Ahead of us was a long stone hallway lit with torches.

"Ok, enough of this bullshit," G said. Then in one fluid motion he hoisted Elijah over his shoulders in a fireman's carry.

Elijah growled. "Giddeon, you mother fucker. Put me down or I will fuck you up."

"Of course you will, big guy," G replied before giving Elijah a hard slap right on his ass.

I could feel my eyes widen as I stared at G in awe. In that instant, he was my hero.

"I really like you," I said to him.

He gave me a dazzling smile and winked at me. "Let's get out of here. I don't want to carry his fat ass any longer than I have to."

I started down the hallway following G, and I noticed Elijah go slack. "Elijah?"

"He's alright. He just needs to rest. It's actually a testament to his strength that he remained conscious for as long as he did," G commented.

I sidled up next to him feeling small. Like Elijah, he was over six and a half feet tall and stacked with muscles. "Are you sure?"

"Yeah. He's tight. Fucking stupid, but tight."

"What do you mean?" I asked.

"Because he pulled you through the *veil* with him."

"That wall of light out in the tunnel?"

"Yeah. A dumb ass move like that would have killed anyone else. He may be one strong son of a bitch, but he could have seriously hurt himself, not to mention how dangerous it was for you as well."

"Why was it dangerous?" We reached the end of the hallway and stood in front of a simple dark wood door. Again, G placed his hand on the door and the light at his palm flared.

The door swung open and I gasped. I had been expecting the door to open into some kind of room or connecting hall. Instead, we walked through the doorway into a forest. Snow blanketed the ground and fell from a dark night's sky. I could see dim flickering lights beyond the trees in front of us.

"We're here," G said simply.

I turned back to look at the door which we had stepped through. It was gone. There was nothing but tall evergreens

58

bathed in snow surrounding us. There was no building, no entryway, no tunnel. Just dark snowy forest. It was as if the door from which we had emerged simply vanished.

"What…? How…?"

"Come on, babydoll. Let's get inside."

I was so tired of all the unknowing and confusion, but most of all the evasiveness, of not getting a simple and direct answer to my questions.

"We can sit down and talk when we get inside." G's voice had gone soft and sympathetic. "Besides, our boy here is going to be okay, but he still needs some tending to."

I looked at Elijah slumped and unconscious over G's shoulders. I nodded.

"Atta girl," he said, flashing another smile at me.

G led us through the trees towards the flickering lights. As we made our way across the virgin snow, I was glad Elijah had given me boots to wear. With each step I took, my feet sunk into the snow until it was past my ankles.

A cottage emerged through the trees before us. It sat nestled in the forest with candles flickering in each of the windows. The little house looked like it may have belonged to Snow White or some equally pure and innocent character—it was that picture perfect.

The cottage was stone with wood trimmed windows and a thatched roof that was covered in a thick layer of snow. Smoke curled and wisped out of the chimney into the midnight sky mingling with the falling snowflakes. The arched wood door was a graceful invitation into the cozy home.

G walked right up to the front door and opened it.

"After you," he insisted.

"Is this your house?" I asked as we walked over the threshold.

G laughed. The deep bell-like laughter was so beautiful it filled me with warmth and gave me a slight high. "No. Absolutely not."

The inside of the cottage was just as rustic as the outside. Vintage furniture filled the place creating a lovely atmosphere. A roaring fire danced and popped merrily in the stone hearth. Although this home was also solely lit with firelight and candles, it was somehow brighter than Elijah's had been.

I followed G into a bedroom. It was cozy, but I got the impression that it was a guest room. There were no effects distinguishing this as someone's personal space.

G placed Elijah on the bed. Elijah groaned but did not wake. He dominated the queen size mattress making it appear as though meant for a child.

"I'll take off his jacket. You stroke his face and hair." G made the command sound like an everyday request.

"You can't be serious," I said.

G snorted. "Trust me. It will help him considerably."

I stood where I was next to the bed with my hands clasped not knowing what to say or do.

G finished removing Elijah's coat and pulled a wood rocking chair behind me. I considered him quite a gentleman as he then helped my coat off and hung it over the back of the chair. Before backing away, he placed his hands on my shoulders and pushed down gently.

'Sit," he said. "You don't have to do anything you don't want to do. I'm going to find our hostess. I'll be back in a few minutes. You can just sit here and keep an eye on him for me."

Without turning to look at G I asked, "Will it really help him?"

"It really will," he responded. "You two might not like it, but you both need each other right now."

Before I could turn back to ask him what he meant by that, I heard the soft click of the door closing behind me.

I sat there staring at Elijah. His skin was pallid and there was still a light sheen of sweat across his brows. His breathing was shallow as well.

When I reached my hand out and touched a strand of his golden hair, Elijah hummed and turned his face towards me.

I felt that magnetic attraction flare between us. Leaning closer to the bed—closer to him—I stroked my fingers through his hair letting my palm make full contact with the side of his head. Heat blossomed under my touch and Elijah moaned.

The intense attraction I felt towards him overwhelmed me as well as the need to comfort and care for him. I found myself closing my eyes and breathing heavily. A pulsing sensation drummed through my core. With both of my hands, I stroked the sides of his face.

A low, pleased purr came from Elijah's chest. Then without any warning, he grabbed me by the arms and dragged me into the bed with him. I was pinned underneath him before I could even process how I had landed there. His eyes were barely open in some state that hindered between unconsciousness and delirium.

His body overwhelmed mine. His massive bulk covered every inch of me. I looked up into his face and my breath hitched. "Elijah?"

He looked at me without seeing me. His eyes were heavy with sensuality. Those gold flecks burned brightly, and his stare left me feeling naked.

My body ignited in response from feeling the weight of him against me. I moistened my lips and shifted so that my breasts were pressing into his hard chest.

His words were slightly slurred. "Need you so badly." His pelvis ground against mine and his head dipped to nuzzle my neck.

I gasped at the sensation, feeling his hard arousal rubbing against my core. Being so close to Elijah was overwhelming my system. There was no room for anything else at the moment. I was immersed in him.

The magnetic pull I felt had me locked into him. I could feel what he was feeling, and the need and desire he was experiencing was brutally devouring.

In that moment, I felt sorry for him. He was consumed by a deep unfulfilled ache, an abyss of longing with no hope for reconciliation. There was a cavernous emptiness within him, an utter loneliness.

I wrapped my arms around him. "Oh, Elijah."

His eyes snapped open as he reared back on his forearms looking down at me, full consciousness slamming into him. He looked confused for a moment, as if he was uncertain of how we ended up in a bed together. Then defiance flared in his eyes.

"Do not pity me," he ground out.

"I'm sorry." I said. "I don't. I just—"

"Please, spare me your babbling." He sat up and swung his legs off the side of the bed, sitting on the edge with his back to me.

"If anyone should be pitied, it's you." His words were cutting—malicious.

I scrambled off the bed backing up until my butt hit the closed door behind me.

Elijah sat, glaring at me. His erratic mood shift threw me, and I was once again confused, not knowing what to feel.

There was a sharp knock, which startled me. I yelped and jumped away from the door before straightening my clothing and hair. Then I took a steadying breath and turned the doorknob.

As soon as the door was open wide enough, G barreled past me, bulldozing his way to Elijah, and punched him straight in the nose.

Elijah's head snapped back and then forward. He brought his hands up and cupped his nose. "Fuck, Giddeon! You're a mother fucking asshole," he shouted.

"You're a cold, sick bastard. Do you know that?" G demanded. "Don't fuck with her like that. Hasn't she been through enough?"

G turned away from Elijah shaking out his hand and muttering, "You selfish jackass."

G walked up to me and put his hand on my upper arm.

Elijah growled low in his throat. "Do not touch her."

G snorted, completely disregarding Elijah. Then he looked at me very seriously and also a touch tenderly. "I apologize on behalf of Elijah. He is a neanderthal with no concept of how to talk to a lady. If you would like to join me in the sitting room, I will introduce you to our hostess. We can all have a little chat." He gave my arm a squeeze. "What do you think?"

I cleared my throat and nodded. "Thank you, G."

He put his arm around my shoulder and hugged me to his side. "Excellent."

Elijah growled once more, and I knew it was because G had put his arm around me.

"Neanderthal," G called out without sparing a glance in Elijah's direction, "you may join us as well once you decide you are ready to behave."

I couldn't help but smile as G and I walked into the main room leaving Elijah stewing on the bed.

CHAPTER 7

A WOMAN WAS IN THE SITTING ROOM. Her back was to us as she stood in front of the stone hearth gazing into the fire. Long blonde hair flowed over her shoulders in waves. Her royal blue dress was snug through the bodice but flared out around her hips and swept the ground. The long sleeves of the dress emphasized slender, graceful arms.

As she turned to face us, I was instantly in awe. She looked like a goddess. Her face was stunning with sharp delicate features. Her eyes sparkled the deepest blue. It was like looking at the surface of the ocean as the sun danced across the waves. I could tell that she was certainly older than me, but beyond that it was impossible to guess at her age. She had a mature, timeless look and demeanor.

In addition to her beauty, she emanated *power*. I could feel the vibrations of it. When she looked at me every candle in the room, as well as the fire in the hearth, flared for an instant, licking higher before settling back into place.

She searched my face seeming to expect something from me. It made me feel uncomfortable but gave me hope that perhaps she knew me and could help me. When I had nothing to offer her but a tight smile, she bowed her head in greeting.

"Welcome."

The one word alone held so much authority it was clear that she was a figure to be respected. I too bowed my head and thanked her.

"Come, dear. Won't you please sit?" She gestured to the large ivory couch in the center of the room.

"Thank you," I replied and took a seat where she had directed. I tried my best to sit up straight and demurely cross my legs at the ankles while resting my hands in my lap.

"Giddeon." She inclined her head to a wingback chair clearly requesting him to take a seat as well. He slid into the chair and plonked his boots up on the coffee table.

The woman raised an eyebrow and G instantly removed his feet, placing them back on the hardwood floor. He even leaned forward from his chair and wiped his hand over the area of the coffee table where his boots had been. Then he flashed a blinding smile at the woman.

I almost sighed at the sight of it. I didn't know if any female on the planet could resist that smile.

"I think that's enough, Giddeon," she said with austerity.

Well, it seemed that there was a female on the planet who could resist him after all.

"Of course, Adriel," he replied as his smile deflated.

"Giddeon?"

"Yes, Adriel."

She assessed him for a long moment before speaking. I wanted to squirm but tamped down the urge. I had a feeling this wasn't going well for G.

"What are you wearing?"

G rubbed the back of his neck. The motion caused his bicep and pectorals to flex beneath the t-shirt which, in turn, caused the *DO IT LIKE A DEVIL* print to become more pronounced.

"Aw, gee, Adriel. I was under the impression that the timeliness of my presence was more important than the formality of my appearance. The summons seemed urgent. I made my way to escort the pr—"

G looked at me and stopped himself. "Err…"

The woman huffed. "Yes. Yes. Fine," she conceded. "But honestly, Giddeon." She gave his shirt a final pointed look and then turned to me.

With the grace of a ballerina, the woman crossed to the couch and sat next to me leaving two feet of space between us.

She angled her body towards me and spoke in a sympathetic tone. "So, my dear, is it true that you have no memory of what has happened to you or even who you are?"

"That's true," I confirmed.

"Are you able to remember anything at all?"

I looked down at my hands, feeling the gravity of my situation. "No, nothing," I said. "The last thing I remember is waking up on Elijah's couch. I can recall everything since then, but nothing before."

I couldn't be sure, but it seemed as though the woman's shoulders sank ever so slightly.

"I see," she said. "Well then, I am Adriel."

Elijah stepped into the sitting room then. All three of us turned to look at him.

"Elijah," Adriel said curtly, "how magnanimous of you to grace us with your presence."

Elijah did not exactly bow his head but rather tilted it down a fraction.

"Please, sit." Adriel did not ask but commanded. It was clear that the "please" was out of formality and not politeness.

"I'll stand," Elijah challenged. He walked to the fireplace, leaned against the surrounding stone, and crossed his arms over his chest.

G made a choking sound and started coughing right as violent thunder crashed outside causing the cottage to shake.

The explosion of sound startled me, and I jumped in my seat. I looked up and saw Elijah's eyes on me before he raised an eyebrow at Adriel.

Adriel smoothed a nonexistent wrinkle out of her dress and turned back to me. "I understand that you are confused right now and that you have many questions. I will try to explain what I believe has happened."

She leaned in to take my hand but seemed to change her mind. Instead she pulled back and settled her hands in her lap. "Do you know what you are?" she asked.

At first, I thought it was an odd question. I was about to tell her that I didn't understand. After all, I was a person, or more specifically, a woman. But then I thought about Elijah's comments. A *nightwalker*, he had called me.

I also thought about passing through the *veil* in the tunnel, about the duality of light and dark which I had experienced. I thought about the glow from my palm when I had first touched Elijah and the same glow I had seen coming from G's palm when opening the doors in that domed foyer.

I didn't know what Elijah was, but he was certainly no mere mortal. I could *feel* the incredible power he possessed. Not to mention that I was connected to him in some unfathomable way.

And I was fairly certain that G was something akin to an angel. He was clearly the same as the woman from the storm—the one who had told Elijah he was wrong. But even if I wasn't a...*nightwalker*, I didn't believe I was an angel either.

When I failed to answer, Adriel took pity on me and continued. "You are an immortal of the Light. As are we. A Radiant. For many years, we have been battling a dark and powerful adversary. It is a war with which our people have been engaged since the beginning of our existence. We believe that you were apprehended by this foe and," she wrung her hands together, "it seems that you have been *infected*, in a way. As a result, you now carry some of our enemy's traits.

"There is a curse spoken of in the mythology of our race. Up until now I believed it to exist only in lore. It is known as The *Umbra Basium* or *The Shadow's Kiss*."

G let out an expletive, but Adriel paid no heed to it. From G's response, however, whatever this infection was, it must be bad.

"Umbra is a dark, ancient evil. It is the antithesis of light, a complete absence of it. Just as radiant energy is a part of the

70

essential makeup of our race, umbra is inherent to those of the Shadow race.

"Normally, those of the Light are immune to such an infection. Our energy serves as a shield of sorts against the taint of the umbra. The only way for one of our kind to become a host to this dark evil is to drain one's wellspring of inner light. However, we as a species are unable to survive without this intrinsic luminescence.

"So, you see the impossibility of *The Umbra Basium*. If one of our kind is stripped of her light, which is the only way to become infected, that individual would perish. And yet here you sit before us, alive, in spite of befalling *The Shadow's Kiss*."

I held up my hand. It seemed as though Adriel was rushing through this explanation in the same way one tries to rip off a bandage. "I'm sorry," I told her, "but I'm not understanding any of this."

Adriel gave me a pitying smile and shook her head. "Of course. I apologize."

She rose, crossing to the fire. After waving a hand in the direction of the flames, the crackling logs sparked and leapt as if stoked. She began to pace. "Allow me to start over."

"Before you do that, can you tell me my name?" I interjected.

She paused, looking startled and uncomfortable, perhaps even pained.

Elijah pushed himself from the wall and took a step towards Adriel. "She has become a *nightwalker*, Adriel. She is no longer that person," he warned.

Adriel dismissed him with a slice of her hand through the air. Anger saturated the space around us. "I will be the one who decides such things," she boomed. It was almost as if the cabin had grown darker and Adriel had grown larger, her voice taking on an echoing quality.

But with just a blink of the eye, the illusion was gone, and all was as it had been. I believed I must have imagined the change around us.

Adriel turned back to me, once again a delicate, lovely woman. "I had failed to consider you would not know your own name. I am sorry, my dear."

She searched my eyes and I was afraid of what she might find. What if Elijah was right. I did not know what a *nightwalker* was, but I was certain it was not something I wanted to be.

When she spoke again, it was with resolve. "You are strong," she told me. "What has happened to you does not define you. Do you understand that?"

It seemed she was expecting a response from me. Not actually sure what she meant, I nodded anyway.

"You do not need to succumb to your circumstances."

Although she didn't ask a question, it felt as though she awaited some kind of confirmation from me once again.

I didn't know what she meant by that exactly. But I did know that I wanted my memories back. I was going to do whatever it took to find myself. So, in that sense, we were in accord.

I nodded again but this time with more conviction.

Adriel looked at me for a long moment and then finally spoke. "Violet…Your name…is *Violet Archer.*"

CHAPTER 8

THE NAME MEANT NOTHING TO ME. I felt neither a sense of recognition, nor any stirrings of memories, but at least it was a start. I was going to have to put one foot in front of the other to reclaim my life, and this was one little piece of information that I had won back.

"Thank you," I said to Adriel. "It doesn't sound familiar to me, but I am glad to know it. Can you tell me what day it is, where we are, where my family is?"

Adriel pressed her lips together into a thin line. With a shade of sadness in her voice that she could not quite hide she said, "You really have lost all recollection."

Smoothing her dress again, she regained her regal composure. "We are in Maine. More specifically, the Allagash wilderness. It is October twenty-eighth. Your family knows of your circumstances and would like for you to accept our care for the time being. It is important you understand why. Please let me try and explain."

I gave Adriel a simple nod and she began once again.

"We are Radiants. Immortals who thrive upon radiant energy—light. We draw power from light and it makes us incredibly strong. It also enables us to manipulate energy." She flicked her hand towards the fire and it roared as if doused with lighter fluid.

"You are a Radiant, yourself. Each of us possess an inner light. It is the wellspring of our powers, of our essential self. You could think of it as a soul.

"Those we fight, the Shadows, are our essential antithesis. Whereas we carry within us light, they house a sinister darkness at the core of their very being. The *umbra*.

"Somehow, you were attacked in a vicious enough manner that your light was drained. With the absence of your light, the *umbra* was able to infect you. As I mentioned, normally for one such as ourselves, we cannot survive without our light, and therefore we could not become infected with the *umbra* because we would die before it had a chance to take hold.

"So you see, when you were attacked and your light drained, you should have perished. Yet somehow you survived. As a result, without your light, you were vulnerable to this infection.

"It also seems that as your light was drained, so too were your memories."

I couldn't stop from interrupting, Adriel. "What does this mean for me?"

Without moving from his relaxed stance by the hearth, Elijah interjected, "It means that Violet is dead, and we are being stupid and reckless by telling you any information. We need to accept the loss of one of our own and move on from it. We also need to

75

realize that we are now in the presence of a *nightwalker* and must treat her as a prisoner of war, not a long-lost Daughter of Light."

Adriel stood and the fury in her voice was chilling. "You will hold your tongue, or I will remove it from you."

Elijah pushed himself from the hearth where he had been leaning and took a step in Adriel's direction. "You are letting your emotions cloud your judgement. We have lost her. Violet is no more."

Adriel closed her eyes taking a deep breath, seeming to gain her composure. In an almost chiding tone she said, "You are the one who is being governed by your emotions. Because of the *Umbra Basium*, you now see her as a Shadow and nothing more. You need to look beyond your hatred and prejudice to see the situation for what it really is. We all felt the *Vinculum*, Elijah. We have felt its surges since you found her. The two of you are connected and for this we must do everything in our power to save her. And you, Elijah, are the only one who can. If for no other reason, do this out of a sense of duty for the survival of our people!"

Although she had begun her response to Elijah with a dignified composure, desperation saturated her last words.

And in hearing what she had to say, I was filled with unease. The last thing that I wanted was to depend on Elijah—for anything.

"It is a ruse." Elijah countered. "Can't you see that? This has all been orchestrated by the Shadow Court. It is a stratagem they have probably been working on for decades if not centuries or even millennia. And you are playing right into their hands. It's the perfect set-up. They've found a way to make her one of their own. Then they send her back to us and we welcome her with open arms. Now they have someone working from the inside to take us all down for good."

"That is a possibility, I will grant you. But she is the last chance we have. The two of you are! If there is even the slightest hope...You must take her to see the Oracle."

Elijah looked incredulous at her last words. "The Oracle?! She rarely grants a petition for audience. And when she does, most don't survive it. Or if they do, they go mad, muttering nonsense and clawing at their eyes. And while that would probably be a fitting outcome for a Shadow, we would have to be granted passage into Aleece to begin with."

Adriel's spine straightened and her gaze was steel. She pointed a finger at me. "*She* will survive it. And she will be healed. You will play your part in the role. This will happen."

The argument between Elijah and Adriel was interrupted by a loud snore. G had fallen asleep where he sat.

"Giddeon Alexander, commander of the Warrior Class and leader of the Archangels, you will rise and attend to your duties!"

At Adriel's command, G let out another snore, still deep in sleep.

"G!" she yelled.

G sprang from his chair in a blaze of light withdrawing a sword of fire, luminescent wings splayed behind him eating up the space of the small room. He was an awe-inspiring vision of light and power.

G scanned the room before realizing there was no threat. The light emanating from him distinguished as he sheathed his sword with a sheepish look.

"I guess I dozed off there."

"I'm sorry. Were we boring you?" Adriel asked with ice frosting each word.

G rubbed the back of his neck. His sculpted arms and chest flexed and strained against the fabric of his shirt. "Cut me some slack, Adriel. It's been a rough few days with all this drama," he gestured towards me and I felt my cheeks heat in embarrassment. "And you and the council in an uproar—Everyone's going nuts and us working stiffs haven't had a break."

Again, Adriel seemed to be grasping for self-control and I had a feeling that she was not used to it being tested. "Perhaps you could escort Violet into the kitchen for some coffee and something to eat as Elijah and I need a few moments for discussion. If that is not too much of a burden for you," she added.

"Yeah, sure. Come on babydoll. Some you and me time will be fun."

I stood from the couch and looked straight at Adriel. "Actually, I'd like to stay."

She returned my look with genuine sympathy. "My dear, I understand we have done very little if anything to clear things up for you and that you are probably more confused now than when you arrived. But Elijah and I must figure some things out before we can properly help you. You have my word that we are going to do everything we can to make things right. I promise I will find a way to fix this situation. Just give us a little time."

G walked over to me, putting his arm around my shoulder. "Come on. If you're a good girl, I might let you touch my abs."

I gave G a half-hearted smile in acknowledgment of his flirty attempt to lighten the mood. But Elijah let out an angry growl.

G turned me around and I let him. As he led me towards the kitchen, he slid his arm down my back, extremely close to my ass, and gave my hip a little pat.

With a crash of thunder and a violent streak of lightning that rocked the cottage, G and Elijah slammed to the floor in an aggressive testosterone fueled brawl on the pristine hardwood. Although the commotion happened faster than I could track, it was obvious Elijah had launched himself at G. I was just surprised that I hadn't been dragged down in the scuffle.

"Enough!" Adriel's voice boomed, echoing through the cabin. She stood motioning her hands in opposing directions as if wrenching apart magnets. Elijah and G went sprawling in two different directions on the floor. G's body slammed into a small decorative table, pulverizing the thing, while Elijah crashed into the wall leaving a gaping hole in the plaster.

G stood up, brushing himself off. "Idiot," he mumbled, as he stalked off down the hall.

Elijah had pulled himself up into a sitting position with his forearms resting on his bent knees, head hanging down. I waited for him to look at me. I didn't know what I was hoping for, but I needed something from him in that moment.

"I'm sorry about all this dear," Adriel said. "If you don't mind following Giddeon..."

I lingered for one moment longer, hoping for something that would not come. Then I gave her a nod, realizing I didn't have much choice in the matter, and left to find G.

CHAPTER 9

L IKE THE REST OF THE COTTAGE, the kitchen was alight with candles and a fire burning in yet another fireplace. It was quaint but modern. G collected two coffee mugs and poured us each a steaming cup from an old-fashioned coffee pot sitting on a metal rack over the fire.

I stood by the island counter with my arms wrapped around my waist feeling cold despite the warm fire.

"Look," G said, handing me a mug, "those two out there would probably piss their pants if they knew I was telling you this, but Adriel is extremely powerful and connected, not to mention tenacious. She will get you sorted out. About that I have no doubt. Just hang in there. You're going through a rough patch but believe me, you'll bounce back."

He took a sip from his mug. "Fuck me, that's hot!" He went over and placed the mug in the freezer grumbling the whole way over about how stupid is was to leave coffee sitting over an open fire.

"It's not Adriel I'm worried about," I confessed to him as he turned back.

"Yeah I get it. Eli is such a grumpy bastard. Not to mention an incredible bore. That guy never wants to have any fun. But here's the thing. I give him a hard time and really try to ruffle his feathers 'cause I get a kick out of it, but he's actually a good guy. He'll come around."

"Does it even matter if he does? I mean, do we really have to have anything to do with each other from here on out? If I have any say in things, I'd rather not see him again."

G let out a heavy exhale. "I'm sorry babydoll, but I've got some bad news for you. This nastiness you got crawling up inside you? It's nasty shit. I mean, it's like the worst thing that could ever happen to you. Seriously. And the only reason that you haven't turned into something that would scare the shit out of all of us is because of that grumpy bastard out there."

"Why?" I heard the fear in my question and struggled to keep my composure. I did not want to depend on Elijah for anything. Not for one minute more. Now that I had met Adriel, I was hopeful that she could help me from here on out and Elijah could go off and make someone else's life miserable.

G came forward until he was standing right in front of me. He took the untouched coffee mug from my grasp and set it on the kitchen island. Then he stepped right into my personal space, looking down at me with such intensity.

The sharp blue of his eyes reminded me of sapphires. And being so close to him, I couldn't help but admire his flawlessly

82

chiseled features. He was the perfect mix of masculinity, gorgeousness, and charming charisma. His towering height and broad chest made me feel diminutive standing next to him.

He reached up and cupped my cheek with his large hand. Although I couldn't help but appreciate and admire his physical appeal, he was making me nervous.

"Violet?" His deep voice was a soft caress and it made me...*uncomfortable*.

I had to clear my throat before I could answer him. "Yes?"

"Do you want to kiss me?"

I paused, looking at his firm perfect lips. "Not exactly. Actually, I would appreciate it if you would give me a little space," I told him in all honesty.

"Dude, what's wrong with you?" he said as he dropped his hand and gave me a light push. The intensity was gone, replaced by his good-natured light-heartedness. "You should be throwing your panties at me. I have to bat women away with a stick."

I knew he was joking (although probably serious too) but he made a good point. Why wasn't I attracted to him in the slightest bit? He was tall and strong, gorgeous, fun and charming. Plus, he had actually been nice to me.

"I bet you've wanted to throw your panties at my boy Eli. I wouldn't be surprised if he's got them in his pocket right now."

I opened my mouth, ready to tell him how wrong he was, but he cut me off.

"Don't even try to deny it. You two are connected and unfortunately it's not something you can hide."

"He tried to kill me! How's that for connected?" I was outraged. It was one thing for me to sense the bond I had with

83

Elijah, but it was entirely upsetting to have someone else confirm the existence of it. Out loud. For the second time in five minutes.

"Lots of relationships start off rocky," was G's breezy response.

I was beginning to see why Elijah didn't care for G's flippant nature. My aggravation must have shown because G wrapped his heavy arm around my shoulders, pulling me into his side. "Sorry. It's the way I deal with things. When you've been alive for as long as I have, you have to find the humor in life or you'll go crazy."

"How old are you?"

He released me and grabbed a few cookies from a plate that sat in the middle of the kitchen island. "Ancient. It's not important. Here's the point. That bond you have with Eli is keeping you connected to the light.

"Think of it this way. You're in a forest at night. You're surrounded by ravenous wolves hell bent on making you their dinner, and the only thing keeping you from being devoured is a weak, sputtering ring of fire around the perimeter of your camp. The wolves are the *Umbra Basium* and the fire is your connection to Eli.

"So yeah. For as unhappy as it makes you, you need that asshole. And if I were you, I would stoke that fire."

"He wants nothing to do with me. He has made it abundantly clear that he loathes me."

"It's a two-way street, baby doll. For as much as you need Eli, he needs you too. The connection you two have is a supernatural one. Don't ask me to explain it, because I don't know the details of it. All I know is that because of the force of the *Vinculum*, Eli is going to have every instinct and cell in his body screaming at him

84

to protect you, possess you, and make you his in every way possible.

"And before you go whining about him trying to kill you, let me spell out the obvious. He's not perfect. That boy out there has some major issues when it comes to Shadow kind. I don't know why or where his hatred stems from, but it's intense and goes way beyond a general ill will towards the enemy. This war between our races is deeply personal for him. So just as the past couple days have been confusing for you, take a moment to consider how confusing it has all been for that grumpy bastard."

"Are you kidding me?" I almost shrieked. "I don't feel sorry for him. Not for one second."

"And I'm not saying you should. Don't get me wrong. I'm not trying to make excuses for him. I just want you to understand *why* things are happening the way they are. Which is why I've shared as much as I have with you. I think you have a right to know. *And* I have complete faith that you are going to recover from all this."

I fought the urge to beg him to tell me everything. "Thank you, G." And I meant it. He had been decent to me. Making me feel like I belonged. Making me feel like everything was going to be okay. And trusting in me enough to provide some explanation, no matter how small.

"Maybe this infection is going away on its own. Aside from the memory loss, I'm feeling much better."

"Have you been listening to anything I've said? It's because of Elijah, dumb-dumb."

I scowled and charged on. "What about my family? Is there someone I should be contacting? Parents or siblings?" I looked at the ring on my hand. "Or a significant other?"

G reached into the fridge to grab a carton of milk and poured himself a glass. "Yeah, I don't know about that. I've already told you way more than Adriel or Eli would have wanted me to. That personal info shit is their call to make."

I didn't bother pressing the issue or asking him why. It was clear from the misgivings Elijah had voiced that they didn't trust me. I guess I couldn't blame them. What reassurance did they have that I hadn't become some spy or whatever? I didn't even know myself.

Music started playing and a deep man's voice sang something about miracles and being sexy.

G pulled out the latest smartphone from his pocket and looked at the screen. "Oh shit. Do you mind if I take this?"

I began to tell him no, but before I could finish the word, he just disappeared into thin air. I looked around the kitchen, confused. When moment by moment passed and he didn't come back, I began to get antsy. Just as I was about to go back into the living room and check on the progress of the discussion out there, Elijah came barreling into the kitchen.

"Where's G?" he demanded.

"I don't know. He got a phone call and just vanished."

"Get your coat. We're leaving."

"What? Why? Where's Adriel?"

He grabbed my arm and began to pull me out of the kitchen.

"Elijah!" I tried to twist out of his grasp as he took me through the cottage. "Let go of me. I'll come with you. You don't need to drag me around."

Completely ignoring me, he shoved me into the guest room. "Put on your coat."

"If you put your hands on me again, I will defend myself," I told him simply and calmly. "I still don't know what is going on here and I am upset that I am not getting any answers. However, I am willing to cooperate with you. There is no need for you to put your hands on me. You do not need to drag and shove me. You *do* need to exercise some simple common courtesy.

"I don't care that you don't like me. Guess what? I don't like you either. But I am willing to suffer your company and if you would like me to continue to cooperate with you, I suggest you do the same."

I was feeling pretty smug about my high-handed speech. I was certain Elijah must be feeling ashamed of himself right about now seeing how I had taken the high road and he was acting so indecently.

I crossed my arms over my chest and raised a brow waiting for his apology or at the very least a conciliatory concession.

Instead that bastard of a brute laughed at me. "Who the fuck do you think I am? Your boyfriend? Get your coat and move your ass or I'll move it for you."

CHAPTER 10

YOU'VE GOT TO BE KIDDING ME." I was walking through the dark woods behind Adriel's house with Elijah. The snow was up to my calves, and it was continuing to fall. "Can't we take your super-secret tunnel or something?"

"No." Elijah did not slow from his vigorous pace to answer me. He didn't even turn his head back in my direction. I was practically jogging to keep up with him.

"You are just the most crotchety, grumpy old man. Aren't you?" I asked him.

This time he didn't even bother with a sharp reply, he just kept plowing through the snow, his powerful legs having no problem covering distance in the virgin powder.

"How do you know where you're going? It's so dark out here." I sounded whiny even to myself, but I didn't care. I wanted to irritate him. I figured if I annoyed him enough, he might decide to slow down and talk to me just to get me off his back.

He finally stopped and turned around, looming over me. His cheeks were ruddy from the freezing temperature and his breath came out in wispy puffs. His voice was steely. "Well you should enjoy yourself then."

I stopped in my tracks. I knew exactly what he meant. It hurt. He was referencing the darkness I had been infected with. And he was purposefully using it against me. Trying to slash at me with it. It was true what G had said. Elijah had a seething hatred of these Shadow people and he was determined to punish me for it.

"What did they do to you?"

"What do you mean?" he snapped at me.

"They must have done something awful to you, for you to want to hurt me the way you do."

His hand flashed from his side and he was gripping my chin, tilting my face up to his. He was only inches away, and his voice was a quiet growl. "You do not talk about things you don't understand. You have no right to ask me questions."

Although he was being aggressive, the instant he made contact with my skin I felt that undeniable pull of attraction to him. It was something greater than my will, and I knew he felt it too. If I had my choice, I would punch him in the face for being such an asshole to me.

Instead, I stepped right into his body, so we were flush against each other. Even through our clothes and coats, I could feel his heat. I felt a similar rush of heat pour out from my own skin.

90

"Goddammit!" he yelled as he released his grip from my face. He stumbled back from me in a hurry before losing control and falling on his ass.

And I finally understood. I finally knew how to handle him. I smiled down at big bad Elijah. "You're going to start answering some questions for me, and you're going to be very nice about it or I'm going to strip off every single piece of my clothing and throw myself all over you."

Elijah's eyes flared with heat at my words. We had a little battle of wills as we stared at each other, neither of us speaking. I knew I had won when Elijah finally tore his lust filled gaze away from mine.

It was so simple. Whatever this sexual compulsion was between us, it was so strong and so base that it overrode any emotions we held towards each other. Regardless of the fact that Elijah hated what I was, and regardless of the fact that I thought he was a deplorable excuse for a man, we were on a razor's edge of self-control. And I was not above using that fact as a weapon.

I threw my shoulders back, notched my chin up and continued in the direction we had been heading without sparing Elijah a second glance. After a pause, I heard him utter a curse and then draw himself up to continue behind me.

Although the woods were as dark as they could be at night, I realized I had excellent vision. It was no problem to navigate around trees and over fallen branches. I also found that I didn't feel frightened in the dark woods, instead I felt an easy peace. Gentle snowflakes fell from the sky and drifted across the thick powder covering the ground before settling in.

Elijah had caught up to me. Of course, he was making sure to walk a step ahead of me so that he was the one leading.

"Where are we going?" I asked him.

"I can't tell you. In fact, you shouldn't even be allowed to see any of this. If I had it my way you'd be unconscious and blindfolded, but Adriel forbade it."

"And you always do what Adriel tells you?"

Although Elijah made no response, I felt an emotional flinch in the air. I had struck a nerve.

"How do you know her anyway?"

"How do you expect me to answer these questions?"

I fell silent. I was hurt. To Elijah, I was the enemy. I understood the *logic* behind why he didn't want to tell me any important or useful information, but emotions are not ruled by logic. G had made me feel like I had someone on my side. I needed that so desperately right now.

We continued on in silence for a time. But when we approached a particularly large tree that had fallen across our path, Elijah placed his hands on each side of my waist to lift me over. He was *gentle*, and I realized it was an apology of sorts.

"We're going somewhere more secure. It's the only place Adriel and I could agree on," he said as we cleared the trunk.

"Adriel's place wasn't safe?" I asked concerned about her.

Elijah gave a humorless laugh. "No, Adriel's cottage is safe— for Adriel. She's incredibly powerful so she only needs certain types of safety nets in place. Where we're going, it's both a stronghold for keeping all types of individuals out as well as keeping them in."

Despite how warm the vigorous walk had made me, I felt a chill creep down my spine. "Are you planning on locking me up somewhere?"

Elijah met my eyes and said, "If it becomes necessary."

Well, I reasoned, at least it wasn't a flat out, *Yes, absofuckinglutely I am!*

"Why are we walking? Are we going to walk the whole way there?" I asked.

"Adriel had to go on ahead without us to get things prepared. She had a vehicle, and a driver left with her. We had the option to wait for another vehicle to pick us up or walk. I chose walk. We should be there in about an hour."

I was about to ask him why he chose to walk, but I realized I was actually enjoying the crisp air, the gently falling snow, and the silence of the sleeping trees. It also dawned on me that it wasn't all that difficult to walk through the deep snow. My legs were powerful. Whatever weakness had been affecting me at Elijah's cabin was gone.

Elijah seemed to be enjoying the walk as well. The churning animosity and contradiction between lust and revulsion were still there, but I had a strong inclination that, for the moment, he was also feeling a sense of peace. With his height and build and the strong angles of his face, he looked like he belonged out in the woods. He had set his pace to match mine and we were walking side by side now.

I pulled my hand out of my pocket to sweep a lock of hair back from my face and the large black diamond on my ring finger sparkled in the moonlight. I held my hand out in front of my face to inspect the stone and was mesmerized by it.

There was something otherworldly about it. Although it was a black stone, it had a kind of inner luminescence that caused it to sparkle and shine, even in the darkness.

"Do you know if I'm married?" I asked Elijah.

I could feel the anger surge through Elijah. At the same time the air around us charged and the hairs on the back of my neck stood on end. A bolt of lightning struck a tree about thirty feet from us. The tree snapped and fell to the ground, smoking.

I didn't bother asking Elijah if he had been the cause of the lightning. It was obvious he had. We both stopped in our tracks. He turned to face me breathing deeply. His massive body jerked with each inhalation. The gold in his eyes was glowing and his entire body was rigid. When he finally spoke, his voice sent chills down my spine.

"Never ask me about that disgusting piece of rock. If you flash it in my face again, I'll remove it from you with the finger still attached."

I was genuinely scared. I didn't want to provoke him any further. I put my hand back in my pocket and nodded.

I angled my body away from his and pretended to be deeply engrossed in the woods around us as Elijah took a minute to calm down.

He started walking again without a word, and I kept a good ten feet between us as I followed along. Neither of us spoke for a while.

After trailing behind Elijah for some time, I realized that we were being followed. I could hear the faint crunch of snow not too far behind. I estimated our tail was approximately fifty feet back.

I couldn't even revel in the fact that I had amazing hearing because instinct took over and I went into a kind of autopilot.

As we passed a tree with a large trunk, I slipped against it instead of continuing on. In doing so, I hid myself from view of the person behind us. I was as silent as the night air, and not even Elijah realized I had stopped as he continued marching forward.

I waited, and just as the individual passed the tree I was pressed against, I gripped his arm and wrenched it behind his back. I used the force of his own momentum to push him face first into the snow and press my knee into his spleen.

Before his face hit the ground though, I locked my free arm around his throat. With my weight on his lower back and my arm around his neck pulling backwards, he was caught in an excruciating hold as I was bending his spine the wrong way. He was completely immobilized, and since I was cutting off his windpipe he couldn't make a peep.

"Elijah!" I called out.

Elijah stopped and turned around. Once he spotted my captive and me, he began to run towards us. As he got close he slowed before stopping completely. He took one good look at me, one good look at my captive, and his face screwed up in puzzlement.

Then he threw his head back and began to...*laugh*.

I was caught so off guard by Elijah's reaction that I let my grip relax just a fraction, but it was all my captive needed to throw me off balance. He shot to his feet and slammed me against the tree trunk.

The wind was knocked out of me and I was pissed that the guy had gotten the upper hand. I looked up about to launch myself straight at him, and instead of seeing a captive, there was G brushing the snow off the front of his clothes and massaging his neck.

"G. I...I'm...I'm sorry, I didn't realize..." I was fumbling for words. I didn't know what to say.

"It's cool. We're all good," G said. "It's nice to see you're getting your strength back," he added dryly.

"What the hell happened?" Elijah demanded.

"She jumped me!" G blamed, pointing a finger at me.

Elijah pinched the bridge of his nose. "You can't be serious."

"It's true! She's like some little forest ninja."

Elijah shook his head. "Maybe you shouldn't be walking the woods unaccompanied anymore. I'll see about putting in a request for a personal bodyguard for you as soon as we're inside the palace, maybe one of the kids graduating from The Queen's Guard."

Although Elijah sounded serious, it was obvious that his comments were taunting.

G didn't get in a huff or try to engage with Elijah in some verbal retaliation. Instead he casually tossed over his shoulder, "Yeah, maybe." Then he put his arm around me and pulled me into his side. "You alright baby doll? I didn't bruise that gorgeous porcelain skin of yours, did I?"

All ribbing from Elijah stopped and he let out a low growl. I realized this was G's way of cutting Elijah off from the teasing comments. It worked like nothing else could have. Elijah had admitted that he felt possessive of me when we had been in the tunnels earlier, and G knew it.

"Let me help you the rest of the way," G said ever so sweetly as he held me tight against his side and ushered me forward.

Elijah let out a frustrated grunt and turned to continue on without us.

I looked up at G. "We made him mad."

G smiled down at me. "We sure did." He held up his hand for a high five.

After I met his palm with my own, I had to get some explanation of what had just happened. "How did I do that?!"

"Yeah, what the hell was that?" G asked.

"I don't know. I didn't even think about any of it. It just happened."

"Don't go off getting a fat head about it. You did catch me off guard. I wasn't exactly expecting that you would jump me." G gave another exaggerated rub of his neck. "Dude. Just what went on in your little world before it all went dark?"

I set my jaw. "I don't know, G. But I'm going to find out."

G gave me a little nudge. "Come on. Let's go catch up to the grumpy bastard. We'll walk along in stony silence and make his day."

G and I followed behind Elijah. I was on an adrenaline high. I had just kicked ass like nobody's business. I was floored. After everything that had happened to me over the last day, after the onslaught of victimized feelings, after feeling so weak and lost, I finally had a taste of empowerment.

I was still in the dark, and I was still scared, but I could now see the tiniest pinprick of light. Learning something about myself—no—not just learning but actually experiencing a facet of myself gave me hope of discovering more.

I now had a sense of determination. I was going to reclaim who I was. And I was going to do whatever I had to, to make that happen. I was a fighter—and apparently a damn good one.

However, I didn't get to revel in my newly uncovered talents for long. Elijah soon stopped at the base of a large tree. He held his palm against the tree, and I could see a glow of light between his palm and the bark for a moment. Then there was a heavy creak and Elijah released his hand. He grasped the trunk, and to my surprise, a section swung open.

Elijah motioned for G to pass through before directing his hard gaze at me. The muscles in his jaw flexed, and at first I didn't think he was going to say anything. But then he jerked his head to the side and growled, "Follow G."

I didn't hesitate and passed through the trunk. There were steep stairs that caused us to descend rapidly. Although there were no lights, I was able to make my way down without needing to pause. Elijah was following behind me, and I assumed that he had somehow shut the *doorway* of the tree trunk.

At the bottom of the stairs G held his palm to a torch and flames sprang to life. All along the stone wall of the tunnel torches flared, one after another.

We were in a narrow passageway with a dirt floor. It was cold, damp, and dank as one might expect an underground passageway to be.

I sensed something up ahead and became uneasy. I took an involuntary step back which caused me to bump into Elijah. He grabbed my upper arms to steady me but withdrew his hands as soon as I was balanced.

I turned around to face him and I knew my expression was desperate. I grasped the front of his jacket.

"Please, I don't want to go through there. Please, Elijah. *Please*. Can't I go another way?"

Elijah's jaw was tight when he responded. "It won't be the same as last time. You won't feel anything going through."

I didn't believe him. When he had taken me through the veil of light in the tunnel system, part of me enjoyed it. But there was the other part of me that had felt excruciating pain. I would do whatever I could to avoid experiencing that pain again. And I could sense without a doubt there was another veil of that same light a little way down the tunnel. Although I didn't see it yet, I knew it was blocking our path.

"Please, Elijah." I grasped his coat tighter. "I can't go through it."

He grabbed my hands and forced me to let go of him. His face darkened. "You'll be fine. G will take you through."

I glanced behind me to look a G, but he was gone. He had continued down the passageway without us.

I turned back to Elijah. "What does that matter. I don't care who takes me through. I don't want to go."

Elijah was gruff with his words. "You don't understand. G will be able to take you through and you won't feel anything."

"How do you know that?"

Elijah's control started to slip and his volume began to rise. "Because he's made of the damn stuff. He's essentially the same pure damn energy as the veil. Okay? He can take you through and manipulate it. He can protect you from feeling anything unpleasant. He can take you through."

Clearly Elijah didn't like the fact that G was my hero in this situation.

"But if he's made from the '*damn stuff*', then why haven't I been in pain when I'm around him?" I had barely finished my sentence before Elijah began cutting me off.

He ran his hands through his hair, on his last straw. "Did you hear what I just said? He can manipulate it. Control it. Although you've been around him, he hasn't let it touch you. Now come on." He grabbed my hand and pulled me forward.

We passed a bend in the passageway and G was around the corner waiting for us. Elijah just continued on. I stopped next to G and looked up at him.

"Come on. Let's go." G took a step in front of me. He squatted slightly and patted his back. "Let papa G give you a ride."

I hesitated. I didn't care what Elijah said. I was not going through another veil. I was about to turn around, leave this godforsaken tunnel, and go my own way. I didn't need this bullshit. If G tried to stop me, I would just kick his ass again.

But then I thought about what I had done. How I had taken down someone twice my size. I may not remember any of the details about myself, but I now knew I was someone to be reckoned with. Adriel had said I was strong. She was right. It hadn't merely been a pep talk.

These people knew things about me. If I left now, I might never know who I truly was. Perhaps G was right; perhaps I needed Elijah. But even if I didn't, even if it was a lie to keep me agreeable, Elijah, Adriel, and G were all keys to uncovering my past.

And I planned on using every tool available to me.

I accepted the lift G offered and let him hoist me onto his back.

"Take me to the other side," I told him. "I'm ready."

CHAPTER 11

OUR FINAL DESTINATION WAS not what I expected at all. It was a large mansion. I hadn't seen the facade of the building since we arrived through an underground passageway, but I could tell from the interior that we were in a huge structure.

It seemed to be an old building with ancient looking stone walls, however everything else—the hardwood floors, large windows and French doors—were all modern, as were the stylish and elegant furnishings.

The thing which was most strange was the fact that rivulets of rain streamed down the oversized, uncovered windows. It had been snowing in the woods on our walk from Adriel's cottage. Although the last portion of our walk had been underground, we couldn't have traveled more than a mile and a half through the subterranean passageway. The gnashing rain was accompanied by bouts of violent thunder and lightning.

And of course, just like Elijah's cabin and Adriel's cottage, the mansion was lit with only firelight. Although we didn't walk through each room, the majority lining the massive hall had their double doors open and I was able to peer in as we passed by. Crystal chandeliers hung from the ceilings, setting the place aglow with candlelight. Sconces lined the walls, and at least one giant fireplace graced each room.

Elijah and G flanked my sides as we walked down the cavernous main hallway. I looked over at G. "It was snowing at Adriel's cottage and in the woods just outside. Did we pass through another type of portal like the one outside Adriel's place?"

"Giddeon," Elijah said warningly.

And that's when G lost it. "Holy crap. Cool your jets, man. I wasn't going to tell her anything important. Dude. I'm sick of your bullshit. I'm like thousands of years older than you. Plus, I'm a fucking archangel. Show a little respect, man. Where do you get off chastising me like I'm a little kid? Chill. You know we really have to make an appointment for you to have the Court's physician surgically remove that stick from your ass."

G stopped walking and took my hand in his. "Sorry, babydoll. If I don't take a break from this guy, I'm going to lose my shit." G gestured to the grand staircase ahead of us. "Your room is just a few flights up. Hopefully, this asshole can show you to it without being a total dick. I'll be back to check on you later. Okay?"

G gave me a quick hug and then turned to Elijah. "Don't screw everything up," he told him and with that, he vanished.

I suddenly felt colder. G was such a warm presence. I instantly wanted him back. He had been a raft, helping to keep me afloat.

But it looked like I was going to have to tread water on my own for a while.

I looked up at Elijah and his jaw was tight. A muscle ticked under his eye before he began to charge forward again. And, as seemed to be our way, I went scuffling after him.

We climbed three floors before Elijah led me down a hallway of closed doors. When we paused in front of the last one, I was genuinely hoping there was a bed with my name on it on the other side. I was emotionally and physically exhausted.

After opening the door, Elijah passed through without a backward glance. I stepped in after him, noticing that the room was dim with a small fire burning in the hearth. This room too, had large uncovered windows which held the violent storm on display, but the fire was cozy and gave off little pops and cracks.

Without warning, Elijah abruptly turned to face me. The gold flecks in his eyes burned just as brightly as stars. He was breathing heavy and his fists were clenched. He seemed to be struggling with his self-control.

I was so startled I took a step back, knocking into the door and causing it to close. Elijah took a menacing step forward and I backed up again until I was pressed against the closed door.

In a rush, I became aware of the emotions pouring out of Elijah. A maddening jealousy overwhelmed him. When I had realized we were being followed in the woods, I had tuned everything out to focus on the approaching person, including Elijah. But now I was painfully aware of him.

In that moment, I realized that every touch, every hug, every interaction with G had driven Elijah crazy. I also realized that all the positive emotions I had felt towards G as well as my disappointment of him leaving, would have been evident to Elijah through the connection we shared. He had warned me earlier that he was feeling extremely possessive of me, but I hadn't gathered just how serious his feelings were.

Elijah took another step towards me with a murderous look in his eyes, and I held out a shaking hand. "Elijah," I used the same tone one probably would with a wild animal, "Now let's just take a minute and calm down."

His response was another angry step towards me.

I fumbled around behind my back trying to find the doorknob, but it was too late. He punched each of his fists into the door by my shoulders, caging me in.

He drew in one heaving breath for longer than the rest, smelling my hair, and a bolt of lust exploded from him, hitting me square in the chest. It was just as before. The uncontrollable need and want. I felt his desire and it fueled my own.

There was also the need to possess me. To make me his. Another man had touched me. Had embraced me. Had held my hand and won my affection.

Elijah's need to erase every trace of G was driving him mad.

And I...*liked* it.

No. No. That wasn't me. It wasn't me wanting to be wanted by Elijah. I tried to remind myself that I hated him. That he had tried to *kill* me. Whatever this connection was between us, I was being forced against my will to want him because of it.

But really, how senseless of me. How often does logic win when pitted against passion? I was a fool to try and reason with myself, even if just for a moment.

Between clenched teeth Elijah growled, "Take off your coat."

Without looking away from him, I reached up to the top button of my coat. But my hands were shaking too much, and it took me what seemed like a small eternity to finally undo it.

When I went to reach for the second button Elijah's hands flew to each side of the coat at the top of my chest, grabbing the material in his fists and giving me a good shake against the door.

He didn't utter a word, but then again, he didn't need to. His expression said it all.

Other males do not touch you.

He ripped the front of my coat open, buttons scattering across the hardwood floor. And Light help me, I arched against the door in response.

Then he turned me around so my chest was pressed into the door, my head turned to the side. He yanked my wrists together behind my back and held them captured there while he leaned into me so that his erection pressed into my ass. With his free hand, I heard him undo his own coat and drop it to the floor. Then he was pulling my coat down my shoulders and off my wrists letting it drop as well.

When he turned me around again, Elijah grasped my ass lifting me up and pressing me into the closed door so that my back banged against it. My legs wrapped around his waist and I rubbed my core against him.

"Take your sweater off." He snarled his words at me and it sent a shiver all the way down my spine.

I grabbed the hem of the sweater and pulled it over my head in one swift motion. He slammed me back against the door and my breasts bounced at the top of the bra I wore. Then he sucked at my neck, and I threw my head back to let him. He continued to lick and suck all along my neck from the tops of my breasts to the bottom of my jaw until I felt an aching slipperiness at my center.

I reached down to the collar of his shirt and yanked the two sides apart. I scratched my nails down his chest and he groaned. His arousal pressed into me and I tried to grind my hips against him.

With my legs still wrapped around him, Elijah took a couple long strides and tossed me onto the bed. Then he was on top of me, covering every inch of me with his big body. I reached down to undo the button on his pants when a bell rang in the room. Ignoring the ring, I freed the button, but the bell clanged a second time.

I looked up at Elijah. "What is that?" I breathed.

He looked down at me. The foggy lust cleared from his eyes and was replaced by shock.

"What? What's wrong?" I asked concerned by his sudden look of confusion.

That damn bell rang for a third time. "What the hell is that?!" I asked him. "And why the hell does it have to ring right now?"

He rolled off of me and reached to the side of the bed where his coat had landed. He pulled his phone from a pocket and turned it off.

And he just sat there on the edge of the bed with his back to me.

I also sat up and clutched one of the pillows to my chest. "Elijah?"

He said nothing and I glanced at the mirror on the bureau, trying to see his face.

But what drew my attention instead was my own reflection. Just as Elijah's eyes had glittered with light, so did mine. They did not glow as intensely as Elijah's and it was barely perceptible, but still, there was definitely a faint violet light radiating from my irises.

"It's Adriel. She's demanding to see me now." He got up from the bed, picked his jacket up from the floor, and buttoned it over his torn shirt. He turned around and took a step towards me. He looked like he was about to say something, but he stopped himself.

Instead he turned back towards the door and said, "This is your room for the night. I'll have someone bring you something to eat."

He gave me one quick glance over his shoulder before leaving. It was just a brief meeting of our eyes, but I saw it there.

Sad. Elijah was a very sad soul. I couldn't help but wonder why.

CHAPTER 12

*I*LOVED HIM. *I would love him in any lifetime. But he didn't find himself worthy and I was afraid he never would.*

I ran down a dark decrepit corridor. The scarlet gown I wore billowed behind me as I ran. The dank rotting wood of the door frames I passed looked as though they would crumble at any moment.

I had to find him, had to convince him, to show him. I had to save him. I was the only one who could and if I failed we would both be lost.

But there was no end to the hallway. No end to the dirt floor. The one door I searched for was nowhere to be found.

I stopped and willed myself not to pant. I strained to be quiet and still, searching for the sound.

There.

It was faint and very far off, but I could hear it. Lonely desolate notes from a piano.

I wouldn't give up. I would run until my heart exploded if I had to, but I would find the room with the piano.

A chill stirred the air behind me. I turned slowly and in the darkness of the corridor I saw that I was not alone. Inky shadows chased me.

I sent a flare of my own light in their direction before turning to run again, hungry whispers nipping at my heels.

I called his name. Again and again I called his name. But it was useless. He was no longer that person. Try as I might I hadn't been able to remind him of who he was.

A hand shot out and yanked me into a dark room. The decrepit door was slammed behind me, the shadows that chased me barred from entry. I stood where I was, breathing hard, unsure as to whether I had been safer out in the corridor with the shadows that hunted me or in this room with the one I had sought.

"Where are you?" I demanded.

No reply. But I felt the air stir behind me and a feather light touch skim my bare shoulder. I spun around but could see nothing.

"You should run from me," came the velvety purr from the darkness.

Chills ran down my spine at the sound of the voice and I swallowed thickly, throwing my shoulders back and lifting my chin.

"You know I won't." I tried for a stoic response, but my voice held a betraying waver.

At my ear, I felt his lips brush my lobe as he replied, "You can't save me."

One sinewy arm wrapped around my waist from behind and my back was pressed flush against his granite torso. His other arm snaked up to grab my chin and push it to the side, exposing the column of my neck.

The lethal strength in his grip was evident, latent power sitting there readily available just below the surface. His power was unlike any other's. His strength unparalleled. I doubted he was even aware of it. But I was. And in spite of his incredible strength, he held me with only a graceful firmness. I could break free if I chose to.

Instead I thrust my chin to the side even more, straining the tendons in my neck. It was an invitation and he was unable to deny his need.

With incalculable speed he struck, sucking at my pulse point and tapping into my essence. I was assailed with lustful need so raw my knees buckled. Somewhere in the deep recesses of my mind, my last coherent thought was about how wrong he was.

***

I awoke to a knock at my door the next morning and slipped into a robe that had been provided for me. It, along with pajamas and slippers, had been sent to my room with dinner the night before. Now a beautiful woman was standing in the hallway with a garment bag draped over her arm and a breakfast tray in her hands.

"Good morning," she said. Her voice was stunning. There was something melodious in it as if she was singing although she wasn't. It reminded me of the way G spoke, just much more feminine.

"I've got breakfast and clothes," she said as she passed into the room.

I assumed she meant for me. "Oh. Thank you," I said, uncertain.

The man who had brought up dinner and pajamas the night before had been stiff and formal, so I was a little thrown by this beautiful woman's personable demeanor.

She placed the tray down on the table in front of the fire. The fire was still the main source of light for the room since the dark storm continued on the other side of the window. It was incredibly odd how there was no change outside, just an unending storm in an unending night.

The woman plucked a bagel from the uncovered food tray, and then she flopped the garment bag down on the bed and perched herself right beside it.

I didn't know what to say or do so I just stood where I was, probably looking like an idiot.

The woman confirmed this suspicion when she said, "Well don't just stand there. Close the door and sit down to eat."

I didn't know what to do other than follow her instructions. When I sat down at the table I looked over at her. She had pale blond hair that swept down her shoulders and back with an unbelievable shine as well as luminescent, pearly skin. Her delicate bone features made her look sophisticated and elegant. She had an air of nonchalance and almost—boredom, even, that only heightened her aristocratic demeanor.

She looked to be in her twenties or early thirties. It was hard to tell exactly. Although she wore well fitted jeans and a button up blouse with the sleeves rolled just below her elbows, she still managed to look high society. With her tall, thin frame and the way she moved, I decided the word that best described her was willowy.

It struck me that she was familiar somehow. For a moment, excitement took over and I believed that I was remembering her from my past. Perhaps my memories were starting to return, and it would just be a matter of time before I reclaimed them all.

"I look familiar and you're trying to ascertain just where you know me from, right?" Her tone made it sound like this was the most boring conversation she had ever had.

I was a little embarrassed that my thoughts had been so transparent, and not to mention that I was boring the hell out of her, but I nodded at her comment while chewing a big bite of pancake.

"I have to wear the most dreadful robe when I'm working. It makes me look like a house. I mean really, there's no shape to it at all. Anyhow, just imagine me in an ugly, boxy robe saving your life from a lunatic about two nights ago. The name's Daphne."

I choked on the bite I was chewing and started to cough violently trying to hide the bits of pancake flying out of my mouth.

In spite of the fact that I was choking and spraying the table with crumbs, she just sat there daintily picking at her bagel and looking completely disinterested.

When I finally stopped coughing, and took a drink of orange juice, she said, "He really is such a brute. You certainly got the short end of the stick being paired with him."

"You mean Elijah?" I asked.

She looked at me like I was a moron. "Yes, darling. Elijah."

"How was I paired with him? What exactly is going on between us?"

She let out a bored sigh. "Oh, that's right. I'm not supposed to discuss these matters with you. Elijah was sure to make that very clear in that brutish manner of his. I mean really, I don't know what he's so afraid of. So what if it does turn out that you're up to some awful ploy with the Dark Ones. It's not as though you would be a serious threat to us. We handle all sorts of unsavory characters on a regular basis."

I had absolutely no idea whether I should be offended that she would *handle* me if I turned on them or relieved that she thought I should be let in on all this information that I was dying to get a hold of.

I decided to just overlook her comment completely. "Yes, he is difficult to deal with," I finally agreed.

"Yes, well, it's not your fault. It's something beyond your control."

"I don't understand any of it. How is it that we have this connection? The *Vinculum*."

"Does the how of it really matter? The fact is that you do."

"I don't want it," I told her.

"Well, no. I mean who would want to be stuck with Elijah?" She paused and tapped a long elegant finger on her plump lips. "He's a bit of a mystery, that one. You know he disappeared for a thousand years or so? Went off and hermited himself away somewhere." She shrugged her delicate shoulders. "It's no wonder he lacks interpersonal skills."

"What happened to him?" I asked, suddenly finding Elijah more interesting.

"No one knows. He was quite young at the time, probably still in his twenties. None of us knew what happened to him. And then after almost a thousand years he just reappeared at court one day a few months ago as if it was the most normal thing in the world. And he refuses to tell anyone where he was or what he was doing."

The fact that Elijah was so old, didn't really startle me. After G had made a comment about age at Adriel's cottage, I had wondered about Elijah. I also wondered if Daphne realized how much she was sharing with me, but I didn't dare point it out to her. I wanted to find out everything I could. No detail was too small or unimportant.

"How strange," I commented.

"Quite," she agreed.

"Do you know Giddeon?" I asked.

She made a strangled sound and I had no idea if it was and affirmation or a negation.

"He said Elijah's a good guy. But if Elijah's been gone the last thousand years, how can he attest to that?"

"These past few months Giddeon is the only one Elijah will tolerate. So Giddeon knows Elijah better than anyone else comparatively. It's not saying much, mind you, but it's something."

"But you don't care for him?"

A beautiful blush stained Daphne's cheeks, and her bored mien turned panicked.

"Giddeon's fine. I mean, I'm not saying he's *fine*. He's just…Nothing. I think nothing of him. We work together and that's all."

I smiled inwardly. Daphne was *flustered*. Over *G*. I didn't blame her. If I was normal and not wrapped up in this weird connection with Elijah, I'm sure I would have fawned over G too.

"I meant Elijah," I corrected.

The relief on Daphne's face was comical. "I am indifferent in regard to Elijah. Maybe somewhat intrigued. But as far as forming an opinion on him, I have nothing more to offer than he is a brute. Although..." she trailed off staring out the large window at the dark storm.

"Yes?" I said trying not to sound too eager.

"Well I guess I would be extremely grumpy if I hadn't passed on and was stuck as the *Prism*. So I'm not without sympathy for him."

"How so?" I baited, not wanting to outright ask what the Prism was or why one would *pass on*, but wanting her to continue talking.

"Well, I mean it's rather dreadful being the *Prism*, isn't it? Having only one fated mate? Not being able to be intimate or even have feelings for anyone else? Dreadful.

"Believe me, I know firsthand. Just as I was without the other half of my coupling when I was Prism so too has been Elijah. But I, at least, was able to pass on through the Light after my thousand years of service and become an archangel—which eases some of the emptiness, albeit not nearly enough.

"Elijah, though, hasn't passed on. It's been quite a scandal among the archangels. Here he comes returned after an almost thousand-year absence. We find out he's alive after all this time, but he hasn't passed on. So very odd and unexpected. He's the first ever to not pass over. Quite a black mark.

"But then slowly the archangels all realize what this means. For the first time, there is both a male and female Prism. And my, you can imagine how that rankles. The rest of us have lived half an existence and yet Elijah of all people gets to have his counterpart. And as if that wasn't dramatic enough, he tries to end her life!

"So while he's a brute—without question—he is also causing quite an uproar and turning the Council upside down and inside out."

"And all of this is being kept from me!" I exploded. I felt a surge of anger erupt from inside my chest and an incredible charge crackled over my skin. A bolt of lightning struck just outside the window as the fire in the hearth flared dangerously, leaping a good foot out from the fireplace.

"And what the hell is a *Prism*?! And are you really telling me that I'm his *counterpart*?! Or is there someone else he has recently tried to kill as well?!"

I stormed to the door and flung it open. "Where is that son of a bitch? He can't keep all of this from me! I'm getting answers."

I had only taken three stomping steps out the door before Daphne appeared in front of me, ablaze in white light with radiant wings outstretched behind her filling the narrow hallway.

"Violet Archer, you will return to your quarters," she commanded.

I was in an angry, disturbed state and my negative emotions awoke the darkness that prowled deep within, the darkness they had told me I was infected with. It eagerly lapped at the anger, finding strength. It uncoiled and began to branch through my system. I let out an involuntary hiss.

Daphne's radiance, along with her wings, quickly extinguished.

"Oh shit." She backed up a step giving me some space. "Violet, I need you to rein it in."

I took a step towards her, narrowing my eyes at her. Eyes that I knew were now branched with black. The darkness iced my blood as it spread through my veins. Power. There was so much

119

dark power welling inside me just beckoning to be used. There was nothing I couldn't do with it.

"Please! I don't want to get Elijah. Just pull it back in."

I hissed at her and felt the darkness spread and flex around me. The air became icy and I reveled in the feel of it.

"This isn't you. You want to know who you are? This isn't it."

I took another step towards her. She was in my way. I was going to end her for it. And I would enjoy extinguishing the light she carried within.

This is what I had been needing. What I had been missing. With this power awakening—responding to my call—I would destroy them all. Those who had tried to control me, to manipulate me, all under the guise of *helping* me—they were obstacles easily disposed of.

They were *wary* of me. The fools. They should *cower* from me.

This pretty little angel backing away from me should have let Elijah take my head, because now I was going to end her.

"Think about it. Do you really want to hurt me right now? Please don't make me get Elijah. You know what an animal he is," she huffed.

I took one last deep breath, allowing the darkness to expand even more before striking out.

However, I didn't have a chance. I went hurtling down the hallway in a blast of scalding white light. I slammed onto my back and let out a moan of pure pain.

But it wasn't pure pain. Not entirely. The part of me that had been stuffed behind the expanding darkness, the part of me that had been my essential self a moment ago—that part of me basked in the light.

120

Daphne was standing above me. "Last chance, Violet. Either push it back or I'm getting Elijah. You're going to prove him right. He'll have you locked up. If any part of you wants to reclaim your life, you better take control."

She was...*right*, I realized. She was right. I didn't want to hurt her. I wanted answers. I wanted to know who I was. I wanted to remember. If I gave into the darkness that was trying to take over, I wasn't going to get the answers I sought.

I closed my eyes and took a deep breath, fighting the roiling dark energy. But it had spread too much, had gotten into my veins. I needed help. I needed Elijah.

I thought about him. I thought about the connection I had with him. And I was startled to find that I was actually able to pick up on a chord of his energy. He was somewhere here in the manor and I could feel him.

I drew on his strong bright frequency. I tugged until I felt it begin to saturate me. Elijah's energy began to recharge my own. And as my own internal radiance sparked, the darkness recoiled, retreating to the darkest recesses of my soul.

"You drew on him, didn't you?" Daphne asked in accusation.

I opened my eyes, feeling incredibly weak after our exchange. "I had to," I said defensively. "Why does it matter?"

"He's going to want to know why. He's going to know something was wrong."

I sat up. "Good," I told her. "Something is wrong. He owes me some major answers."

"Yes. Fine. Of course. But not now," she insisted helping me to my feet.

"He's here somewhere," I responded. "I'm finding him." And I was going to let him have it.

Daphne gave a distasteful look as she raked her gaze over me. "Really? Like that? You don't even want to get dressed and comb your hair before you go off to castrate Elijah?"

I looked down at myself and ran my hands through my hair. She was right. I was still in pajamas and a robe and my hair was a wild rat's nest from a fitful night's sleep.

"Fine. But I'm getting some answers!" I insisted, making my way back into the room.

Daphne ignored my comment as she followed in behind me asking, "Besides, don't you even want to see what I brought you?" She crossed to the bed and picked up the garment bag. With the barest hint of interest, she said, "I'm going to make you pretty."

I sighed. I had a feeling it was going to be a very long day.

CHAPTER 13

I FOUND MYSELF in a stylish and elegant parlor later that evening with a glass of champagne in my hand and a fervent desire to escape to my appointed bedroom as soon as possible. I didn't know whether the gathering was a meeting, a cocktail party, or some strange hybrid of the two, but whatever it was, it was a terse, uncomfortable situation.

I was in a tasteful navy cocktail dress that very successfully walked the line between classy and sexy. My legs were a mile long thanks to a combination of high heels and high hem. My curves and tiny waist were gracefully highlighted and all the while I appeared sophisticated as the high neckline and short sleeves of the garment compensated for the rest of my skin on display.

And I hated it.

Daphne had spent the day babysitting me. She had flat out admitted that was why she had been sent to see me. She refused to tell me any more about Elijah, myself, or the *Vinculum*. She just promised over and over again that we would discuss it tonight with Adriel.

It wasn't all bad, though. She had arranged for massages, haircuts, facials, manicures, pedicures, and lots of gossip magazines.

Finally, after she had my hair and makeup professionally done, she stuffed me into the designer dress and mile high heels. Of course, she had seemed bored to tears throughout the entire day, but overlooking that fact, she was actually very pleasant to be around and even kind of fun.

However, this part—this miserable gathering—was awful. I was incredibly uncomfortable both because of the tiny dress and painful heels I was packed into as well as the company I found myself in.

Daphne had told me that we would have a drink in the parlor before sitting down to dinner. But once we had entered the room, I realized she had forgotten to mention that others would be joining us.

G sat on an elegant sofa looking as comfortable as could be, leaning back with his large arms draping the couch back. Elijah was standing in a corner of the room with his arms crossed over his chest. The heartbreaker from the tunnel was pacing in front of the crackling fireplace.

And to the side of the fireplace stood a man I did not recognize. He wore the same type of white robe which Daphne had appeared in the night outside Elijah's cabin. As Daphne had been that night, this man was aglow with wings of light flaring behind him. He seemed to stand at attention in a rather detached sort of manner.

The instant we walked into the room, three pairs of eyes landed on us with such intensity, I thought I would stumble backwards from the impact. Elijah raked his gaze over me so possessively, I shivered. And the heartbreaker from the tunnel looked utterly concerned as well as relieved as he halted to a stop. G, however, was staring only at Daphne and he almost looked confused. The angel didn't bother with either of us. He just continued to stand at attention.

If Daphne noticed the look from G or was uncomfortable at all, she didn't show it.

"Evening, boys," she said as she crossed over to a tray of full champagne glasses set out on a sideboard. She gracefully lifted two and held one out for me. I didn't want the glass, but I also didn't want to be rude, so I was forced to cross the room and take it from her. I secretly cursed her the entire trip over as I tried to keep from falling in the massive heels I wore.

"So," she said to the room as a whole after handing me the glass, "what were we talking about?"

Elijah glared at her. The heartbreaker looked nonplused and G guffawed. Once he finally got his laughter under control, G said, "First I had to hear Eli and Killian bitch and moan over who should be where, to get to do what, to say what, to be in charge, to be the one protecting, blah blah blah. And then Cord, ever the life of the party, finally put an end to their cat fight with some old and stuffy council law business.

"So basically, I've been sitting here in painful silence with these two drama queens," he gestured to Elijah and the heartbreaker before nodding at the angel, "And the ice princess. Thank the

126

Light you ladies have arrived. I don't think I could have taken a minute more of it. But I almost forgot the best part—"

G broke out into uncontrollable laughter. "Did you see what they're wearing?!"

I had noticed the angel's robe, but I took a closer look at Elijah and the heartbreaker. Although the exact colors and cuts varied slightly, they were both dressed in dark well-tailored pants and a gray cashmere pullover that accentuated their sculpted physique. Either they had planned to dress as twins or they were victims of coincidence.

Despite how grouchy I was feeling, I had to hold back a laugh—as well as a sigh. G was so great to be around. He was giving us that brilliant smile of his. He looked so relaxed and comfortable. He exuded a sexy confidence. His expensive looking tailored black jacket and white collared shirt made him look like a movie star at a red-carpet event. He was just so dreamy.

A loud crack had us all looking in Elijah's direction. The back of a beautiful antique chair that had been sitting next to him had split down the middle where his hand rested. And he looked like he wanted to throttle me.

I made a note to myself that I needed to learn how to check my emotions when around him. Once again, he had picked up on my general feelings and once again it had enraged him.

G shook his head and gave an exaggerated eye roll.

Daphne held out her glass in Elijah's direction and toasted. "To your defeat of the furniture, Elijah. May you win many more battles before the night is through." Then she tossed back her glass, draining the champagne, before throwing it into the fireplace with a shatter. And of course, she did it all with the most blasé of attitudes.

The heartbreaker muttered, "You're all fucking crazy."

"Daphne, I'll thank you not to destroy my crystal." Adriel's stern reprimand was a surprise to us all. She had entered unnoticed during Daphne's sarcastic toast and now stood in front of the closed door.

G swung his thumb towards the corner where Elijah stood. "He started it."

"Giddeon, do you always remain seated when a lady enters?" Although Adriel seemed to be asking a genuine question, if you were paying attention, you could hear the ice underlying her words.

At that, G stood up and gave a slight bow. "My apologies." And of course, I found another thing to admire about him. He was so good natured that his apology seemed quite genuine.

When Adriel looked behind G to the heartbreaker, she frowned. "Killian, what are you doing here?" She turned to the stranger next. "And you, archangel. I did not send for you."

"I should be a part of this." Killian said. Unlike G, he clearly understood Adriel's preference for formality and added, "Lady of the Court," as he bowed his head. But before Adriel had a chance to respond, he continued, "As too should Davis. Why is he not here?"

"Killian, I understand this is difficult for you, but you go too far and assume too much. This is not your place."

"I respectfully disagree. I am her personal guard and while she is here, this is exactly my place. I have brought a council representative to enforce my position."

The angel was tall and broad just like G and Elijah with brown hair and golden skin, appearing in his mid-thirties. G had referred to him as *Cord* and I supposed that was his name. He finally broke his unmoving (and from what I could tell unblinking) stance to address Adriel.

"Lady of the Court, do you acknowledge this warrior as the girl's *senterium*?"

Adriel's features were pinched as she replied, "Yes."

"As her *senterium*, he is to be available to her. By law she is not to be kept from him while at court, and he is to have access of knowledge that concerns her safety and wellbeing. Must I remain here to enforce council law?"

"No. That will not be necessary."

With a single nod to Adriel, the angel disappeared.

My personal guard. I knew he was talking about me. I swayed where I stood, and Daphne grabbed my elbow. She took the glass of champagne from my hand, downed it in one graceful gulp, and then ushered me to sit. In spite of how light headed I was feeling, I still managed to notice that she sat me in a wingback chair away from G instead of the closer option which was next to him on the couch. Daphne then took the spot on the couch for herself.

Elijah growled, "Adriel. Get him out of here. Or I will personally remove him."

"Adriel. *Please.*" Killian's supplication was quiet. Although he only spoke two words, it was obvious that an entire history lay behind them and from the softening of Adriel's eyes, she knew that history all too well.

Adriel let out a defeated sigh and said, "You are not to speak unless spoken to." Then she turned to Elijah and looked pointedly at the spilt chair. "I will kindly ask you not to break my furniture, Elijah."

Elijah glowered but didn't respond.

I looked back at Killian and found him staring intently at me. It was so odd to have the knowledge that he had been a figure in my life but to have no recognition of him. Why would I have had a personal guard? And if he had been my personal guard, he probably had known me fairly well. I couldn't help but wonder what he would be able to tell me. I needed to keep tabs on him.

"If you are going to be joining us, Killian, you need to know that Violet is not well."

"She is the—"

"Killian!" Adriel's voice boomed through the room. "I have made a concession for you. Do not disrespect that. Say one more unsolicited word, and I will not only allow Elijah to escort you from this room but I will, in fact, assist him."

Although his eyes blazed, Killian nodded once.

"As I was saying, she is not well and has suffered a very severe and life-threatening illness. Along with becoming ill, she does not have any memories prior to two days ago. I'm sure you can understand that this is a confusing time for her. We are doing our best to try and discover what happened.

"However, since she cannot remember, it may take a while to get a timeline of events sorted. It will take some time for her to recuperate, as well. I do believe that it is possible for her to recover but we must take things slowly.

"We do not want to bombard her with information. It is possible that could have a negative effect. That is why we are not rushing into details about her life and why we are trying to let her gradually adjust and make a full recovery. She is safe and stable at the moment. And that is all that matters."

I assumed that Killian had not been told any of these details yet, as Adriel was taking the time to fill him in. And from the whole show with the angel, it seemed that Adriel had not wanted him to know. I wondered as to what kind of relationship Killian and I had had if he was willing to go to such extremes to be a part of this.

I also noticed that Adriel was being very vague with her explanation. She didn't mention the *Umbra Basium*. And she glossed over the fact that they were afraid I might turn on them.

Adriel turned to look at me then. "I can only imagine how difficult it is to be in her situation right now. But she is a strong individual."

Her last two sentences caught me off guard and I was touched. I gave her a tight smile, not sure how exactly to respond.

"Adriel, if I may?" Killian spoke up.

"Do not test my patience, Killian," Adriel warned.

He continued in spite of her cautioning. "I have some information that I think you should hear. It may be directly related to whatever has happened to the…to Violet."

The room became very quiet. All fidgeting, grumbling, and bored disinterest came to a halt.

Sounding like she was walking across a precarious old bridge, Adriel asked, "What is it?"

"She was there to take him out."

"What?"

"She went with the intention of assassinating the Dark Prince."

131

A collective burst of sighs, groans, and expletives filled the room.

"She said it was an opportunity to finally end the war. To take control of the Shadow House and find an accord under Radiant Rule."

"And you let her?" Elijah's angered outrage had him stalking up to Killian. G intervened by hopping over the back of the couch and stepping between the two men, placing a hand against Elijah's chest.

Killian's own anger fueled his response. "I tried to stop her. But she was going to do it regardless of what I or anyone else had to say. It's not as though you were around to do something about it. Why the hell are you here now?"

"You fucking idiot. You've destroyed her. She's ruined and it's all because of you. Your schoolboy crush had you so pussy whipped that you didn't even come close to doing your *job* of protecting her."

Killian's temper redlined and he lunged for Elijah. However, G was an impenetrable wall.

"You pompous asshole. I don't give a shit what you say about me, but you will not insult her like that."

Killian was right. Elijah's *ruined* comment had sparked a humiliation so thick, I choked on it. Dealing internally with the situation was difficult enough. But having my ruination verbalized to the full room was shaming.

"*Enough.*" Adriel's command boomed through the room filling every corner of it. "You will end this. Now."

Elijah and Killian stood there staring each other down. Killian was the one to look away first. He glanced my way and then retreated to the opposite side of the fireplace. G and Elijah remained standing where they were while Daphne was still on the couch generally looking bored and unconcerned throughout the whole ordeal.

I stayed put in my chair when all I really wanted to do was go somewhere private with Killian and hear everything he had to say. I was reeling with this turn of events. I now knew that I had gone someplace to try and assassinate a prince to end a war. Which was such an extreme, dramatic notion, that I found it difficult to take seriously.

The news didn't jar any memories either. It did, however, raise so many questions. If it was true, then where did I go? How did I get there? Who is the Dark Prince? What was my plan and where had it gone wrong? Or had it gone right? Was there a dead prince somewhere out there because of me?

Adriel took command of the room once again. "Killian," she didn't sound pleased at all, "we will speak in private. You are dismissed. Go directly to my office and wait for me there."

"I am staying with Violet and carrying out my duty."

Adriel was clearly flustered and losing her cool. She flung her arms up into the air exclaiming, "For Light's sake she isn't going anywhere. You. And I. Need. To. Talk."

Killian gave me an assessing look before gravely nodding and heading out.

"Daphne. Giddeon." She gave them a meaningful look without saying more. They both nodded as if understanding completely and stood to leave.

With one of his killer smiles, G extended his bent elbow in offering to Daphne. "Shall we?" She looked utterly taken aback before blushing and finally slipping her arm through his.

G looked back at me before the two of them left the room. "Don't worry. We'll get everything sorted out." He patted Daphne's hand. "There's nothing this girl can't do."

Daphne's eyes rounded in surprise at the compliment and her cheeks reddened even more. I almost wanted to laugh. I wasn't surprised in the slightest by G's flirting, but what was unexpected was Daphne's reaction to it.

Adriel turned back to me. "I'm sorry. I…I need to go and…" She had been distant, professional, and businesslike with me up until this point. But this news had her rattled and there was now a crack in her polished demeanor.

"What were you thinking!?" she exclaimed before turning on her heels and leaving.

CHAPTER 14

Violet's Playlist:
Over My Shoulder, Mika
Help Me, Maximilian Hecker
Cut, Plumb
I Wish I Was The Moon, Neko Case

ELIJAH AND I WERE ALONE IN THE PARLOR. As I sat on the plush chair, I looked out the floor to ceiling windows. Like Elijah's cabin and Adriel's cottage, I had noticed the windows in this place were numerous, large, and uncovered. The unending rain poured from a dark sky. Intermittent bouts of thunder rumbled in the distance and every now and then lightning cracked.

Despite the way the uncovered windows welcomed in the storm, it was warm in the parlor. The fire in the hearth was generous. It provided the room with light and heat. Still, I wished I was wrapped in a blanket. Things were happening so quickly. I felt like my only option was to hold on tight and observe while someone else was steering.

Elijah hadn't moved, but I knew he was still standing behind the couch. I could sense him there. Looking out of the windows, I asked, "Why?"

I knew he would understand. I didn't have to say more. We were connected. It wasn't that he could read my mind, thought for thought. But we were tuned into the same frequency.

Elijah walked over to the windows and also looked out into the storm with his back to me. "If you turn, it could be damaging information. You could use it against us."

"Do you really think that's going to happen?"

He shook his head and turned to face me. "No. Not while we're together."

Elijah stood there, studying me. The fire cast a flattering light on him. The strong features of his face were highlighted. The deeper shades of blond in his hair and stubble were accentuated and the powerful build of his frame was outlined by the backdrop of the towering window. He looked larger than life, standing there.

The pull was there too. It was always there. I had to constantly fight the urge I felt to go to him. To be next to him. To touch him.

He turned back to the window and I knew it was because he didn't want to look at me. "To let the sunlight in," he explained. "That's why there are so many windows. Why they are usually uncovered and oversized. It's to let in the light. And before you bother me with more of your questions—"

He was right. I was about to ask why that was.

"It's because the sunlight is our energy source. It's what fuels our power and recharges our inner light. We derive our strength from it."

"The storm…"

"It's been six days. With no break, no change. We don't know how long it will continue. I think whatever happened to you… we think it might all be connected."

"If you need the sun—"

"We're all a little weaker because of it, but we can go months before things get drastic. We'll have this resolved by then."

"Well, I can see why you're suspicious of me."

Elijah turned from the window to look back at me. I had surprised him.

"It makes sense. If I was near these Shadows and became infected with something, and at the same time all of you are weakened upon my cryptic return…well I can see how I seem suspicious. And I honestly can't say what happened, Elijah. All that I know is that I don't want to hurt you or anyone else that I've met. I just want my memories back. To know who I am."

I paused, unsure how to play my hand. Unsure how much to reveal, how much to push. During the day with Daphne, I had replayed and processed the details of what she had let slip. I had been so focused on the fact that I was an apparent threat to others, that I had not taken the time to consider who was a threat to me.

When I truly thought about it, I didn't know who *I* could trust. Information was being kept from me.

Why? Was it truly because of the dangers I could inflict upon these people? Or did more brew beneath the surface?

I had decided during the day that I would not outright question Elijah about what I had learned from Daphne. Instead I was going to begin collecting information. And every time I came across another puzzle piece I would tuck it away until I could see the complete picture. *Then* I would decide who I could trust.

I might have some supernatural connection to Elijah, but that didn't mean I had to trust him.

I needed him. I knew that. And my body wanted his, desperately. So I decided I would bide my time. And even if I couldn't stop myself from giving in to him physically, I didn't have to give in to him emotionally. I could use Elijah, just as I was sure he was using me.

I would not make the mistake of forgetting that Elijah had secrets. And out of anyone I had met thus far, he was the most adamant that I not be told my past.

Standing there in front of the window with the storm raging behind him, he gave me a measuring look before assessing everything about me. He started at my heels, worked his way up my crossed, bare legs, took in my hips, waist, and chest draped in the navy silk, before lingering at my neck. I took in a sharp breath, actually feeling the escalating lust brewing between us as crackling energy began to vibrate in the room.

When Elijah met my gaze again, I could see those golden sparks in his hazel eyes glowing like embers. He began to stalk towards me, the closer he came, the larger he grew until he was towering over my chair. His big body was all I could see any longer. Every inch of his massive shoulders, chest and arms was in front of me. I was forced to crane my head back to look up at him.

He leaned down, placing each hand on the arms of the chair until his face was at my neck. He inhaled deeply before brushing my ear with his lips and saying, "Then we're on the same page, princess."

He began to pull away, but I couldn't let him. I needed more of him. I grabbed the back of his neck and slipped my fingers into his hair, pressing my own face against his cheek.

Feeling him, smelling him, being close to him was essential. It was everything and the only thing I had to do in that moment. The energy between us intensified at the contact and I felt a bolt of it run straight to my core. I cried out as Elijah groaned.

"It's time for her to go." The words were grated, seething with anger.

Elijah and I both looked to the door. Killian was standing there, barely keeping himself from charging Elijah.

Elijah slowly and deliberately stood to his full height before stepping in front of the chair, blocking Killian's view of me.

"Leave now and I won't tear you apart in front of her." Elijah sounded deadly.

"She's coming with me. *Now*."

"Like hell, she is." Elijah took a step in Killian's direction and I grabbed his wrist. He turned to me, looking startled as though he had forgotten I was there.

I wasn't aware of what my touch was doing until he looked down at his wrist. There was a glow under my palm. It was the same way I had touched Elijah in his cabin the first night I woke there. As it had that night, the touch seemed to have a calming effect on him.

I stood and faced Elijah. "I should go."

Although he had calmed, he wasn't agreeable. "Not with him. I'll take you to your room."

"Elijah," Adriel appeared in the doorway, "We need to talk."

"I will come to your office after *I* take Violet to her room," he answered her with no room for discussion.

However, Adriel was not about to be ordered around. "This is urgent, and it cannot wait. We need to discuss tomorrow night. Killian will have supper brought up for her. And then will dismiss himself." She said the last part as a warning and it was clearly a reminder of instructions she had already given.

Elijah gave Killian a menacing snarl before barreling past him and Adriel.

Adriel turned to follow Elijah and I was left alone with Killian in the parlor. He wasn't distant with me the way everyone else had been. He charged right up to me and pressed me into his chest wrapping his arms around me. He squeezed me so tight and for so long, I didn't know if he would willingly release me.

While still holding on to me he said, "I'm so sorry. I shouldn't have let you go. This is all my fault." Then he finally pulled back to look down at me, but kept his arms wrapped around my waist.

Just like with G, my heart didn't skip a beat and I didn't feel anything other than slightly uncomfortable that Killian was so close. But that didn't mean that I was blind. He was *gorgeous*. Just so pretty—and yet still masculine. A total sigh and bat your eyelashes at him heartbreaker. Although he was not quite as large as Elijah and G, he was still huge, and he still towered over me. The torso I was pressed against was sculpted with rock hard muscles…and I felt zero attraction to him.

I tried to gracefully untangle myself from his embrace and he let me go.

"How are you feeling?" he asked. Before I could respond he added in a low whisper, "No, don't answer. Let's get you to your quarters and we can talk there, otherwise Adriel will be on my case."

Once we reached my room, Killian opened the door and stood back to let me enter. He followed behind me and closed the door. Then he pulled out a chair from the small table and waited for me to sit. The fire was alight in the fireplace, popping and crackling. The chandelier in the center of the room was also lit with candles and as a result, the room was warm and glowing.

A knock sounded at the door and Killian said, "Stay right here. I'll get it." After only opening the door a crack and a polite thanks, Killian returned to the table and set down a silver tray while removing the cover. Dinner.

"Adriel is pretty formal. I think you were meant to have dinner in the dining hall with her and the others. But I guess I interrupted those plans." He grinned at his last comment and Light help me, he had dimples.

Killian pulled out the chair across from me and sat at the table. "And you're welcome. I know you hate the formal stuff."

"How do you know me? I heard you say you were my personal guard. What is that?"

He shook his head looking incredibly irritated. "Adriel has issued a petition to the Council for you to be placed under her guardianship. Until they respond with a ruling, I can't speak with you about anything that could influence your current *state*, as she put it"

"I won't say anything to her, honestly. Please, you clearly know me. I'm so lost right now. You have no idea what it's like to be a stranger to yourself. To have no clue what has happened to you and to not know the people around you."

"Vi, there is nothing I wouldn't do for you. But this isn't something I would just be reprimanded for and it isn't something that we could keep a secret. The Council is ancient and powerful. They have their ways. If I have so much as the intention of breaking the laws of Adriel's petition, they will know, and they will send an archangel to take my head. I can't let that happen while you need me."

I hung my head and closed my eyes. I had thought I would find answers here with him and it was just another dead end.

Killian reached out and tucked my hair behind my ear. "Everything is going to be okay. Regardless of the petition, no one can keep me away from you. I am your *senterium*. And just as I can't break the council laws of the petition, those same council laws mean that no one can stop me from protecting you."

A loud, ceaseless banging started at the door.

"Damn." Killian stood up. He opened the door only a crack before slipping out and shutting the door behind him.

I could hear him talking to someone right outside the door, but all I could make out were muffled male voices. Then Killian came back in.

"I'm sorry. I have to go. Eat your dinner. Take a nice bath. I had the cleaning staff put a few of the books you like on the night table."

He was pulling a small device out of his pocket. "Here I brought you your music library."

He handed me the small device but the moment I took it the screen flared on before extinguishing with a little pop. An angry black cloud puffed out of it.

"I guess you don't remember how to handle electronics," he began fishing in his other pocket, "Which is why it's a good thing I made you a backup." He set another small device down on the table. "I only brought the two with me so make sure not to break this one."

"I didn't do anything to the other one," I said with incredulity (and maybe a little defensiveness).

He smiled sadly, "You really don't remember anything, do you?"

I shook my head.

"We store a lot of energy in our bodies. So, it's difficult for us to be around electronics because we overload them with electricity and they short. We're able to use them, though, we just need to be very careful and conscientious of them. It's why you generally don't find light fixtures or modern appliances in Radiant dwellings. It takes too much effort to rein in our energy all the time. Not to mention that everything would explode at any emotional outbursts.

"Just concentrate on the energy you feel flowing through your body."

I looked at him like he was crazy. "How am I supposed to do that?"

"Close your eyes."

When I kept looking at him he said, "If you want your music, you need to close your eyes."

"Fine," I grumbled.

"Listen to the hum in your veins. Keep focusing on it until you pick up the frequency and then notice the vibration of it. You will be able to feel it. Grab on to it and once you have a hold of it rein it in from your hands."

I sucked in a startled breath when I realized I could do exactly as he described. I could feel the energy pulsing through me and I *could* pull it back. It was amazing. I got so excited that I tried to do the opposite and extend the energy outwards.

Killian cleared his throat. "Uh, Violet?"

I opened my eyes smiling at the incredible ability I had. I saw Killian standing next to me looking very uncomfortable. He was rubbing the back of his neck, the muscles in his arm and chest flexing. "I can, ah, feel that." He shifted uncomfortably. "Do you mind pulling back?"

"Sorry. I didn't realize…"

"It's okay. Clearly you don't remember, but," he cleared his throat, "that kind of caress is pretty intimate. You might not want to do that around others."

The pounding sounded on the door and a man's voice bellowed, "Killian!"

"I'm coming," Killian reassured whoever was out there. I wondered if it was his blond partner from the tunnel, the Viking god.

"Just be sure to pull back your energy if you want to play any music." He pulled me out of my chair and into his arms as if it was the most natural thing in the world. He held me tight against his chest and buried his face in my hair.

"I'm so glad you're back. Get a good night's rest. I'll be back tomorrow morning."

He gave me a kiss on the top of my head and then released me to open the door a crack and slip out. A deep male voice was questioning him as they walked away.

I honestly couldn't decide how I felt about Killian. He was so close and familiar with me. He made me feel like we were dating. It was nice to have that kind of care and support from someone. But he was still a stranger to me. And his intimate embraces and overall possessiveness towards me were a little overwhelming.

I took a deep breath, closed my eyes, and found that hum of energy coursing through my veins. I pulled it back from my hands and then picked up the small electronic. No pop and fizzle. No smoke.

I was able to turn it on and browse the playlists. I made sure to be aware of keeping my energy from touching the device. It seemed like there was a playlist for any possible mood. I hit play on the one titled *Melancholy* and went to start a bath in the adjoining washroom.

Music can be a soothing balm at times. It can put into expression your feelings in a way that you never could. And I was ever grateful to Killian that evening for his consideration.

I listened to the entire playlist once. Songs like Mika's *Over My Shoulder*, Maximilian Hecker's *Help Me*, and Plumb's *Cut* were a cathartic release. But there was one song in particular that I listened to on repeat long after my bath had turned cold.

After I dried and dressed in the pajamas I had been given, I sat in front of the fire staring out of the large uncovered window. I searched in vain through the black storm clouds hunting for a light I couldn't find as Neko Case's *I Wish I was the Moon Tonight* played over and over again.

CHAPTER 15

*H*E WAS COMING FOR ME. *Nothing in this world or the next would stop him. His fury towards me consumed him, and he was going to make me pay for what I had done.*

His thoughts continually centered around finding me. He was envisioning what he would do when he finally captured me.

With my hands bound behind my back he would throw me onto his bed, following close behind. With one brutal rip, the shirt I wore was torn down the center and my uncovered breasts were bare to him. A second rip and my skirt fell away, leaving nothing between his gaze and my naked flesh.

He would give my breast a covetous squeeze with his large hand before trailing down my flat stomach to grasp possessively between my thighs. I would cry out. A surge of male satisfaction would course through him, and the agony he had endured would be replaced by triumph.

He would make a vow to himself that he would never let me escape him. He would keep me chained to his bed for eternity. And with that vow, he would press my head to the side and sink his teeth into my neck.

I screamed and opened my eyes, sitting up in bed. The dwindling fire burst in a small explosion, while every candle in the room flared to life. My heart was pounding in my chest, I was drenched in sweat, and the pulse drumming between my thighs was as intense as a second heartbeat.

My hand flew to my neck. The skin there was unbroken. It had just been a dream. Only it wasn't a dream. Maybe it was more accurate to call it a vision.

Those had not been my thoughts, those images and ideas not from my own mind. They had been another's and somehow, I was privy to them. The intense ferocity of anger, lust, and possession were so overwhelming, so extreme, I knew I did not have the ability to comprehend them, let alone issue them.

The door sprang open and Killian charged forward with daggers in hand. After taking a calculated assessment of the room and finding no threat, he asked, "What happened?" Although his voice was calm and level, he didn't lower his weapons.

"Dream. I had a bad dream," I told him.

After taking another scan of the room, Killian relaxed, holstering his daggers. He walked over to me and looked shocked but had the manners not to say anything. Instead, he altered course and fetched a damp hand towel from the bathroom.

"I'm so sorry, Vi," he said sitting on the edge of the bed. "This is all my fault. This shouldn't have happened to you." He began to dab my face and neck with the towel. "Did you remember something in your dream?"

"Get the fuck away from her."

Killian sprang off the bed and withdrew his daggers in a practiced move.

Elijah laughed without humor. "If you think those will save you, you're even dumber than I thought."

When Killian saw who it was he lowered his weapons but did not put them away. "She doesn't need this. Leave."

"You should take your own advice, kid."

Killian stashed his knives and squared his shoulders. "What you don't get is that I'm her friend. I *care* about her. Can you say the same? I can only imagine the hell she's been through. It's giving her nightmares. Do you really think she needs you pushing her around right now?"

Elijah said nothing. Instead he walked over to the bed, opposite from Killian. Reaching down, he cupped the back of my neck. The warm glow from his palm sent a soothing sensation through my entire body. I shuddered; I could feel myself relax and my turbulent emotions calm.

I let out an involuntary sigh. Not realizing it, I had closed my eyes. When I opened them again, I was disconcerted.

Killian was looking at me with such surprised distaste, I immediately felt embarrassed. His eyes flicked back and forth between me and Elijah. "Are you...? Is he...? You haven't..."

"Enough. Leave us," Elijah interjected.

I looked at Elijah then. "I'd like for you to both leave." Killian had been so kind to me, I didn't want to direct the challenge to him, but I had no problem letting Elijah know I didn't want him there.

Elijah clenched his jaw, a muscle ticking on the side. He just stood there staring at me.

I became incredibly irritated. That dream had flooded me with intense feelings. I was hot and flushed, with my body still experiencing tremors.

The truth was, I hadn't cried out only in fear upon waking from the dream. When the man bit me, I had come in my sleep. And it had carried over into real life as I woke.

Now I had these two men *hovering*. And I honestly didn't know if I wanted to punch them or...make out with them.

The desire to do both kept building the longer I met Elijah's stare. Between clenched teeth I ground, "Get. Out."

Elijah's reply was just as clinched. "Not. While. He's. Here."

I let out a jagged breath. I was about to launch myself at him. To do what, I didn't know. But I didn't want to find out.

I ripped my gaze from Elijah's and snapped my attention towards Killian. Before I even began to speak, Killian nodded. "Of course, Vi. Whatever you need." He was filled with such genuine concern, that I immediately softened. "I've been keeping watch outside your door. I want you to know you're safe. No one can hurt you."

He looked over at Elijah and his words hardened. "Or bother you." Looking back at me again he finished, "Just let me know if you need anything." Then he made his way to the door. But he didn't leave. He stood there waiting for Elijah.

I turned to Elijah and didn't bother with saying anything. I just flung my hand in the direction of the door.

His eyes sparked. Those gold flecks glowing. His body tensed. And he moved forward a fraction of an inch.

I knew with absolute certainty that he wanted to grab my shoulders and shove me against the headboard.

I let my hand drop and pulled the covers up. I was growing wet at the thought of his hands on me and his body covering mine.

Elijah smiled. Slowly. A wolf's smile. With mocking sincerity, he murmured, "Sweet dreams, princess," before turning to leave.

Once the door was shut, I collapsed against the headboard. But it wasn't Elijah or even Killian who I thought about. It was the man from the dream.

Yes, I had been terrified of him. He was a dark shadowy figure with so much coldness and emptiness inside of himself, that I had felt all hope and warmth being sucked away as if meeting an event horizon. But there had been something else there. Something I couldn't quite grasp, but I knew it had been exigent.

It was some time before I was able to sleep again. But right before I did, I thought about what would have happened if Killian had not been there. I knew it was only because of his presence that Elijah and I had not ended up in some fiery—and very physical—interaction.

I made a note to myself to see who I had to talk to in the morning about sending a huge fruit basket with a thank you card to Killian.

CHAPTER 16

I REALLY DON'T THINK this is a good idea, Daphne."

"Would you rather sit alone in your room all night?"

"Yes."

She waved an unconcerned hand in the air. "Well instead of sitting and doing nothing here," she explained, "sit and do nothing there."

Once again, I had been babysat by Daphne all day. And once again it was evening and I was stuffed into a dress complete with complementing heels, hair, and make-up. Only the way I was dressed tonight, made me realize I had looked like a hobo the previous night.

The dress I wore was the palest of peachy pinks. The bodice of the gown was sheer with hundreds of tiny crystals arcing across the chest and down to the waist. The crystals just covered the swell of my breasts. They winked and twinkled in the firelight. The multiple layers of the chiffon skirt danced light as air around my legs and brushed the floor. However, a long, hidden slit ran up the front of the skirt so that with each step I took the smooth toned skin of my left leg peeked out.

My hair had been left down but my natural waves had been enhanced. One side was pinned back behind my ear with a crystal pin. The chestnut waves shined as they flowed down my back and over my shoulder.

What enhanced my appearance most, though, was the make-up. My skin had a fresh dewy glow and my lips looked plumped and a little glossy but neutral in color. In fact, they were very similar in color to my dress. My already large eyes however, appeared even larger. My lashes swept out in long strokes and the violet color in my irises popped.

Daphne was more simply dressed. She wore a sleek, long black gown that swept along her willowy frame. Whereas the dress I wore enhanced my curves and the rosy hue to my skin, Daphne's dress highlighted her slim frame and alabaster complexion.

Her hair was loosely knotted at the back of her head. She had no need to do much to her appearance because she radiated with that internal incandescence. She was simple but breathtaking.

"Perfect. Utterly perfect," Daphne said when she saw me complete with gown, hair, and makeup.

"You look beautiful, Daphne," I replied.

"I suppose I do," she said without much interest. "Now let's get going. You will be expected in the great hall. And I'm sure your very pretty *senterium* is waiting for you. He is yummy by the way. I wish I had had a personal guard like him. It was all I could do not to swoon yesterday."

When I opened my mouth to protest she said, "You don't have to talk to anyone. The only thing you need to do is sit at a table with Adriel and Killian. You can eat if you like—or don't. Adriel believes it's important for you to be there. And before you ask again for the hundredth time, no, I cannot tell you anything about it."

Daphne crossed to open the door of the suite. When I didn't move to follow, she said, "You can either walk on your own or I can pulse you there."

I figured she meant she could just vanish into thin air and take me with her, which was something I did not want to experience at the moment. So, like a good little soldier, I followed her out of the room and down the hall.

As we turned the corner for the grand staircase, I saw Elijah pacing the landing, and I stopped where I was.

Elijah looked over at me and froze. His gaze burned. I could feel a slight heat blush across my cheeks and I looked down at myself.

Daphne cleared her throat with a feminine hem. She turned to me and gave me a kiss on the cheek along with a squeeze on my arm. "I'll see you down at the banquet, darling."

She continued to the staircase and gave a nod to Elijah. "Good evening, Elijah," she said as she passed him.

Elijah nodded back in acknowledgment but didn't take his eyes off me. After Daphne made her way down the first flight of stairs, I started towards Elijah. He was wearing a modern, perfectly tailored tux and his golden hair was combed off his face.

I realized just how handsome he was; he could give G a run for his money.

It occurred to me how influencing my first impression of Elijah had been. I had been terrified of him at our initial

157

encounter and he had continued to be a complete jackass to me since. But turning the corner and seeing him in a new light, it was like seeing him for the first time.

I took a breath, willing myself to remain calm and in control. Then I began to cross to Elijah. But with each step I took, the candles lining the hall flickered, and I knew that Elijah was struggling with his own self-control.

Once I joined him at the landing he snapped his eyes away from me, gazing down the stairs. Without a word or any further acknowledgement, he gestured for me to begin my descent.

I gathered the airy skirt of my gown and took the steps slowly. "I thought—" I began, but I realized I didn't want to infuriate him with my wording. So instead I said, "I wasn't expecting to see you."

Since I wobbled on the tall heels of my shoes, Elijah placed a steadying hand on my elbow. "Things changed. I am now your escort for the night and will serve as your personal guard." The last part was said with derision, and it was clearly a shot at Killian.

I wanted to ask why but, once again, I thought better of it. Besides, whether it was Killian or Elijah, it didn't matter. I flat out did not want to attend this event, regardless of who I sat next to.

"I don't think this is a good idea, Elijah."

But no reply came my way. Ever stoic, Elijah simply continued to escort me down the stairs.

I indulged in a good hearty sigh and thought, *well fuck it.*

CHAPTER 17

THE CAVERNOUS BALLROOM WAS BREATHTAKING.

Grandiose chandeliers sparkled with the glow of hundreds of candles from the cathedral ceiling. Trees with white bark lined the sides of the room. Their branches—covered in white, pink, and peach blossoms—arched towards the center of the ceiling and twined around the chandeliers creating a flowery canopy above. Here and there petals rained down upon the guests and the floor.

The thrum of frivolous conversations was garnished with the tinkling of crystal and soft laughter. The hall was packed with hundreds of people, men in tuxes and perfectly coiffed women in ball gowns.

Elijah and I had entered the hall from a side door that blended into the wall when shut. It led us directly onto a dais with a long formal banquet table at the head of the room. Adriel sat at one end of the table looking elegant and regal as she conversed with a man to her right. They spoke with their heads bowed and close together as if sharing secrets.

He was an older gentleman with white hair and a cropped white beard. In spite of his apparent age, he was quite handsome and fit. The term *silver fox* sprang to mind. Although he had a distinguished air about him, he looked like he would be capable in a trying situation.

Elijah directed me to a seat at the center of the table, holding out my chair. As I sat down, an excited murmur began to ebb through the crowd below. I noticed that most eyes were now staring at me. Then much to my dismay a smattering of applause began which tore through the crowd like an infection.

I looked back at Elijah in alarm. He wore a broad smile across his handsome face, but it did not reach his eyes.

He spoke out of the corner of his mouth. "Stand back up. Just give them a nod and wave. Try not to look so startled."

"Try not to look so startled?!" I whispered.

"Just do it!" Elijah gritted through his fake smile, his eyes smoldering with rebuke.

I awkwardly rose to my feet and did as I was told. The crowd erupted in cheers and whistles. I gave them an uncertain smile and sat back down. The attention was quickly removed from me when Adriel stood raising her hands causing the candle light to flicker.

"My dear friends," she began in her elegant voice and the crowd hushed, "If you would be so kind as to take your seats." She paused as the crowd shuffled around and sat at the luxurious tables which filled the hall. "It is with the greatest honor that I share this evening with you all. As you know, tonight is a celebration of a historic coupling."

Here and there guests from the crowd glanced my way. Wondering what Adriel meant, I looked to Elijah who had taken the seat to my left. He ignored me as he continued to stare at Adriel in polite attention.

What coupling was she referring to? Was Adriel about to announce to everyone here that Elijah and I had this damned connection?

My gaze was burning furious holes in the back of Elijah's head. He exhaled in clear annoyance but wouldn't give me the satisfaction of turning to look at me.

"This new union between the Radiants and the Shadows bestows hope upon us all for an end to these dark times. We have finally reached a brighter future and a finale to this long-standing war. Let us celebrate and all raise a glass to peace and prosperity!"

The crowd applauded and cheered raising their overflowing champagne glasses.

I had no idea what she was talking about. A union between the Radiants and the Shadows? She had told me at her cottage that they were engaged in an endless war with the Shadows. Had they made some announcement that I was now a Shadow? Was that paired with the fact that I was connected to Elijah the union she spoke of?

After everyone had clinked glasses and gulped champagne, Adriel continued. "I was sincerely hoping I would not need to make this next announcement. But it seems our honored guest is delayed this evening."

An anxious murmur passed through the crowd. Adriel raised her hand and spoke over the various chattering. "However, while one guest is delayed, another, unexpected guest, has arrived."

She looked at Elijah then and I could feel how incredibly uncomfortable he was.

"Tonight, we have the last Prism, Elijah Stone." Adriel crossed to Elijah and he stood, actually giving her a slight bow before they exchanged two formal kisses, one on each cheek.

Sitting right next to them and having spent the last couple days in their presence, it was obvious how staged this exchange was. But the crowd ate it up clapping, whistling, and cheering all while giving a standing ovation. Elijah gave a nod of acknowledgment to the crowd before returning to his seat.

As the wait staff began to swarm the tables Adriel announced, "Dinner is served. Let us dine and dance in celebration of this momentous time."

Attentions were turned to the plates being presented and the hall was filled with socializing chatter once again. I didn't bother with more than a glance at the leafy green salad placed in front of me before turning to Elijah.

Under my breath I demanded, "What is this all about?"

Adriel had referred to Elijah as the last known *Prism*, but Daphne had implied that I was his counterpart, and also a *Prism*—which I still didn't understand the meaning of. However, the way Adriel had phrased her introduction, it seemed as if Elijah was the only one. I was completely in the dark about what this ball was for, and I was scrambling to put the pieces together.

In a low voice Elijah snapped back, "I don't like this any more than you do."

I blinked in mock confusion before responding in an angry whisper. "I didn't ask you how you were feeling. In case you hadn't noticed, we can read each other in the most intrusive, creepiest, distressing, *intrusive* way. I don't need an update on how you feel."

Elijah took an aggressive bite of his salad. "Eat your lettuce."

All of a sudden, an orchestra began playing. I looked to the opposite end of the hall and noticed musicians had filed in and taken up instruments.

Elijah swore under his breath before wiping his mouth with his napkin and standing up. He held out his hand to me and plastered that phony smile on his face again while his eyes seethed. "We have to dance now."

My eyes rounded and I faked a smile of my own. Knowing that all eyes were once again upon us, I gritted, "I am absolutely not dancing with you."

By this point, Adriel had made her way over to us. I can only imagine that we looked like a trio of lunatics with manic grins across our lips and murder in our eyes.

"Everyone is expecting a dance. You two will give it to them right now or so help me I will lock you both in the dungeons for three months where you will have to relieve yourselves in a bucket in the corner and trap rats if you want to eat!"

For whatever reason, Adriel's words struck something deep within Elijah. I could feel violence erupt just below the surface. The golden flecks in his irises blazed to life, but he quickly shut his eyes and somehow gained control of his emotions.

I stood up and took his hand, hating them both, as well as all the people gathered in the ballroom and most especially the orchestra. Then Elijah bent his arm and I threaded my own through it. We crossed the dais and descended the stairs to the petal covered dance floor as though we were a fairytale prince and princess having our first wedding dance.

Surprisingly, Elijah was quite adept and led me around the floor like it was the most natural thing in the world. However, he dug his fingers into my waist where his hand rested and directed, "Don't look down. Look at me."

I looked at him then, alright. And I gathered all the anger I could and blasted it at him knowing he would feel it through our bond.

He gave me a smile that reminded me of a wolf's snarl.

And all the while the crowd looked on at us adoringly.

Just when I was wondering if the song would ever end, someone pushed me. Hard. Inhumanely hard.

I was launched into Elijah's chest and we went careening towards the floor. I was embarrassed that we were tumbling with everyone watching. But at least we were falling gracefully, thanks to Elijah. He wrapped his arms around me, taking the impact of the floor on his back. Then he rolled on top of me tucking me into his chest.

Even though we had stopped falling, I couldn't understand why the floor was shaking. And why people had started screaming.

"Let me up," I grumbled, pushing on Elijah. When he didn't budge, I tried to peek out from under him.

I realized then that the entire ballroom was rocking in a shattering earthquake. A deafening boom sounded through the hall and the chandeliers went crashing to the ground. The one closest to the door was now blocking the exit.

I could also see Daphne and G, as well as a few others at their table. Each of them stood and were suddenly ablaze, appearing to be more light than corporeal form. Expansive radiant wings flared behind them and in their hands, each held a sword of fire. I saw them like that for only the briefest of moments because G shouted something at them and in the blink of an eye, they were gone.

As chaos swelled in the ballroom, Elijah swept me up off the floor and charged for the hidden door from which we originally entered. As soon as we were through and back in the grand hallway, he set me on my feet.

He began yanking off his jacket and bow tie. He was also saying something, and it was most likely directed at me, but I wasn't paying attention. I had turned to face the large front door that was framed by two floor to ceiling windows.

Through the windows, I could see that the violence of the storm had escalated. The rain beat against the glass and incredible gusts of wind battered the entire facade of the mansion rattling the panes to a distressing degree.

Angry red lightning lit the black sky while a bomb blast of thunder rocked the foundation mimicking another earthquake. Yet over all the noise, someone was whispering.

Something had come. For me. I knew it unerringly. I had to go out there. I needed to. I took a step towards the door. Then another. The whispering grew louder. And that's when the evil burrowing deep in my soul...began to whisper back.

But before I could get any closer, a hand clamped over my arm yanking me to a halt. I didn't take my eyes from the door though. Making my way out that door was the only thing that mattered.

There was a shake on my arm and I think someone said something, but it was hazy and seemed far away.

Elijah turned me and grabbed my face with both hands, forcing me to look at him. Inspecting my eyes, he swore and then ripped open his shirt. He grabbed both of my hands in his and pressed them to his chest before wrapping his arms around me and pressing his face into my hair.

A golden glow flared between us and I could feel his energy wash over me. I took in a gulping breath of air as if I had been without oxygen for too long. I was overwhelmed by him; every inch of my body was pressed against his. Feeling him so close, there was no room for anything else.

I breathed him in. I felt his hard planes, the warmth and strength of him. I was momentarily wrenched from the pull beyond the front door. But I knew it was a temporary reprieve. I could still feel the whispering tug out in the darkness just beyond the shelter of Elijah's embrace.

He spoke rapidly at my ear. "We have to leave here now. We're going to run to the right of the staircase. You are going to follow me. We don't have time for questions or arguments. You will have to do exactly as I say. If anything happens to me, fight anyone and anything that comes your way and run as far and fast into the woods beyond the gardens. If what's out there gets a hold of you, you could be lost forever."

Most of the candles in the chandeliers had been extinguished. But another flash of lightning exploded, momentarily lighting the hall with a sinister red glow as thunder shook the walls. One of the gigantic chandeliers crashed to the floor behind us and I hunkered into Elijah while he covered the back of my head with one large palm.

"We have to go now."

He led me to a specific spot by the side of the staircase. His grip on my hand was bruising, but I was glad for it. I knew it meant he wasn't going to let me go easily. The minute he had released me from his embrace, I had felt the need to turn for the front door again, but I had fought it.

Elijah pushed against a panel at the bottom of the stairs and we entered another small hidden hallway. It was dark in the passageway, but the floor was even and clear of any debris. After taking various twists and turns we eventually reached an old oak door that was boarded with planks of wood across it.

Two packs lay in the corner. I wouldn't have noticed them except for the fact that Elijah bent down to retrieve them. He strapped one to his back. Before helping me with the other, he had me remove my shoes, saying that I wouldn't be able to run in them.

Lowering his shoulder, Elijah broke through the planks and even the door itself. I scrambled through the opening after him, and we emerged into the gardens at the back of the mansion.

The torrent of rain drenched us immediately and the forceful winds made it so that the rain stung us from all sides. Strands of wet hair lashed all around my neck and face.

I knew we were heading for the woods that bordered the property. But the expanse of lawn between the gardens and the woods was massive. We would be exposed in the open before reaching the cover of the dense trees. Shouts and what sounded like bomb blasts carried from the other side of the mansion, echoing through the opening between the sloping roofs of the two wings.

But out here in the back of the property, we were alone. Without hesitation, Elijah had us sprinting through the gardens and onto the lawn. I kept expecting something or someone to stop us, but we made it to the line of trees and ran headlong over fallen branches and soggy leaves.

Something inside screamed at me to turn around and go back. This instinct wasn't sinister and dark. It was something else. Something that I didn't understand. I faltered for a moment, but Elijah squeezed my hand and released a blast of energy that went pumping through my veins, flooding me with charged light.

With the storm still raging around us and the earth still trembling at our feet, we ran deep into the forest.

CHAPTER 18

I DON'T KNOW HOW FAR we ran or for how long. But I didn't care. The farther we got from the Radiant Court, the less I felt the darkness within trying to rise and answer the seductive call from the front of the mansion. After a certain point, the impulse was completely gone.

What seemed like hours passed and then we finally came upon a small wood cabin. There was no clearing, no space around the structure, just trees and leaves right up to the very walls. Only then did we stop running.

Elijah ran up to the door and opened it, ushering me in, before slamming it shut behind us. He finally let go of my hand. After flicking his wrist to the side, a small blaze sprang to life in the scrawny fireplace.

I stood where I was, shivering, but incredibly thankful for the shelter from the stinging rain. I could see that this one windowless room was all there was to the structure—no bathroom, bedroom, or kitchen. A sleeping pallet was on the floor and that was it. The space looked clean, but completely empty.

Elijah slid the pack from my shoulders and placed it on the hardwood in front of us. Then he did the same with his own before ripping his soaked shirt off. "Take off your dress."

I thought about protesting but the dress was drenched and completely covered in mud and debris. It was also ripped and plastered to my body. I decided I would rather be in my tiny panties and strapless bra, exposed to Elijah, than in the ruined garment one minute longer.

I tore the thing off and turned to face Elijah. However, he was turning back to me at the same moment and we bumped into each other. His nostrils flared as he raked his gaze over my body.

"Put these on," he snarled as he shoved a bundle of clothes from the pack into my arms.

The only problem was that I was a little busy staring at his damp skin in the firelight. His broad shoulders and muscled chest were too much to take in. And because of the damn attraction I had to him, I had to focus all my energy and attention on not reaching out to trail a finger down his rigid abdomen.

So the bundle of clothes ended up falling to the floor.

"Violet," he growled quietly, "I need you to get dressed." Each word was an exercise in control.

I tore my eyes from his perfect body to look at him. Those gold flecks blazed in his irises as I knew they would. But his burning gaze was pulled from me and refocused on the center of the room where a sudden noise erupted.

Daphne and G had appeared out of nowhere in the middle of the cabin. G was hanging onto Daphne's shoulder for just an instant before he collapsed to the ground. He was covered in blood, and he was unconscious. Daphne's wet hair was wild and disheveled having come undone, and her dress was ripped around her thighs as if haphazardly converted from floor length to mini.

Instead of a sword of light, which I had seen her holding earlier, she now grasped a solid steel one which she dropped to the floor. The clatter of the steel upon the hardwood, rang through the small cabin as Daphne knelt beside G.

"Help him Elijah!" The unaffected air of sophistication she usually conveyed had been replaced by wild desperation.

Elijah took a few swift strides to kneel on the other side of G. His eyes flashed to Daphne's. "What happened?"

"It was The Dark One. He was able to reach the mansion. I can't explain it. I don't know how, but he was able to reach us. We cut him off in the courtyard while Adriel had everyone evacuated. We did what we could before falling back. This idiot tried to take him on alone while the rest of us retreated." She gulped in a breath before pleading, "Help him."

Elijah tore off G's bloody shirt. "If they're just surface wounds, he'll heal on his own."

"It's not just the surface wounds. He was covered in the umbra. I could barely reach him to pulse him out."

Daphne grabbed Elijah's hands and tried to thrust them towards G's chest. "Help him," she urged again.

Elijah snapped his hands back. "I can't. Ours are too similar. He needs energy from a complementing source. He needs female energy, not another male's." He looked up at Daphne. "You heal him."

Daphne moaned. "I don't know how. I've never connected with another."

I thought about how G had encouraged me to stroke Elijah when he had been ill. I was embarrassed to be clad in only my underwear, but I cleared my throat and stepped forward. "Maybe just try touching him?" I offered.

Daphne's head whipped around. "You." She jumped to her feet and lunged towards me. My reflexes kicked in and I side stepped her attack. She spun around to face me, and Elijah stepped between us, blocking Daphne.

"Back off, Daphne," he warned.

Daphne's voice was low and mean. "Elijah, step aside."

"I'm afraid I can't do that, Daphne."

"This is all because of her. G is *dying* because of her. Two archangels are dead tonight because of her. The Radiant Court was attacked, and innocent civilians could have died. Her life is not worth the death of so many others. She is no longer who she once was. She ceased being one of us the moment she left the Court of Light. Now move out of my way because I'm handing her over. If the Throne of Evil wants her, he can have her."

"Daphne, think about what you're saying. Think about who she is."

But Daphne was done thinking and done talking. In a blur of motion, she sent Elijah sprawling across the floor. She was on top of me before Elijah had even stopped sliding. In the split second before she had me pinned and immobile, I was able to use her body's momentum to roll her off to the side so that I landed on top of her. I straddled her hips with my knees digging into each of her thighs, and I pinned her shoulders down with my forearms. She bucked her hips sending me rocking on top of her, but I refused to budge. She bucked a second time and my breasts bounced threatening to spill out of my bra.

"Oh, fuck yeah." The words were faint and weak. We both whipped our heads towards G. He was watching us through one eye while the other remained swollen shut.

"Giddeon!" Daphne cried.

Then I was being hoisted into the air and onto my feet by Elijah while Daphne scrambled out from under me and over to G.

"Go back to straddling each other," G croaked. "And Eli, make yourself useful and count raindrops outside."

Daphne knelt next to G with her hands hovering near his chest. "I'm not sure what to do," she whispered to him.

"You don't have to, Daph." G spoke to her with a sweet gentleness that was uncharacteristic of his usual cocky swagger.

"I want to." Her hands began to shake slightly but she rested them on G's perfect, although bloody, chest.

G moaned and arched his back off the floor. His hands shot up, grabbing Daphne and pulling her body on top of his.

Daphne's gasp of surprise was utterly feminine. Then just as suddenly as they had appeared, they were gone.

"Fucking angels," Elijah muttered.

I slipped to the floor and sat with my knees drawn into my chest and my arms wrapped around my legs. I didn't care that I was practically naked. I was so over all of this.

Elijah continued to change, taking off the wet and muddy pants he still wore and replacing them with solid black fatigue pants from his dropped pack. He also procured a black shirt and a tactical vest as well as boots.

"You need to get up and get dressed."

I was tired. I was tired of the running. Of not receiving answers. Of not knowing where I was going but most especially of not knowing where I was coming from.

"Why? Apparently, people died tonight. Because of me. Daphne's right. If someone or something is coming for me then why not just let it take me. I'm not worth all this death and destruction. I've already lost whatever life I had. If what Killian said is true, then I made my choice. If I went into harm willingly then I need to pay the cost for it. Not others."

Elijah squatted down in front of me. "You cannot even begin to comprehend what you're talking about. All the information that you're aware of, that you've heard and pieced together over the last few days, is only the tip of the iceberg. There is incredible mass below, the likes of which you cannot begin to imagine. So before you decide to go all virgin martyr on me, take the time to consider the fact that some very powerful individuals are doing all they can to protect you. And let me tell you princess, it's not out of the goodness of their hearts. Like it or not, you've got a role in all this."

Then he took a shirt similar to the one he was wearing and began to shove my arms into it before angrily pulling it over my head.

"What are you doing?"

176

"You're not going to dress yourself? Fine. I'll do it for you." He pulled me up to my feet and began stuffing my legs into black leather pants. "Even though it goes against every fucking instinct I have at the moment, even though I want nothing more than to shove those little panties down your thighs and bend you over, I am going to get these goddamn clothes on you and we are going somewhere safe."

He gave the pants a final yank over my hips and stormed back to our packs on the floor. "Because the only thing stronger than the instinct to take you," one boot came flying at me, hitting me on the side of my ass, "Is the drive to protect you." Another boot came sailing for my head, but I caught it.

I didn't want him trying to put my shoes on as well, so I bent to shove my feet in them. The black leather boots were tight and knee high. Once again, Elijah somehow managed to provide clothes and shoes that fit me.

I didn't know what to do other than ignore his sex driven comments. "Did you have these bags packed and placed in that passageway?"

He came over to me and began to buckle straps on each of my thighs. "When you make enemies, you learn to be prepared. Based on the information we learned from your drooling little boyfriend yesterday, we knew an attack was a possibility. Daphne and G went to gather information on the outcome of your little vigilante attempt. They could neither confirm nor deny the death of the Dark One. But since he deigned to pay us a visit tonight, apparently he lives."

Elijah sheathed knives into the holsters attached to the thigh straps. "A nightwalker, even the most powerful of them,

177

shouldn't have been able to reach the mansion. The packs were an overly cautious maneuver. They shouldn't have come into play." He gave the straps a final tug with more force than necessary.

"Oww."

"You have a dagger in each holster. Stab anyone who comes near you. At this point, don't trust a soul. If the Dark One was able to breach our veils, there's no telling who or what to trust."

Elijah began affixing various weapons from the pack to his own body. "You heard what Killian said. You decided to make an attempt on the Dark Prince. Here's a little tip for the future. If you plan on assassinating the most powerful Shadow, land a killing blow, because otherwise you're just going to piss him off. Now he's after you and my bet is, he wants revenge.

"No one knows who he is or where he came from. We just recently learned about his rise to power. We have no idea what he's capable of, but if the prophecies about him are true, he will be the greatest enemy our kind has ever faced.

"We can't let him get ahold of you. You have your own destiny in all this to fulfill. I don't have time to go into details now, but just know that an entire race of people—your people—are depending on you. You can't give up and you can't surrender. You are going to have to run when I tell you to and fight when there's no escape."

Elijah picked up the sword Daphne had discarded and slid it through the back of his vest. Then he came up to me and placed his hands on my shoulders. "I get that this is difficult. But I've heard about you from Adriel. Apparently, you were a very capable individual. If any part of that remains, I need you to dig down deep and find it."

I looked up at him. "Are you being nice to me?"

He let go of my shoulders and took a step back. "Don't confuse self-preservation with affection. Because of the connection between us, I am bound to protect you. If you're confident and are able to take care of yourself in a trying situation, my job becomes easier and the chances that I stay alive increase."

"That's a relief. For a minute there I thought we were going to become friends."

Of course, Elijah ignored my comment. Instead of a reply, he knelt and began zipping the packs back up.

"I need to get you somewhere safe. I don't know if there is anywhere on this plane of existence that the Dark One can't find you. But I do know a place on another plane that is protected. It's called Aleece, and it's where the Council of Elders resides. It's also where The Oracle takes residence. If you're able to petition her, she may be able to restore you—that is if the meeting doesn't kill you. Adriel seems to think you're strong enough for it. Maybe you can prove her right."

He walked to the center of the room and slipped a knife under one of the floor boards, prying open a trapdoor. "We are going to take this tunnel to another *Vestibule*. It will be like the one we entered on our way to Adriel's cottage—the circular structure with all the doors. One of the doors will have a tall triangle intertwined with a circle. That is the entry to Aleece."

He stepped away to pick up a torch by the hearth and lit it in the fire before crossing back. "If anything happens down in this

179

tunnel, you need to run, find that door, and make your way through it. Do you understand?"

"Yes, but what do I do once I get there?"

"Ask for Davis. He'll know what to do." Elijah stepped into the trapdoor. "Now let's go. We can't spare any more time."

And I followed Elijah down into the darkness.

CHAPTER 19

~Violet's Playlist: Howl, Florence + The Machine~

THE TUNNEL WAS VERY SIMILAR to the one we had driven through when leaving Elijah's house to meet Adriel. Without the aid of car headlights, hollow empty blackness surrounded us on all sides. The light from the torch Elijah carried illuminated the path just a couple feet in front of us before being consumed by the dark. To say it was unsettling would be an understatement.

I was being hunted and I knew it.

Although Elijah wanted to keep any pertinent information from me initially, I had come to learn quite a few details. I knew that Radiants were immortals who had an inner light, and they drew strength and power from the sun. They were governed by the Council of Elders and various angels were somehow involved with carrying out council orders. The Radiants had been warring with the Shadows for an untold amount of time.

I didn't know much about the Shadows, but apparently the most powerful among them was the Shadow Prince who was also known as the *Dark One,* the *Prince of Darkness,* or as Daphne had referred to him, the *Throne of Evil.* I had heard Shadows referred to as *nightwalkers* as well.

However, beyond knowing of their existence and their alleged prince, I didn't know much about them other than the fact that they couldn't (or weren't supposed to be able to) pass through the veils of light.

Killian said that I had intentionally gone to try and assassinate the Dark Prince. But where I went, how I got there, what my plan had been, and what had happened were all mysteries. Yet, I did know that somehow my own inner light had been drained which resulted in an infection of darkness, called the *Shadow's Kiss.* And connecting to Elijah had been the only way to keep the darkness at bay and recharge my own luminescence.

According to Adriel, my family was aware of my situation. But as much as I wanted to trust her, I just didn't know if I could. I mean really. Where were they?

However, none of those things drove me as crazy as the ring on my finger. So many different scenarios had passed through my mind concerning the ring (from the mundane to the outrageous), that I was just at a loss. There was simply no thread to follow.

The one thing I did know for certain was that I did not want to take it off. It was the only thing that was my own. Everything else that I wore or carried, where I slept at night, what I ate, those were all things provided by others. None of it was mine. The ring was my sole possession.

And all of that put me here. In a dark tunnel, dependent upon Elijah while being hunted by some evil and apparently powerful being.

After traveling along in silence for some time, Elijah interrupted my mental breakdown of the situation. "I'm going to warn you now. We will have to pass through a Veil. I can't afford to take you through. You're going to have to cross it on your own. I believe you will be able to pass through the light. Your own light had been steadily recharging. But it may be difficult. You need to start mentally preparing yourself. We won't have any extra time once we reach it. You are not safe here and we need to get to Aleece. That means that when we reach the Veil we cannot stop outside of it. I don't think it will be like it was the last time we went through together. I think it will be easier for you now, but that isn't saying much."

I was listening to Elijah, but I kept looking over my shoulder. I couldn't help but feel as though we were being followed. However, there were no sounds behind us and I knew the darkness of the tunnel was getting to me.

"Elijah, don't you think it's about time you told me everything? Hasn't this all gone too far?"

"Perhaps. But this is not the time and place. I need to get you to a secure location. It was a mistake to stay at court."

He picked up the pace. "The Oracle might be able to help you. To heal you. There's a chance for you now. I didn't see that at first. If I can just get you fixed, get you better—that would change everything."

His words sent a chill down my spine. I supposed they were meant as comforting, in a way, but they just made me feel less than worthy.

There wasn't time to focus on Elijah's comment, though. We were approaching the Veil. I could feel it then. It brought the duality of the light and dark I carried within myself into sharp focus.

Thankfully, Elijah was right. This time was different. I wasn't brought to my knees in agony. My energy was charged from being with him. It was difficult, but I was able to pass through. I didn't pause and I didn't hesitate.

Two towering stone doors stood in front of us carved with intricate script and symbols. It took great effort on Elijah's part to move the huge slab of stone. The groan of rock grinding against rock echoed through the dark tunnel. He made progress inch by inch as his muscles bulged with strain. The doors seemed to shimmer, and I got the impression that they were even heavier than their incredible mass implied.

My skin began to prickle at the sound and I was overcome with an ominous sense of foreboding. We needed to get inside the Vestibule and through the connecting door.

Once the rock was displaced just enough for us to slip through, Elijah dashed into the Vestibule pulling me behind him. I believe he felt a similar urgency as though our time was running out.

The cavernous space inside was almost identical to the one I had been in previously with Elijah and G. It was another circular area with a high domed ceiling and what looked like a small bright star floating in the center. Doors lined the continuous curving wall in various shapes, sizes, materials and colors. Elijah began to run across the stone floor headlong for the opposite side of the cavern, pulling me with him.

"It's the old wood one. Straight ahead," he directed. "Do not let go of me once we pass through."

And that's when I looked back.

I don't know why I did. He had been as silent as a shadow would be.

He had come for me. I knew then that he would not rest until he had me. That he would hunt me until the end of his days. There had been a Florence + The Machine song in my music library, *Howl*, and it was everything he was.

Dense black shadows surrounded the Dark Prince, swirling and shifting, as if restless and haunted. They seemed to be sucking the light from the burning little star overhead. The star sputtered and flickered fighting to remain intact, which caused an eerie strobe light effect all around us.

I felt it stir again. The infection. I couldn't control my response.

As I tried to stop and turn back towards the Dark Prince, Elijah increased his speed. My sudden stop paired with Elijah's momentum had me falling to the floor, and the unexpected dead weight from my tumble caused Elijah to trip.

Shadows branched out from the Dark Prince then in a ring all along the curving wall of the Vestibule. We were surrounded by them and all the doors were effectively blocked.

I didn't know if the shadows served only as a visual barrier and we could pass through them or if they would physically prevent us from passing. The way they moaned and wailed, I didn't want to find out.

Elijah lifted me up off my butt and onto my feet, sending an intense wave of energy over me.

"You have to fight the dark pull," he commanded. Then he pushed me behind him saying, "If you can make it to the door, go through it. If not that door, then any one. Just get away. Do *not* let him take you."

Elijah turned to the Dark Prince and drew the sword from his back. "You shouldn't have come here," he growled. As he spoke golden rays of light gleamed around him. He wasn't illuminated in the same way Daphne or G had been. While they radiated a pure white light, appearing more light than corporeal form, Elijah appeared still very much himself. It was no less awing, though.

The shadows around the Dark Prince billowed and screeched, and an icy blast filled the room. Elijah took off, charging the prince.

I knew I had to remain in control and I honestly fought to, but a frenzy was brewing inside me. The dark beast I housed rattled its cage and howled to be released. The shadows surrounding us answered in tortured wails. I clamped my hands over my ears, reminding myself of Elijah's words. The only reason I was able to even attempt staying in control was because of the strong pulse of energy Elijah had directed at me.

But taking a step towards the door through which we needed passage, I realized we couldn't make it. The shadows that barred our path whispered to me in gruesome detail. They told me that they would gobble us up and spit out our bones if we tried to pass.

The beast inside me stopped rattling its cage. Instead, it began to caress the bars with its silky black head. Purring and rubbing, back and forth, back and forth. It was a black panther all lethal grace and velvety darkness. It wanted to be stroked by its master.

I needed to go to him. Elijah was poisoning me with lies and omissions. If I just went to him, to the one I belonged to, all would be made right. I looked towards him with worship in my eyes. I needed him and no other. The connection I had with Elijah was a paltry thread compared to what I felt for the one who commanded the darkness.

I shook my head. Trying desperately to dislodge the dark thoughts creeping in from the recesses of my mind.

Turning back, I saw Elijah swing the sword at the Dark Prince. With incalculable speed the Dark Prince's shadowed hand whipped out and grabbed the sword by the blade, yanking it from Elijah and throwing it to the ground. His other hand shot out and connected with Elijah's solar plexus, sending him flying off his feet and landing on his back.

Despite the debilitating blow, Elijah immediately sprang onto his feet in a kick-up. He showed no signs of weakness, but his light was extinguished.

"You're pathetic," Elijah spat. "Is this the only way you can get a woman? Torturing her and then hunting her?" He cracked his knuckles. "Come on, why don't you fight me like a man? No light. No shadows. Just you and me."

The shadows around the Dark One climbed higher and shrieked in response. That was when I learned something detrimental about both of them.

I was sickened.

I shared a connection with the wailing shadows. We were of the same ilk. I could feel them. And I knew that they would never be caged. Not again. Not after being imprisoned for the eternal night. The Dark One did not control them. They controlled the Dark One. And it was only a matter of time before they freed and empowered the piece of themselves that lived inside me.

I also knew that Elijah was incredibly weakened. Only now did I realize the toll I had taken on him. I had been draining him these last few days and he had not seen the sun in just as long. He had shared most of his strength with me before charging the Dark Prince. And that effort had taken the last of his power. I could feel how empty he was now. He was weakened because he had been strengthening me.

Although, he wasn't entirely drained. He still held light, a low glimmer, that continued to trickle and recharge from some transcendental wellspring. It was as though it came from his very soul. And the only way he could ever be completely devoid of light would be if his very soul was ripped from him.

Challenging the Dark Prince to fight without their gifts was Elijah's only option. But those shadows would not be contained. We were trapped and there was no way out.

"Well what the fuck are you waiting for," Elijah challenged. "Come the fuck on."

Again, those awful shrieks tore through the air, and then the shadowed form of the prince began stalking towards us. In a quiet voice Elijah murmured, "Run for the door when he strikes."

"Elijah, no!"

"Damnit, Violet. Do it!"

189

Elijah began charging to meet the Dark One. This needed to end. My prince would finish this Light One for good and then I would be free to return to the darkness with him.

No. *No.* I shook my head again, fighting to stay in control. I began backing towards the door inch by inch. It took all the strength I had to force my feet away from the Dark Prince.

Elijah bulldozed into the hazy form of the Dark Prince, driving his shoulder into the prince's midsection. The Dark One took a few stumbling steps back but did not go down.

The shadows blocking the doors around us, flickered and wisped, becoming smoky. I had the opportunity. I could run through them and not be harmed. I could feel how they condensed back around the prince to stave off the oncoming attack.

But I couldn't leave Elijah. I had to do something.

"I'll go with you!" I shouted.

Although he was cloaked in shadows, I could tell that the prince whipped his head in my direction.

Elijah, too, turned back to me. "Violet, no! Run now!"

The prince grabbed Elijah by the neck and flung him across the cavernous space until Elijah's big body crashed into the far wall. He landed on the stone floor in an unconscious heap.

"Stop!" I screamed. I took an unsteady breath. "I'll go with you. Willingly. Just leave him be."

The lingering shadows surrounding the Vestibule receded and condensed around the Shadow Prince. The Dark One turned to me. Waiting. I still couldn't see him under all the shifting darkness. I didn't know who or what I was approaching exactly, but I began to cross to him without hesitation.

As I reached him I felt the temperature in the air around me plummet. Those shadows lapped at me eagerly. I felt an answering dark call within but managed to keep a tight focus on the need to help Elijah. Within those shadows, just a few feet from the Dark Prince, I slammed into a wall of turbulent emotions.

His chaotic, frenzied thoughts were those of a rabid animal and not a rational man. He was maddened. There was such anger and animosity. Such emptiness and desideratum. All spiraling around him in a destructive cyclone. I wanted to shrink back from the onslaught of feelings, but instead I steeled myself pulling on all the strength I could draw from my connection with Elijah.

Then I walked right up to the Dark Prince...and stabbed him.

In an almost undetectable motion, I grabbed the handles of each dagger strapped to my thighs, flipped them out of the holsters and drove them into the Dark Prince's gut. I didn't even have to think about the motion. Muscle memory drove the movement.

I was surprised when I felt the knives sink into flesh. I was afraid they would just slash through air, but I had to try something. As quickly as I plunged the blades into his abdomen, I yanked them out. Then I followed up with a kick between his legs and turned to sprint back to Elijah.

The anger of red hot betrayal saturated the air. It was tinged with a note of...*anguish?*

It didn't matter. I had to get Elijah and myself out of there.

I didn't know how my actions had affected the Dark Prince. I didn't know if he was doubled over on the floor where he had stood or if he was right behind me just about to reach out and grab me. I didn't bother to glance back and check. I had to focus on getting Elijah and myself through the door and to safety.

Elijah had said Aleece was the one place he knew the Dark Prince couldn't reach. I had to try and get us there. Drawing again on the energy connection from Elijah, I ran for the door. By some miracle, Elijah had landed directly in front of it. I slammed both palms against the wood praying with all my might for it to open.

What happened next was so unexpected that I was dazed for a moment. An incredible bomb blast of light erupted between my palms and the door. The entire vestibule was flooded with bright blinding light. I threw my forearm up to cover my eyes.

I don't know why, but I expected to hear a wail of agony or at least a hiss of annoyance from the Dark Prince. There was nothing but silence, though. Even if I had wanted to check on what had happened to the Dark Prince—to find out how much distance I had between us—the solar flare filling the cavern prevented me from being able to see anything.

I reached down by my feet and groped for Elijah. When my hand made contact with his back, I crouched next to him and pushed with all my might.

At first, I only managed to budge him a mere inch, unable to find traction on the stone floor. But I kept trying. I was determined that we would make it through the threshold.

All of a sudden, a force other than myself was helping him through. While I was pushing at his limp body, it was as though someone else was pulling him through the door from the other side.

A furious roar sounded behind us vibrating the very floor. But it was abruptly cut off, because sooner than I expected, or was prepared for, Elijah and I both went tumbling through the open door.

CHAPTER 20

I FOUND MYSELF SPRAWLED OUT and sliding over cold ice. I scrambled to my feet and looked for Elijah, fearful I would also find the Shadow Prince had followed us through the door.

I turned in a circle. There was no Shadow Prince and no Elijah. I turned a second time, much slower, straining to see where Elijah might have landed. But I was alone.

I called for Elijah and the sound of my voice echoed even though I was in a flat open space. The icy surface stretched all around me as far as I could see. It was solid and thick under my boots, and a fine dusting of snow danced across the surface with each gust of arctic air. I realized I was standing on a frozen lake.

There was no moon in the inky night sky and no clouds, but the light of stars and planets seemed to surround me with an incredible smattering of galaxies sprinkled throughout. My breath fogged out from my lips with each exhale.

A small hooded figure approached. The cowl of the figure's robe hid the individual's face completely. A gnarled finger was pointed in my direction.

"You are a foolish child, you are." The voice was that of an old crone.

"I beg your pardon?" I asked in reply.

"To be acting weak, when so strong. To be letting it control you, when you control it. Bah!" she spat to the side, "A fool."

"I'm sorry. I don't know what you're talking about," I told her.

"What a waste, it be. Given a gift of great means and you don't even bother. Just let yourself drown, you do. Needs you, he does. His time is running out."

A gust of arctic wind blew sending the dusting of snow that covered the frozen lake swirling into the air around us. My hair blew across my face and I had to sweep it away.

When I looked back at the hooded figure she was wobbling away into the darkness.

"Wait!" I called. "Who are you talking about?"

Her old crone voice floated on the air back to me. "Running out of your own time, as well."

"I'm looking for someone named Davis. Can you direct me to him? Please. I've lost my guide. I think he might be hurt," I desperately tried.

I began to follow after her, but she was quickly putting distance between us. Although she limped slowly, with arthritic movements, I somehow couldn't catch up to her and she eventually blended into the dark night horizon.

I ran after her—after where she had disappeared—but there was nothing. I spun in a circle again. The lake stretched out to the horizon in each direction. It was infinite. I would walk forever in whichever direction I chose and would never reach the surrounding banks.

I could see a faint glow in what I knew to be the very center of the lake. I began to walk towards it. As I got closer to the heart of the lake, I realized the glow was coming from under the frozen surface, and a large smooth rock jutted out of the ice illuminated from the light below.

The rock was shaped like a tombstone. It even had elegant script engraved across the flat surface.

Knock to find your weakness.
Knock to find your fear.
Knock to find your strength.
Knock to find your dear.

I paused for only a moment, gathering my courage. Instinctual knowledge was somehow being conveyed to me in this surreal setting. And without a doubt I knew that this was the only way out.

If I tried to walk away, I would walk forever getting nowhere. If I sat down and waited for something to happen, I would sit and wait forever. The only way to move forward was to follow the directions engraved on the rock.

I pulled the dagger strapped to my thigh and banged the hilt against the tombstone four times. Deep rumblings reverberated beneath my feet until there was a loud creak and the ice began to crack in a wide circle around the tombstone, trapping me against it. I had to fight the urge to dash away.

As soon as the crack completed a perfect circle, I was plunged into the icy water. My muscles tightened in shock. I hadn't expected the sudden sinking. I fought to breach the surface of the water, but it was as if someone had a hold of my ankle and was pulling me down through the black icy water.

I struggled not to take a breath, but the instinct was overwhelming. I abruptly reached a point where I stopped sinking and simply floated. Yet when I tried to kick to the surface, I made no upward progress.

A small pinpoint of light appeared. Instead of offering me reassurance I was inexplicably fearful of it. It rapidly grew in size and I realized it wasn't getting larger but nearer. When the light was a foot away from me, I saw it was a small child.

A little girl floated in the depths of the icy black water. Her pale hair floated around her deathly white face just as her dress floated around her small body. She was lifeless but she emitted a soft golden glow of light.

I began to choke. My lungs filled with water. Again, I made an attempt to swim to the surface, and again I went nowhere, simply floating in place.

Without warning the little girl's eyes flashed open, light beaming from her irises. I tried to swim away from her. Choking and drowning. I knew I would lose consciousness at any moment.

She reached out her small delicate hands and placed them on each side of my face, holding me still with her touch. She pressed her lips together and it looked like she was exhaling although no bubbles left her blue lips. And then I could breathe.

Air filled my lungs and although I was sunken amidst the depths of the lake, I could somehow breathe. The little girl's lips moved as if she was talking but no sound traveled through the water. Instead, I could hear her voice inside my head.

It's coming closer, she warned.

What is, I thought. I didn't know how to communicate with her. I opened my mouth to try and speak but she had already read my mind.

You will see.

What are you doing here? I thought at her. *Do you need help?*

No. But you do. You could die here, you know. You are drowning right now. The small child's voice that sounded in my mind was devoid of any emotion.

How do I get out?

You swim. But will you take him with you? She wasn't asking a favor of me but pondering my actions with a detached curiosity.

At her comment, I noticed a little boy who had not been in my field of vision a moment ago. His small limp body floated about twelve feet below us near the bottom of the lake. He had dark hair and wore no clothes. His pale white back was curled in the fetal position and I could see the peaks and valleys of his fragile spine.

What is he doing here?

He followed you in.

There was no little boy. It was the Shadow Prince who chased us.

He was a little boy once. Just as you were a little girl. How quickly people forget, she mused.

Will he die here?

Eventually. The light does not reach the darkest of depths. You must swim to the surface in order to reach it. You made that mistake once and it cost you dearly. Do not make the same mistake again. You cannot send light to places it does not reach.

I don't understand.

No, you do not. And now you must leave. It's coming closer.

Without warning the little girl disappeared in an implosion of water. I was sucked towards the epicenter, trapped in the vacuum of the current. But just as quickly, the force that had held me in place was lifted and I knew I had a matter of seconds to swim to the surface before being imprisoned in this icy lake for eternity.

I couldn't leave the little boy, though. Something had resonated when I had seen him. Some forgotten memory had pinged. The memory did not play or flash like an old home movie or photograph. The memory was still locked away, but I knew it was there buried somewhere. Waiting.

I wanted to reach the little child, but a new force was now sending me towards the surface of the lake. I was swimming against a strong current as I tried to reach the bottom of the lake. There was no light any longer. Once the little girl had disappeared, the light had extinguished with her.

I was kicking with all my might in total icy blackness. I had stopped needing breath when the little girl had appeared, but now I desperately needed to breathe. With my hands outstretched I reached, trying to find the little boy where I thought he had been.

But I couldn't. I was going to take an inhalation any second, unable to fight the urge to breathe. And I would drown. Even knowing this and being terrified in the total blackness as well as unsure any longer which direction the surface lay, I couldn't leave him.

And then a little hand grasped mine. He had found me. Somehow in the chilling inky depths, he had found me.

I squeezed my hand around his in an iron grip and began to kick furiously in the direction of the current. I believed it was shooting us upward to the surface.

When I breached the surface of the water, I sucked in an agonizing breath. The frozen air stabbed at my lungs. I coughed and spluttered and sucked in more painful air as I kicked to the shore which was now within reach.

A person stood on the bank, reaching out to me. I threw my arm up and felt a strong warm hand clasp around my wrist before being hauled out.

I lay on my back staring up at a blue cloudless sky, just trying to catch my breath. A face appeared above me, and as I squinted up at it, I realized the man who pulled me out of the lake was the same man I had seen with Adriel at the Radiant gala.

The neatly trimmed white hair and beard complimented his tanned taut features just as they had the other evening. I noticed now that he also had piercing silver eyes. He wore a long white caftan that somehow managed to accentuate his solid frame.

"Are you alright?" His voice was deep and pleasant.

"The boy," I gasped frantically, "Help the little boy!"

"It's alright," he said reassuringly. "Here, just sit up and breathe for a moment."

He helped me sit up and I looked around. Gone was the icy infinite lake. In its place was a tranquil reflecting pool that couldn't have been more than two feet deep. And instead of the darkness of night, I blinked my eyes at what was a picturesque bright afternoon. On the opposite side of the pool, amid luscious cliffs and waterfalls, stood an imposing tower which spired up into the atmosphere.

I had to blink a few times to comprehend what I saw. The tower looked as though it had been cleaved in two right down the middle and somehow remained standing. The left half was ivory and shone brightly in the sunlight. The right half was a glossy onyx. The rooms which had been at the heart of the split hung exposed, simply dangling precariously in the sky.

"I don't understand what happened," I said looking up at the man. "How did I get here?" I looked around. "Where's the little boy?"

"All are tested when they visit Aleece."

"There was a little boy. I was holding his hand. He was in the lake. At the bottom. And I pulled him up with me. He needs help."

The man put his hands on my shoulders. "Please, Violet, you must understand. It wasn't real. It was a test. There is no little boy. You do not need to fear for him."

"Yes, there was!" I was desperate to find him. To make him feel safe. Happy. Protected. Loved. More than anything I needed to make him feel loved.

"Look at where you are, Violet. There is no lake. Only the reflecting pool."

I cast my eyes around wildly before scrambling into the tranquil water. I knew the surface must be an illusion. I had just experienced the deathly chill and total darkness of what lay beneath.

But I was not plunged back into agonizing icy pain. The temperate water rose only to my thighs and no higher. I looked down into the clear water, searching the basin for any signs of the little boy or of some trench that opened up into dark depths below. But there was nothing.

"It was a test, Violet. Those who enter Aleece are tested," he repeated. Gentling his tone, he said, "There was no little boy. He existed only in your mind."

I opened my mouth to argue. The little boy had been real. I had known him somehow. He needed me. Needed me desperately and I had failed him. That was real. And no one could convince me otherwise. However, I realized there wasn't any more I could say to the man. He would simply repeat that it had not been real. So I closed my mouth.

But I couldn't help but consider his explanation. If this man was right, if it had in fact been a test, had I passed? What exactly were the parameters of the test? Had the little girl implied that the dark-haired child was the Shadow Prince? Was the point of the test to see past the innocent facade and abandon him there? Thereby defeating an evil being and preventing more innocent death and destruction? Or was the point of the test to show compassion and help him out of that dark icy grave?

"Let me take you inside where you can dry off and rest." The man stepped into the reflecting pool, paying no heed to the water that soaked the bottom of his robe. He placed one hand on my back and with the other he took my hand in his. Then he began ushering me out of the pool.

He helped me remove my waterlogged boots. He hadn't been wearing any shoes to begin with. So now we were both barefoot.

After we had begun walking down a small path that meandered through tall grasses and wildflowers, my head began to clear, and I stopped—startled and fearful all over again.

"Wait! I need to find my, ah—" I didn't know what the hell to refer to Elijah as, "—my traveling companion!"

The man smiled kindly, "Elijah must be tested as well."

"But we crossed the threshold together and he wasn't at the lake with me. I lost him somehow."

"He must face his test alone, just as you had to."

"He was so weakened when we crossed the threshold. I had to push him through. He wasn't even conscious. I don't know how badly injured he was. Please, we need to find him."

The man looked a little troubled, but maintained a kind look in his eyes. "Elijah must prove virtuous. There is nothing any of us can do for him."

This guy was really starting to piss me off. I pulled away from him. "Look, thanks for your help but I need to find someone named Davis. He'll know what to do."

The man smiled a deep genuine smile with a touch of sly fox at the eyes. He held out his hand, "I'm Davis. It's nice to meet you, Violet."

I sighed and shook his extended hand. Well he was the man Elijah wanted me to find, and if Davis wasn't stressed about Elijah, then I guessed I didn't need to be either. Although I was still worried. When I thought about what had happened in the *Vestibule*, I couldn't help but wonder if I had weakened Elijah even more by pulling on the connection we had. I almost felt like each time I had, I was taking strength from him.

"When will Elijah *arrive?*"

I wasn't surprised that Davis knew my name. He had been sitting with Adriel at the banquet and Elijah had told me to specifically seek out Davis, so whether he had known me previously or this was a first-time meeting, he clearly was already aware of me.

In his irritatingly relaxed and vague manner he replied, "It is different for everyone. No one can say."

I didn't know what to say other than a begrudging, "Okaaay."

"Would you like some dry clothes and a place to rest?" He stood there next to me in the beautiful green valley dappled with wildflowers, patiently waiting.

I glanced at the small path. It lazily wound through the valley to the split tower that was framed by snowcapped mountains and cascading waterfalls.

"I can tell you of this place as we walk," he added.

I sighed. Once again, I was in an unfamiliar place dependent upon a stranger. What else was there for me to do? Was I going to jump back in that shallow reflecting pool and search for Elijah or a way back to the vestibule in two feet of water?

I was wet and tired. I may have, allegedly, provoked a terrifyingly evil monster by making an attempt on his life and lost my memories in the process—but I wasn't a total fool.

I gave Davis the brightest smile I was capable of. "That would be lovely."

CHAPTER 21

A LEECE IS A VERY SPECIAL PLACE," Davis informed me as we walked along the path. "As you can see, it is the home of the Ivory Tower. The Tower is where the Council of Elders resides and officiates."

I looked at the imposing structure and was awed by it. The way it stood with the jagged split down the middle was like something out of a surrealist painting. What made the split so eye catching was the fact that the tower was two different colors on each side of the split. One side was pure alabaster while the other was onyx. Both sides gleamed in the sunlight. Yet between the two sides, along the massive split, those exposed rooms sat dangling precariously.

"What happened to it?" I asked Davis.

"No one can say for certain. You see, Aleece was the land of the Originals. And the Ivory Tower was erected by them and served as their home. According to legend, the Originals were a perfect race in all ways. They had highly advanced intelligence, superior physical strength and form, as well as perfectly developed interpersonal abilities.

"In perfection, there is balance. The Originals were wholly balanced in all ways. They were a utopian society.

"However, with all their incredible perfection came incredible arrogance. After a time, they deemed themselves to be more reverent than the very gods who made them. The gods were displeased. As punishment, they sent down a lightning bolt which split the Originals in two.

"The Originals were separated into light and dark, no longer in perfect balance. The light half remained here at the Ivory Tower while the dark half fled to another plane where they could retreat into the comfort of darkness and shadows.

"It is said that the lightning bolt which separated the Originals was the cause for the split of the tower. According to legend, the tower was a true ivory and turned to the alabaster and onyx that it is today when the split occurred."

"The Radiants and the Shadows," I commented. "The light and the dark."

Davis smiled at me and it was like the sun shining. "Very good."

"What exactly is the Council of Elders?" I asked.

Davis stopped to pluck a wildflower and then stood to hand it to me. "The light half of the Originals, of course."

I begrudgingly took the violet flower from him. "How much of this is myth and how much is truth?"

Davis shrugged his broad shoulders and began walking again. "Who can say? How does myth propagate? It is a story told from one generation to the next. The Elders themselves are so old that they can no longer remember their beginnings."

"How old are they?" I asked.

"Old enough that counting the passing time has become meaningless."

"Who are you, Davis?"

He bestowed me with that shining smile again. "I am a *voluntarius*, a volunteer. I work in the tower tending to the garden and maintaining the structure. There are thirteen of us who tend the grounds and the structure. We consider ourselves humble servants. Thirteen servants. Thirteen Elders."

"But you were at the Radiant Court, at the gala, last night."

He placed a heavy hand on my shoulder and gave me that kind look again. "My dear, the dinner at the Court was three days ago."

"But," I tried to replay the events since then in my mind.

"The journey to Aleece varies for everyone."

"I only spent a matter of minutes at that lake."

"Time is not rigid. It ebbs and flows. It is different for all who journey here."

I let out an exaggerated sigh and Davis laughed.

"Everything is just spiraling out of control around me," I confessed to him.

"Hmm, so it seems," he replied. "But what will you do about it?"

"Well I don't know what choice I have other than to follow along." I gestured down the path we were walking.

"Hmm."

"That isn't a helpful response," I told him.

"I suppose not," he agreed.

We walked for a time in silence, the tower growing ever larger as we approached. I began to hear the waterfalls from the cliffs behind the tower, and I could see a large garden in the front of the structure. A few men and women were tending to the plants. They all had gray hair and they were all dressed in white caftans as Davis was.

Something had been bothering me about the myth Davis had told me. I hadn't been able to articulate the thought, but I felt desperate to get an answer before we arrived at the tower.

"If the light half of the Originals is here at the Ivory Tower, then where is the shadow half? And why do the Radiants and Shadows war?"

"Indeed."

"Davis—"

But he cut me off as the path led us to a freestanding stone archway. It was a simple, crude structure that was crumbling in places. It looked as though it had been standing there since the dawn of time. And if Davis' story had any merit to it, then perhaps it had. But aside from its imposing size and age, the oddest thing about it was that the keystone was missing. Yet the arch remained standing.

"All those who enter must agree to a vow of silence when traversing through the Ivory Tower. You may speak in your private room or in the surrounding grounds, but not in the common space and not in the gardens. Appropriate attire is required and there are no shoes permitted in the tower. You will find an acceptable dressing gown in your washroom."

Davis promptly passed through the large arch without allowing me a response. I followed after him and we passed the gardens which lay on either side of the path, closed in by white picket fences. The handful of people scattered throughout were tending to the grounds. However, as we passed, each one turned to us. They did not speak or wave, but each wore the same kind of serene smile Davis had.

I wasn't sure how to react and I glanced at Davis. He was simply returning the tranquil look to each one in kind. I tried to mimic the slight upturn of the lips in response, but knew I was failing miserably.

Luckily, we came upon the wide entrance of the Tower and I no longer had to engage in the strange greetings. There was no need to open the double doors however, as they too were split down the center. We simply stepped right through the gaping cleft.

Being inside the tower was aweing. It was like hiking inside a narrow chasm with a wide base. The ruptured rooms climbed up into the atmosphere on either side of us and high above was the open sky.

The rooms were empty from what I could tell, but they made for a startling juxtaposition. While they dangled in a haunted and forgotten way, the airy light that seeped from the open sky above was almost holy.

Even the floor in the entryway was split down the center with an alabaster stone comprising the left half and an onyx stone making up the right half. What was most fascinating was the scorch mark that lined the center divide. It certainly did look as though the floor had been struck by lightning. It wasn't proof that Davis' tale was truth, but I could see how it would help perpetuate the myth.

Davis led me off to the left, to the alabaster side, and we entered a cramped elevator. The door was manually shut and instead of a panel of buttons, the small car had an exposed rope that was clearly part of a pulley system. Davis began to tug on it and we rose in a jerky but fairly quick fashion.

I took his vow of silence comment to heart and didn't try to speak to him. The tower exuded an air of solemnity that I couldn't bring myself to defy.

After ascending for quite some time, Davis slowed the car and brought us to a stop. He opened the elevator doors and led me into a plain hallway. Without a word, he opened one of the closed doors and gestured for me to enter. Then after a quick bow and gracious smile, he turned and started for the elevator. No instructions. No goodbye.

I stepped back into the hallway feeling abandoned. I almost called after him, but the air was heavy with that same reverent pressure that seemed to sink throughout the structure. I didn't dare disrupt the silence. I thought about chasing him, but I just didn't have the heart to.

Regardless of what Davis said about my experience at the lake. It had been very real to me. I had physically experienced every moment of it. I was wet, cold, and fatigued.

So I didn't know how to find Davis. Or when he would be back. Or what I should be doing in this place. What did it really matter? I would figure it out.

I stepped into the bedroom and shut the door behind me. It was spartan with a simple single bed and a basic wooden desk with matching chair. There were no embellishments or decor pieces. Just four white walls and the three pieces of wood furniture. The bed had a white cotton sheet over the mattress and a second turned down sheet, but no pillows or blankets.

There was a connecting door in the room that led to a private bathroom. The bathroom was also simple, but there was a tub and I found that hot water was an option. There were a couple towels laid out on a shelf and a plain white bar of soap. And it was all the luxury I needed.

***

After I bathed and dried, I dressed in the white caftan which hung upon the backside of the bathroom door. It was the same as Davis had worn, just in a smaller size.

There was a knock at the door as soon as I had finished dressing. I began to make my way over to answer when the door was flung open. G walked in as if he was expected, shutting the door behind him.

"Hey," he said. He looked completely healed from whatever wounds had afflicted him back in the cabin, but his greeting lacked any enthusiasm and he seemed pretty downtrodden with his shoulders slumped and his bare feet shuffling the floor.

Like Davis, and now me, G wore a white caftan. He was clearly uncomfortable in it, shifting around in the robe and tugging at the neck and sleeves as he sat on the modest bed.

"Wow, you look a lot better from the last time I saw you. Nice threads," I mocked. "What's this all about anyway?" I asked, gesturing to my own outfit.

"Stupid fucking Elder shit," he huffed.

I raised my eyebrows at him, not understanding.

He huffed again and the exhale was so cute on him. Here he was this big gorgeous male and he was sulking like a little school boy.

"The Elders—" He stopped and started over. "This is the Ivory Tower. It's where the Elders reside. And everything has to be all formal and old school. So we all have to wear these fucked up dresses."

He tugged the front of the caftan. I don't know if it was to drive home his point or just out of irritability, but apparently, he tugged a little too hard because the back of the robe ripped down the middle.

He froze and looked at me with wide eyes.

I winced.

It was all the confirmation he needed. He threw his head back and cursed to the ceiling.

"Man, I'm going to get so much shit for this." He looked at his feet resting on the wood floor. "We can't even wear shoes." Reaching down and grabbing a foot he sniffled, "And my feet get cold."

I sighed. G reminded me of a golden retriever. He was nice to look at, sweet, friendly, loyal, powerful and athletic. Why couldn't I have strong inexplicable feelings for him? Which reminded me.

"Where's Daphne?"

A pained expression passed over his face. "That cold fish? Who cares."

That hadn't been the response I was expecting.

"You do. Don't you?" I asked gently.

He stared at me for a long moment looking defiant and then looked away. His big hand rubbed his chest right above his heart.

"Yeah...I do."

G stood up and crossed over to me, pulling me in for a side hug. He rested his chin on the top of my head.

"Trouble in paradise?" I asked.

"Yeah. Something like that. Honestly, I don't know where she is right now. It doesn't matter." He let out a heavy breath. "I'm sorry for what happened at the cabin. What she said to you wasn't fair."

I wrapped my arm around his waist and gave a return squeeze. "Thanks, G." I pulled back from him. "But she was right. My life isn't worth the lives of others. I don't even know who I am. Where's the point in that?"

"Help an angel out. Knot the material back together for me?" He gestured to the back of his robe.

I sighed. "G, you can't just ignore what I'm saying."

"Ah, yeah. I sure can. We're not having this discussion, babydoll. Now hop to it."

"Fine." I reached up and tied the two ripped sides together at the base of his neck, making the knot as inconspicuous as possible. It didn't look too bad.

"So, you decided to go for a dip, huh? I heard you were flopping around the reflecting pool like a fish out of water earlier."

"Davis told you that?" I scowled. But it reminded me of another thing. I turned back to G. "The Shadow Prince found us just before we reached the threshold for Aleece. Elijah tried to fight him and was severely injured. We managed to get away, but I had to push him through the threshold while he was unconscious and we were separated. I told Davis about it and he said not to worry. But Elijah was so weak. I'm afraid for him."

"How the hell is that boogey man getting through the veils?" G mumbled to himself.

"I don't know. What does it matter. He just is. G, what about Elijah?" I insisted.

He snapped out of his personal musings and folded his large arms across his chest. Peering down at me he said, "Let me get this straight. The Dark One kicked Elijah's ass and you saved him?"

"It wasn't like that. We did what we could, and things just happened."

"Man, you are something else. That Shadow bastard almost ended me outside the Radiant Court. If it wasn't for Daphne pulling me out..." He let out a breath. "So how did you get away from him?"

I didn't know why, but I felt guilty about what I had done. I curled my toes and examined the floor. "I...I kind of...well...I stabbed him. I don't think he was expecting it. I lied to him about going with him willingly and I think he believed me."

G shook his head. "Something else," he repeated.

"What about Elijah?"

"There's nothing we can do. We just have to wait. He'll be fine. Don't stress over him."

G gave me another big hug. "I know you're tired. Get some rest. You're safe here. If you get hungry the kitchen is on the first floor. It's in the back on the white side of the tower. Stay away from the dark side. There is always bread and water available down there. The voluntarius hold a communal dinner at five, if

216

you're up for it. It's pretty lame since everyone sits in total silence, but they ring one of the tower bells as a notice. I have some stuff I have to do, but I'll be back tomorrow."

Thanks, G," I said stifling a yawn.

He nodded and gave me a quick kiss on the head before leaving.

Everyone kept telling me not to worry about Elijah. But as I lay down in the borrowed bed, I knew better.

CHAPTER 22

A BOY. *A MAN. SHADOWS. A lonely life. A melancholy melody. Strong, graceful hands. Ice blue eyes. I loved him. I would love him in any lifetime. Broken. I wanted to save him. Dying.*

He wants to touch me, but he knows one single touch will scorch him. I am everything he can never have and everything he can never know. I am light and air and sunshine. I am the happy tinkling of chimes. I am self-confidence. I am loved and treasured. These things he can't even begin to comprehend. We are not two different people. We are two different things.

He is a thing that lurks in the forgotten shadows of the night. And I am a thing of warmth and beauty and eternal sunlight dappling through the leaves of the trees.

My laugh. He hears it echoing down a hall and it disturbs him. He wants to hear it again. He never wants to hear it again. He wants to understand it. To understand how something could be so free. He wants to hear another version of it. A softer more seductive version of it in his ear late at night while

I'm wrapped around him. He wants to know what it feels like to laugh. He is angered by it. By the fact that I share something—something to him that seems incredibly special—with others.

My laugh floating through the corridor pains him. It is a sharp reminder that I could never be with someone like him. He is dark and cold and empty. My laughter would be sucked away—absorbed entirely by the yawning abyss of darkness within him.

I loved him. I would love him in any lifetime.

I knew he watched me. I let him think I was unaware. I let him keep the shield of distance that he needed. I stretched and arched in my white cotton camisole and panties. It was wrong to tease him, but I wanted him to see what he could have. Could have if he would just find a way to climb out of the dark pit he had buried himself in.

I wanted to touch him. To soothe him. I wanted to wrap my arms around him and press my body to his. To show him how I saw him. I wanted to be enough for him. I wanted him to see me as a worthy reason to break free from the bonds which tethered him.

I purposefully dropped my brush. I bent over slowly, letting my hair cascade down my arms and sweep the floor. I stayed like that longer than necessary before languidly standing back up.

Just knowing he watched me was incredibly arousing. My nipples stiffened under the thin cotton of my camisole and my panties grew wet. I rolled my head to the side and let my fingers trail across my collarbone. Then down over one breast and lower still across my midriff. Wishing it was his hand that touched me, I let my fingers trail over the front of my panties and then graze at my core over the delicate cotton.

Electricity crackled in the air and I let a sensual smile brush across my lips. I was willing to bet he wasn't even aware of the radiant energy he was exuding.

***

I had slept right through the dinner bell. But in the early morning hours I found myself tossing and turning. Vivid dreams had left me sweating, panting and unable to fall back asleep. Unsure what to do with myself, I simply lay there for a time.

And then out of nowhere, I felt his energy. He pinged onto my radar and I knew that he needed me. Something was very wrong.

Elijah. I had been right to fear for him.

I tore from my room in a panic, running down the dark and empty hall until I reached the elevator. It was easy to operate after having watched Davis and I descended in a hurry.

Out the front entry and down the path, I followed the pull beckoning me towards the edge of the forest off in the distance. I was choking on fear as I ran. It was close. Too close. And I might not get to him in time. He was *fading.*

After what seemed like a small eternity, I knew I was almost to him. I ran unerringly towards one tree. Under the moonlight, I could see a figure there, collapsed on the ground.

"Elijah!" I screamed.

There was no response.

I scrambled to the ground turning him from his side onto his back. He let out a barely audible moan and I gasped.

He was badly beaten—much worse than when I had last seen him in the vestibule. One eye was swollen shut and his other eye, as well as his jaw, were blackened with bruises. His lip was split open and I couldn't even begin to guess at the extent of injuries that must have damaged other parts of his body.

221

"Elijah," I whispered. I stroked the hair from his damp fever drenched forehead. "What happened to you?"

And even through all the pain, I could feel the relief that swept over him when he cracked open the one eye he could and saw me. "Violet," he croaked. My heart softened for him then. I knew that he wasn't relieved because someone had come to help him. He was relieved because I was safe. Because I had made it to Aleece.

"Oh, Elijah." I couldn't keep the sadness from my voice. He was going to die here on the ground.

I could gauge Elijah's inner light through the connection we shared, and it was weak and faint. He was dying. The bond screamed at me to save him and I knew there wasn't any time to try and get help. Although I lacked my own free will in this matter, I would have wanted to try and help him even without the compulsion of the bond. He had risked his life to protect me. I felt gratitude as well as guilt. I would do whatever I could to save him.

I placed one hand on his cheek and he winced at the gentle touch.

"Shh. It's okay. Everything's alright. I'm going to help." I placed my other hand on his chest. I had no idea how to go about this, but I willed all the energy and light that I had directly into Elijah.

He moaned and his big body jerked at the flush of light that erupted from my palms. I felt the pulse of his life force momentarily flicker before settling back into a dying ember. It wasn't enough. He needed more.

I tore open the front of his ripped and dirty shirt. The golden skin of his muscled chest and abdomen was covered in black bruises. I fought back a cry, willing myself to be strong and calm. I pulled my own caftan up over my head and tossed it to the side before lying as gently as I could on top of him so that our chests were pressed together, bare skin to bare skin. I lay on him willing my own energy to cover him.

Elijah's spine arched on the ground and he let out another moan as light flared between us again. I could feel it working but it was still not enough. He needed more. More of me. All of me. But I didn't know what to do.

"Elijah, I don't—"

My words were abruptly cut off as Elijah rolled me over onto my back covering me with his large broken body. He buried his face in my neck and wrapped his arms around my back pinning me between him and the earth below. His hips were cradled in the valley between my thighs and he gave a slight rocking motion.

I let out a gasp at the sensation. It felt so right. It was exactly what he needed. What we both needed. We had to be as physically connected as possible. I understood that. There would be no greater way to exchange energy than by being physically bound.

He bucked against me again. "Need you, Violet," he groaned, his voice raw from whatever calamity he had been through. "I've never needed anything as bad as I need you right now." He sucked on the pulse point at my neck and I could feel a flare of energy there.

I cried out at the incredible sensation and forgot any discord I had been feeling. All at once, I was hot and wet and throbbing.

223

Every inch of my skin was vibrating with the energy Elijah was pulling from me. Each moment was torturous ecstasy. He sucked harder at my neck and began to thrust against me through the jeans he still wore.

I wanted to free him from the denim, but I couldn't get my hands between us. His massive chest and rigid abdomen were pressed flush against me.

"Elijah," I moaned. But he was too far gone to hear me. Every thrust hit me in exactly the right spot, each suck on my neck ratcheted me higher. A tidal wave was building and when it was just about to break, I moaned his name again. Then it came crashing over me breaking into a million little pieces again and again before eventually receding.

At the same time, Elijah paused his rhythmic thrusts before jerking above me and groaning hoarsely. His big body shuddered over me before slowly easing still. He grazed his lips and nose all along my neck and jaw.

I could feel his energy replenished. It was nowhere near enough, though. He was still in a critical state, but he was stabilized for the moment.

Still caging me in his arms and pinning me to the earth, he grazed one final kiss on my neck and passed out.

CHAPTER 23

ELIJAH," I hissed. "Elijah wake up!"

When Elijah first lost consciousness, I was too stunned to know what to think. I felt amazing, like I had just had the longest most replenishing sleep of my life. In being so close and physical and intimate with each other, somehow the energy between us had flared and recharged leaving Elijah stabilized and me completely revitalized.

I also felt more connected to Elijah than before. We were becoming more tightly bound and I honestly didn't know what to think about that.

I wanted him healed and well, but I also realized that we were in quite a precarious position and dawn would approach soon. He was so solid, so massive, that I couldn't push him off of me. He still wore his jeans, but I was totally naked. I had no idea if someone might be strolling along and find us sprawled in such a compromised entanglement.

"Elijah!" I tried tapping his back. Nothing. I began wriggling underneath him trying to shimmy my way out. If only his arms weren't caged around my back I would be able to slide out from under him, but he had me pinned.

I either needed Elijah to move on his own or I needed someone to help me. But I could read Elijah more now than ever. I could feel that he was out cold in a healing state and would not be woken. I thought of G. I had seen G and Daphne at the cabin, had seen them go through something similar when G was badly injured. If anyone could understand my predicament it would be him, right?

Feeling incredibly foolish I timidly called out, "G?"

There was no response. I don't know why I did it. I guess I just thought that being an angel he might have some omniscient abilities.

I began wriggling under Elijah again in the hopes that I could get one of his arms loosened and free myself.

Great booming laughter cut through the quiet predawn air and I yelped. When I picked my head up to peer over Elijah's bulky shoulder I saw G standing a few feet away lit like a firefly and guffawing.

"It isn't funny!" I snapped at him. "He was going to die, you know."

More laughter.

"You probably did the same thing to Daphne," I huffed.

Between gasping breaths, he heaved, "I so did."

"Just get him off of me!"

Still chuckling G said, "Okay." He used that tone that says *I think that's a mistake and you'll regret it but if you said so...*

He reached down to pull Elijah up and I realized why he had used that warning tone. I was going to be lying naked flat on my back and I would never be able to look G in the eye again. I would probably spontaneously combust from total humiliation.

"Wait. Don't!"

G started hooting all over again.

"Just loosen his arms out from under my back," I amended.

He pulled Elijah's arms out from under me.

"Now hand me my robe."

"Wow, you're bossy."

I tacked on an impatient, "Please."

G reached down and placed the robe in my hand.

"Turn around for a minute—*please*."

G dutifully turned his back and I shimmied out from under Elijah. I put on the robe as fast as I possibly could, feeling utterly exposed and embarrassed.

"Alright. Thank you."

G turned back around with a huge smile on his face. "You owe me. *Big time*, baby doll."

"Yeah, yeah, fine," I grumbled. I kneeled down and tried to gently roll Elijah over onto his back.

G kneeled down to help me. He sucked in a breath and his internal luminescent distinguished when he saw Elijah's face, torso, and arms. All good-natured lightheartedness left him.

"He's healing. It was worse when I found him," I told G.

"Let me take him to the tower. I'll be right back for you."

"No just take care of him. I can walk back."

G disappeared with Elijah and a moment later he returned. Before I could even voice a protest, we were in the room I had been given. A single candle was lit on the desk, and Elijah was lying on his back in the small bed still unconscious.

I pulled the chair from the desk over to the bed. "Can you get me a wash cloth and some towels as well as a basin of water?"

G nodded and disappeared.

I smoothed my hand over Elijah's forehead inspecting his wounds. He did look better, but only slightly. He had dried blood caked down the side of one ear as well as on his lip. The skin around his swollen eye was split and needed cleaning. He also had some dirt from the forest floor smudged on his skin.

I had no idea what had caused the mottled black bruises across his abdomen and arms and I shuddered looking at them thinking that I probably did not want to know.

G returned with the clean towels and water as well as a fresh robe for me and a larger one for Elijah.

"I can feel his energy," I told him. "I can feel that he's stable. But he's still so weak. So injured. Is there anything that we need to do for him? Does he need a doctor?"

G placed his hand on my shoulder. "You can do more for him than any doctor right now. The bond you feel with him? It's an energy bond. It's called the Vinculum. Your energy and his energy feed each other. Recharge each other. And it's only between the two of you. You can't have this connection with anyone else and neither can he."

G squeezed my shoulder. "Look, it's not my place and it's not my business, but I think you two need to make this work and not fight it. You're good for each other. Elijah needs to get over his prejudices and you need to let go of your resentment. He's a good man Violet. Just give him a chance. Show him why he's been so wrong."

G leaned down to place a big brotherly type kiss on the top of my head. "I'm sorry. There's something I have to do. But I'll be back to check on you two. Take care of him," he said just before he pulsed away.

I set about trying to clean Elijah as best I could. Over and over again I dabbed the washcloth in the small basin of water and gently wiped away the blood and dirt on him. I emptied and refilled the basin twice because of how dirty the water was becoming.

I already knew that Elijah was large and muscular, but gently washing every inch of his arms and torso, I developed an appreciation for his physique. The rigid peaks and valleys

I didn't know what to do about his jeans. They were filthy with more dried blood and dirt, as well as what looked like dark oil. I didn't think I could take them off him easily, if at all. If they were coming off, I would need to cut them.

The clothes I had worn when I arrived in Aleece were hanging in the bathroom. And I fetched one of the knives from the holster that Elijah had strapped to my thigh before we had begun our trek.

I slipped the knife between Elijah's ankle and the cuff of his jeans. I pierced the denim and sliced through the fabric, effectively cutting a small slit along the side. Continuing the process all the way up, I eventually had a full-length tear along the side of his right leg. Doing the same on his left side, I was able to slide the pants out from under him fairly easily. His legs looked the same as his arms and torso, covered in sickening black bruises. But there were no open wounds.

I did a gentle wash over his legs with the wet cloth and then a thorough scrub of his shoeless feet, which were filthy. I covered him with the sheet once he was as clean and dry as I could manage.

Then I took all the supplies into the bathroom. I knew I needed another bath myself after having been naked on the forest floor and covered by the grime from Elijah, but I didn't want to leave him alone. Instead I did a quick cleaning as best I could with a wet washcloth and dressed in the fresh caftan G had brought before putting away the basin and soiled towels.

I settled back into the chair next to the bed to watch over Elijah and contemplate what G had said. I don't know how much time passed like that, with me keeping watch over Elijah and the thoughts of everything we had been through in our short time together playing through my mind like a movie reel. But I was startled from my reverie when Elijah began to shift restlessly.

I leaned forward to gently shush him and stroke his hair. He opened one bleary eye and looked at me before muscling his way up onto his elbows.

"Lie back down," I whispered, "Go to sleep. Everything's alright."

He looked at the chair I was sitting in and then forced himself to sit up fully, the large muscles in his shoulders, chest, and abdomen flexing and bunching with the movement. Next, he moved his legs over the side of the bed.

"What are you doing? You need to lie down."

I stood trying to usher him back into bed. I knew he was weak. But I knew it only because of our connection. He planted his feet on the floor and stood, a vision of powerful, albeit bruised, golden male towering above me in the candlelight.

He was and would always be strong and stern. He would never show weakness. And looking at his big muscled body and determined mien, I knew it was foolish to try and force him to do anything.

But then that determined expression of his shifted. To say it softened would be inaccurate. Nothing about him was soft. But it lessened.

"Take off the robe." It was a request, and for once, not a demand. In his own way, it was a supplication. His voice was still gravelly and hoarse, barely usable.

In that moment, I could deny him nothing. I gathered the hem of the robe in my hands, lifted it over my head, and pulled it off. My hair swished down over my shoulders, chest, and back from the motion.

Elijah looked at me with such a longing ache that my heart broke a little for him. Then he picked me up, laying me down in the bed, and settled back into it himself. He wrapped his arms around me so that my back was pressed firmly against his chest. A thrum of soothing energy immediately began to hum between us. He draped a possessive leg over mine and began stroking my hair.

I was taken aback by the tenderness he was showing me. I hadn't thought him capable of gentleness, but he stroked my hair as if I was the most fragile thing he had ever held.

After a time, Elijah's broken voice parted the silence. "They killed my family."

I held my breath, not knowing what to say.

"You asked what they did to me," he continued. "They killed my family when I was ten. I was there when it happened. My mother had shoved me into a closet. I could see things through the slats of the closet door. They were brutal."

I remained quiet, not wanting to interrupt.

"I couldn't handle having the feelings I did for you. To feel that way for a Shadow, it was…difficult. I don't want to talk about my trial to get here. But I had a choice and I fought to get to you."

I slowly turned to face him. I searched his eyes. There was so much there. Pain. Vulnerability. Need. I knew I was seeing a side of him he shared with no one.

I laid a gentle hand on his cheek and barely brushed my lips over his. Then I pulled back to look at him.

His large hand cupped the back of my head and he crushed his lips over mine in a possessive kiss. He was claiming me. Accepting me.

My tongue found his over and over again as my fingers slipped into his hair. Then he was rolling me onto my back as he covered me with his body. His hard chest pressed against my breasts and his solid thighs sank in between my own, forcing them open.

He pulled back to look down at me. Even with the swollen cuts and bruises, he was perfect. I would always remember the way he looked in that moment, gazing down at me, with his golden hair, tanned skin, and blazing eyes.

I knew Elijah was giving me a chance to say no. But I'm not sure if I had a choice then. The compulsion to be with him. The intimate connection I shared with him. The things I felt for him. I'm not certain I could have fought any of it. But the truth was, I didn't want to fight it. Becoming lost in another and having them lose themselves in you—it's an indulgence that any of us rarely get.

I reached up cupping his jaw and ran my thumb over his lips. Elijah closed his eyes and turned his head to kiss my palm. And I knew I had sealed my fate.

I threaded my fingers through his hair and he leaned down to kiss me while he pressed into me. He had to rock back and forth, over and over again, just to fit the head of his shaft. I was slick and throbbing and the motion alone was sending me to the brink of an orgasm. Then he began longer strokes, going slowly, allowing me to accommodate his massive size. His kisses were filled with the same languid sensuality as his thrusts and I got lost in him.

Everything and everyone drifted away. All that existed was me and him in this small simple room with a single candle burning. His hands were in my hair and every inch of his massive body was covering, possessing, and owning my own.

The energy exchange between us was less explosive this time. It was like a spring of light slowly being filled, gently rising higher until it was brimming with liquid sunshine.

I refused to let myself come. I didn't want to interrupt what was happening. I wanted to make love like this to Elijah until the sun inevitably rose.

But I couldn't. The pleasure was building behind the wall I had erected, and I couldn't hold it back for much longer.

"Elijah," I moaned.

"I know," he answered.

Then he sucked on the pulse point at my neck and I came in a wet rush that went on and on. Elijah jerked over me moaning my name and crushing me to him. He buried his face in my hair and continued to come, thrusting, over and over again. Just when I thought I was being released from the paralyzing pleasure of my orgasm, I began to come again from Elijah's ceaseless thrusts.

With one last groan, he finally stilled over me. The weight of his big body grounding me, keeping me in the here and now. He began to rub his nose all along my neck and side of my face. I laced my fingers through his hair and kissed his cheek. When I turned my head to accept more of his nuzzling, I drew in a startled breath.

All around the room tiny little sparks floated. They were golden and winking, creating a magical glittering effect.

"What is that," I breathed.

Elijah picked his head up to follow my gaze. "It's why we are pulled to each other," he answered. "It's a special kind of magic that strengthens our race." He placed his head down to rest in the curve between my neck and shoulder. When he spoke, I could feel his lips on my skin. "I thought the sparks were just a figurative part of the story. I didn't know they were real." His words began to slow and halt. "It's the energy that forms between the Prisms."

I knew he needed more rest. I reached out and stroked his cheek. "Sleep," I told him.

And with hundreds of tiny stars floating in the air of the dark room, he did.

CHAPTER 24

I QUIETLY GOT DRESSED and splashed cold water over my face in the bathroom. Elijah continued to rest in the small bed. He had begun to shift a little when I left his embrace, but I smoothed a hand through his hair and he settled back to sleep.

He had healed rapidly while he slept. Gone were the lacerations on his face. I didn't want to wake him by trying to inspect the rest of his injuries, but I was fairly certain those would be almost healed as well.

G waited for me outside in the hallway. He had woken me, telling me in hushed tones that my presence was requested by the Council.

My stomach was in knots. G had looked ill at ease and that worried me. In the time I had spent with him, it seemed that nothing could rattle G's carefree nature. But for some reason, this had.

I was dressed in the caftan and was barefoot as I crossed into the hallway. I had braided my hair and then twisted the braid into a knot at my nape trying my best to appear appropriately before the Elders.

G paced in front of the elevator but stopped when he saw me. He forced a pained smile.

I was about to ask him what this was all about, when I remembered the vow of silence. I wanted to whisper to him in spite of the rules of the tower, but the pressure to honor the vow was heavy in the space of the hallway.

He gestured for me to enter the elevator and I complied. I looked at him, trying to find answers in vain.

G gave me a reassuring look and squeezed my shoulder before using the rope in the elevator to drop the car down to the main floor. I followed him through a backdoor into the bright blue morning.

There were flower gardens behind the tower and an awing view of the mountains which surged up in a dramatic grade just beyond the grounds. The various waterfalls cascading from the ridges created a white mist that rose from the base of the peaks.

It was painful not to be able to talk to G but once we were past the gardens, I felt the compulsion to remain silent dissipate.

"What's going on?" I breathed, trying my best not to sound panicked. "What's wrong, G?"

"You have been summoned for trial. I have been ordered to escort you to the Hall of Truth."

"What does that mean?"

"I'm not sure. I don't know the details of it. But I am going to stay with you, don't worry. We'll get this all sorted."

239

"What if I don't want to go?" Yes, I felt like a coward asking the question, but really, how much more of this was I supposed to take? I began to long for Elijah's cabin. Things were different between us now. Maybe we could just go back there and hide from everyone else for a while.

"I'm sorry Violet. It's not an option."

"Fine. Whatever. Let's get this over with." What more could be thrown at me anyway? I suddenly let out a hysterical laugh.

"Everything's going to be fine. Really."

It didn't take some special connection to know G didn't believe what he was saying.

We approached the base of the mountain directly behind the Ivory Tower. In front of us was a large pool where the falling water collected. The spray from the falls misted us as we approached an old bridge. It passed from this side of the pool, between two of the falls, to connect with a cave-like entrance in the mountain face.

Once we passed through the mouth of the cave, we came upon two towering double doors that reminded me of those we had seen in the Vestibules. They too were made from carved ivory stone with elegant script engraved on the surface. In an unsettling fashion, the doors silently opened on their own accord as we approached.

Next was a simple hallway that led to a large chamber. The space was flooded with indirect natural light resulting in an airy setting that took on a dream-like quality.

The hall was cylindrical with curved towering ivory walls on all sides that soared ever upward. I could see no ceiling and no end to the walls. They simply disappeared into the hazy white light. It was impossible not to feel a sense of awe at the majesty of the space. Those soaring walls seemed to glow with their own holy radiance that suffused the place with a heavenly air.

About fifteen feet up, alcoves, just large enough to fit an individual, were carved into the ivory in a perfect ring. In each one of the thirteen alcoves, a white robed figure stood.

The Elders.

They were indistinguishable from each other, appearing identical from one to the next, with hoods drawn concealing their faces. They looked like religious statues and standing perfectly still in their carved niches, they imposed just as much reverent solemnity as any divine relic.

As G and I had just stepped onto a circular dais in the center of the hall a larger than life singular voice sounded.

"The Council does not permit audience. Why do you stand before us, Archangel?" The powerful voice asked. None of the robed figures in the alcoves moved. Although they were still as statues, there was no doubt that the thirteen Elders were somehow behind the voice and speaking as one.

I could feel G's strong hand surreptitiously squeeze my shoulder. "I would like to evoke ancient tradition and serve as the orator for the accused, if it so pleases the Council." His calm confident voice flowed through the space with ease.

A low hum came from the mezzanine above. It was as if many different voices were conferring together from very far away. And then the singular voice responded echoing through the hall. "It will be so."

241

I could feel the tension in G's body relax just a fraction. It seemed that he was past the first hurdle but expecting more to come.

The voice continued. "Who stands against the accused?"

From the shadows of another adjoining tunnel stepped Daphne.

"I do," she declared, her flaxen hair and dewy skin shimmering in the diffused light. She was an incredible sight to behold and I couldn't help but momentarily wonder how G looked standing behind me. Although I did not dare try to turn around.

Whatever sacredness this place held, it was palpable and undeniable. I was willing to bet that even the most deplorable of people would fall to their knees in supplication at the reverence of the Hall.

As soon as the words left Daphne's perfect lips G took a halting step forward shouting, "Daphne, no!"

I could hear the feelings for her entrenched in his plea.

If Daphne flinched at all in response to Giddeon's hurt betrayal, she internalized it. Her demeanor remained fiercely stoic and resolved.

"Silence," the eerie intercom voice of the Council boomed. The command echoed against the ivory walls. As the only sound in the space, it seemed to gobble up all the air leaving none for breath with which to form words. It didn't take a genius to deduce that outbursts were a serious infraction in the Hall.

After a pause the hollow voice of the Council demanded, "Your defense, orator."

Without hesitation, G responded. "The accused is tethered, and the Vinculum has been impelled, as the Council is aware. The very thing for which our race has desperately sought has been attained because of her. She must be protected, healed, and made whole once again. The Lady of the Radiant Court believes it possible."

"The Lady is biased!" Daphne interjected.

The entire hall began to shake as if experiencing a massive earthquake. From behind, G grabbed me to hold me steady, each of his large hands clutching my upper arms.

In what looked to be a begrudging manner, Daphne knelt to the floor and sat on her feet lying her arms and body out before her. Although her face was pressed into the floor and the quaking of the very earth around us threw off a deep rumble, I could hear her say, "I beseech the council to pardon my offense. It will not happen again."

"Rise and speak," the unearthly voice ordered.

Daphne stood once again and began.

"I have come to bear witness. She is *Shadow Kissed*. She carries the *Umbra Bassium*. I request the Council forsake her to her circumstances and return her to the Shadow Court."

"Daphne! Don't do this." G lunged towards her, but he was hurtled against the wall as an invisible force threw him. For just a moment, there was a crack in Daphne's stoic demeanor.

Then the collective voice of the Elders thundered, "Do not approach the witness."

I thought of going to help G stand back up, but I had the impression that the Elders would not like for me to move from where I stood.

"The time for oration is over. We will make our judgement."

At those words, a chill passed over my chest. It was as if an icy hand was pressed against my skin, somehow slipping beneath my robe. I sucked in a startled breath.

The far-off whispering of several voices creeped through the chamber once again before the singular voice rang out, "Her heart is not pure."

There seemed to be a finality to the statement, as if a decision had been made. The invisible hand lifted from my chest, and I let out a shuddering breath, feeling violated. I also couldn't help but feel that my fate had just been sealed.

"You are dismissed. Leave now and await your sentence." And with that each of the statue-like Elders simply faded from their alcoves.

When I looked back down, Daphne was gone. G and I stood alone in the chamber.

"Let's go," he said, his voice void of any emotion.

I followed him down the passageway and out the stone doors, which slid shut behind us as we emerged into the mouth of the cave. As soon as the doors were fully closed, I heard a scratching sound behind us.

I turned and a golden script began to appear across the now blank surface of the ivory doors. The script was in a language I didn't understand.

I stood staring dumbly at the elegant shimmering cursive, not wanting to turn around and see the look of pity I knew must be splashed across G's perfect face.

"I'm—" G began to speak but the sound of heavy footsteps approaching had us both turning to face the opening of the cave.

Even before I laid eyes on him my pulse began to race. When I caught sight of him, his burning gaze was locked on me, those golden flecks alight in his hazel eyes.

I could feel the sudden emotions churning within him like a destructive squall.

He was violently angry. Barreling past G, he came right up to me, stepping into my personal space until our bodies were less than an inch apart. I had to crane my head back to look at him.

"If you ever take off like that again..." he said, letting the implication linger.

He opened and closed his fists at his sides and I knew he was fighting the compulsion to grab me.

"Easy there, fella," G said putting his hand on Elijah's chest and nudging him a step back.

Elijah shot G a murderous look and opened his mouth about to say something, but G cut him off.

"Don't even. Don't fucking even. Look, man. I've got shit I'm dealing with too, alright? You're not the only one being driven crazy by a female. But you don't see me stomping around like a neanderthal, do you? You have got to get a hold of your shit. Things have just gotten real serious, real fast. We don't have time to deal with one of your tantrums. The Council has delivered their ruling."

G grimly nodded towards the script on the stone door.

Elijah followed his gaze and went still at what he read.

"What does it say?" I asked them.

"You're to be delivered to the Shadow Court," G said softly.

Elijah grabbed my hand and started pulling me away. "I'm getting her out of here."

245

"Eli, you can't do that, man. You can't brazenly defy a Council ruling. You can't even begin to imagine how you'll be punished."

Elijah ignored G and began pulling me across the bridge from the entryway of the cave, disregarding whether I wished to go with him or not. I could see a figure approaching us from the other side.

We met Davis in the center of the bridge with the rush of the waterfalls veiling us on either side.

"They ruled." Elijah told him.

"I know."

"I'm getting her out of here."

I expected Davis to object the same way G did, but instead he nodded gravely. "You have to find The Oracle."

With evident frustration, Elijah responded, "That's why we came *here*."

"We found this in her sanctuary, but no one knows what it means." Davis handed Elijah a matchbook.

On the front flap the initials *D.I.* were printed. On the back was scribbled,

Went to take a walk on the wild side. ~O.

"You can't be serious," Elijah scoffed.

"We don't know what it means," Davis replied simply.

Elijah slipped the matchbook into his pocket. "I know the place."

Davis raised his brows but did not comment.

"Will we be able to leave unnoticed?"

"Yes," Davis replied, "The Elders will be in their chambers for the rest of the hour."

G spoke up, clearly unnerved. "I have to stay out of all of this. If the Council finds out I was a part of any transgressions…" He swallowed thickly.

I briefly wondered just what kind of a hold the Council had over G, but he wrapped me in a bear hug before pulling back to wish me good luck.

"Take care of her," he said to Elijah. Then he gave Davis a respectful nod and vanished.

Elijah tugged on my hand. "We're leaving."

I pulled my hand from his grasp. "Maybe I should just accept the ruling." Although the idea terrified me, I couldn't stand the thought of having any more deaths on my hands—of ruining people's lives.

Elijah took a step towards me, and I was fairly certain he was about to throw me over his shoulder and cart me off. However, Davis took my hand in both of his before Elijah had the chance.

He gave me a warm smile. "You are destined to do great things, my dear. Just remember that the phoenix must succumb to the fire before she is able to rise from the ashes."

His look was filled with something. Maybe pride? I couldn't quite tell. But in a strange way, I didn't want to disappoint him.

"I know you, don't I." It was a statement and not a question. I didn't remember him, but the way he looked at me—there was something there. Something familiar.

"Of course, my dear. But right now, you have an Oracle to find."

CHAPTER 25

~Violet's Playlist: Unsteady, X Ambassadors~

THE STENCH OF STALE GARBAGE and urine pervaded the narrow alley we walked down. The passage was a sad, dirty, forgotten crevice between two tall brick buildings. It was just past midnight and I was grateful I did not have to see the place in the light of day. A battered steel door sagged next to a particularly offensive dumpster. Elijah took to pounding on the door when no answer was given to an initial knock.

A woman began speaking over the screech of the door opening. "… gives a good goddamn. A wench has got ta piss ya know. Ye all want me ta jump off the pot just ta welcome yer royal arses."

When the door had finished opening a middle-aged woman stood before us with one hand on her hip and a cigarette precariously dangling from her bottom lip. Her flaming red hair was rolled into curlers placed haphazardly around her head. The 'do was accentuated with frizzy tufts of the coarse mop sticking out between each roller. A yapping little dog put on a show of aggression at the hem of the woman's housecoat letting us know we were not welcome.

The woman peered at Elijah. "Uh, it's you," she said with disinterest. Her phlegmatic gaze turned to me. "Who's the broad?"

Elijah had pulled out a wallet. "She's with me," he responded handing the woman two one hundred-dollar bills.

"Uh," was her only reply, and then she bent down holding out the money. The little dog snatched the bills between his jaws and trotted away into what looked like a small shabby sitting room. He rooted the cash under the cushion of a dog bed before completing a circle atop it and plopping down.

"Well, come on. Do ye expect me ta stand here all day?! Be on yer way."

Elijah took my hand in his and we stepped inside. A rickety elevator sat to the right of the entryway. He pushed the call button and the door opened revealing exactly what I had been expecting, an old, dirty car with a flickering fluorescent light. Elijah pushed the only button, which was noted with the initials *D.I.*, and we began to descend.

We rode in silence which was fine with me. I had no idea how to respond to this place. I was convinced he was taking me to the bowels of the city.

We had arrived in London via a private jet. After departing Aleece—which was much simpler than entering, by the way—we had gone directly to a small runway somewhere back in the Radiant domain where the sleek aircraft had been waiting for us.

For whatever reason, the supernatural storm no longer plagued the area, and our return was met with a clear, cloud free night.

Before boarding the jet, Elijah had been sure to give me a lecture on holding back my energy, on keeping it from touching the electronics and the jet itself. I didn't tell him that Killian had already given me an impromptu lesson. I just nodded along in agreement.

He had also made a call before take-off and within minutes, clothing and shoes had arrived for us. As he handed me a small overnight bag, he pointed to the back of the plane and said, "The bathroom's in the back." Then he turned towards the cockpit to confer with the pilot.

I was grateful to have something other than the flimsy white robe to wear, and after entering the small restroom, I dug into the bag and changed.

The cream-colored pants, peach blouse and taupe heels were elegant yet youthful and quite fashionable. With the clothes was a delicate clutch. I also found a hairbrush, portable curling iron, and makeup bag in the carry-on. I put the items to use and when I was finished, my hair was in glossy chestnut waves and my makeup was fresh and clean.

I opened the clutch thinking I would throw a compact and lip gloss in. I was caught off guard, though, as I found a sleek dagger nestled in the silk lining. After my initial bewilderment, I shrugged. I guessed Elijah couldn't very well strap it to my thigh this time around, and I threw the make-up in to join the weaponry.

Returning to the seating area, I noticed that Elijah had also changed. He was in dark gray pants with a crisp white shirt and mid-tone gray blazer. And just as mine did, his clothes too looked to be designer label and expensive. Although he had begun to heal rapidly, his eye was still bruised and his lip split. However, the marks did not detract from his handsomeness and how well he filled out the clothes.

As soon as Elijah and I had settled across from one another in the supple leather recliners, the plane departed.

"Elijah," I began.

"I know," he cut me off.

There were so many issues to be discussed. I didn't know where to start. I tried for something innocuous. "My family?" I asked. "Who are they? Where are they?"

"Isn't it obvious?"

"No. It's not. Please. No more evasions. No more omissions. Just give me clear answers."

"You're Adriel's daughter," he replied, point blank.

I didn't say anything for a moment. My mouth opened but no words sprang forth. So I closed it and just stared at Elijah. I searched his eyes. His hard, unwavering stare was all I found. And it was clear he was telling the truth.

"Adriel is my *mother*?"

I was reeling. I had been with my mother and I hadn't even known it.

Elijah gave a grave nod.

"Where do I live? With Adriel at her cottage?"

"You both live at the Radiant Court. The cottage is Adriel's private residence. A type of getaway, but as the Lady of the Court

252

and the Heir, you both officially live at Court. At least you did until you went off on your *covert mission*."

"The Heir?" The way everyone had looked at me at the ballroom gala began to make sense.

"Yes, Princess."

My eyes rounded. Elijah had called me that before. "So not a mocking endearment, but a title."

He shrugged. "Both."

"My father? Brothers? Sisters?"

Elijah gave a heavy exhale and rubbed his eyes. "Davis. No siblings."

I shook my head, my ire rising. "Adriel and Davis are my parents? You, I understand not trusting me. But my fucking parents won't even introduce themselves to me?!"

"You're right. I didn't trust you. But it was different for them. They didn't' want to overwhelm you. Think about it. Would it really have made you feel better? To be told people you didn't recognize, knew nothing about, and had no memory of, were your parents? Don't you think that would be a pretty awful, hollow feeling?

"Adriel wanted to make you feel comfortable so she tried to keep a little distance. She was also running around like a woman gone mad trying to figure out how to help you while keeping you safe and the whole thing quiet so that you could have your privacy from anyone not involved. Not to mention that my initial concerns were legitimate, and Adriel knew I had a point. And what the fuck am I doing sitting here defending her?" He let out a frustrated grunt and ran a hand through his hair.

But I knew what he was doing. He was trying to soften the blow. He was explaining her actions for *me*.

He looked at the table between us when he spoke next. "Your Light has steadily charged, but when you first woke, it was undetectable. Radiants don't just go off and come back as Shadows. It would have been reckless and irresponsible to not approach the entire situation with caution."

And I knew he was also trying to explain his own actions as well.

I took a deep breath and looked down at my hand. "The ring?" I wasn't sure if I really wanted to hear an answer, but I couldn't be a coward. I had to piece my life back together.

Devoid of any emotion, Elijah replied, "You're married."

I jumped out of my seat and my hands flew to my mouth. I stared at Elijah in horror, the previous night replaying in my mind.

"It's not what you think," he said in irritation. "Sit down. It was an arranged political marriage. Neither of you had met the other. There wasn't even a ceremony. You both signed papers with your lawyers separately. I don't know if you even met him after it was official.

"Who is he?"

"A stranger to you. It doesn't matter. You're with me now. The Vinculum supersedes all other bonds, legal or otherwise."

And now the anger over the ring made sense. I too felt a possessiveness towards Elijah. It was an intrinsic part of our connection. I couldn't imagine the incredible jealousy I would have felt had another woman laid claim to him. And if I had had to stare at a constant symbol of their union, such as a ring on his finger, I probably would have detested the little piece of metal too.

Which reminded me. "What about you? Does someone live with you?"

"No."

"But all the clothes. The cosmetics. The...You have an entire wardrobe for a woman at your cabin." Not to mention the ring I had found there.

Again, Elijah ran a large hand through his hair as he glanced to the side, averting his eyes. When he looked back at me, it was with an unapologetic mien.

"It was for you."

I shook my head. "I don't understand." I looked back down at the ring again. "You just said I lived at the Radiant Court and married a stranger."

Elijah stood up and began to pace the aisle. He said nothing and after a few moments passed, I began to wonder if he would explain. I was about to give up on any further revelations when he finally spoke.

"About every thousand years two people are born, known as the Prisms. A male and a female. These two are bound to each other through a connection of energy known as the Vinculum. They are unable to connect with anyone else. They can only experience romantic love, lust, sexual desires, hope and happiness, with their counterpart, the other Prism.

"The energy they share, the Vinculum, has ways of helping to strengthen the race. I don't know how it works exactly, but as Radiants, we are all connected by our energy. The Vinculum solidifies and reinforces this connection.

"For millennia, the Shadows have been interfering with the arrival of the Prisms. Either preventing their conception, killing mothers who carry the next Prism to be born, or outright killing the Prism when he or she is a child. As a result, there have been times when the race has gone without both the male and the female Prism or, more commonly, when only one reaches adulthood. After all, why go through the hassle of two assassinations when one will do just fine."

Elijah paused and rubbed his pectoral, just over his heart, before continuing. "That happened to me. The one I would have been bound to—they got to her shortly after we were born.

"I have been alone. It has been...*difficult*."

I thought then of the emotions I had felt from Elijah when he had been recovering at Adriel's cottage after taking me through the Veil that first time. He had been groggy and unguarded, his emotions wide open.

I had felt such an aching loneliness. He had been lost in a sea of longing. Such need. Such want. A lifetime of sadness. And to live with that for a thousand years...

The puzzle that was Elijah began to fall into place. He had lost his family when so young and then never had any hope of loving another. Of starting a life and family of his own. It was tragic. And I thought of a song by the X Ambassadors on the music player Killian had given me. The song was called *Unsteady*, and it was exactly what Elijah was. On the surface he was strong, solid, and secure. But deep within he was unsteady.

I was careful not to let the heartache I felt for him leave my chest. I did not want him to think I pitied him. I knew he would not respond well to that. So instead I simply nodded, and he continued with his confession.

"After a thousand years of service, a Prism *passes on*. It's difficult to explain but essentially one becomes an angel like Giddeon and Daphne. For whatever reason, I haven't.

"I learned of your existence and I..." He trailed off. Either unable or unwilling to finish his sentence.

I looked down at the ring again. "Elijah, are you telling me...I mean, are you the arranged...? Are we...?"

"No." He cut me off and I was grateful I didn't have to ask him outright if he was my husband.

"I was too late." He looked at me then and I saw regret. "You had already gone. If I had just been there sooner. How could I have possibly known you would go off and..." He shook his head. "It was for you. The cabin. The clothes. I wanted something to offer you. A gift."

I opened my mouth, but no words came out. I was...Well, I didn't know. I didn't know how to feel.

All of a sudden, a wave of exhaustion swept over me, and it wasn't my own. Elijah was still recovering from his injuries and needed to rest. No one would know from looking at him, but he was still far from well. "Elijah, why don't you sit down?"

He shook his head in negation.

I reached out and grabbed his hand before he could begin pacing again. I sent a gentle wash of energy through our joined hands and scooted over a seat as I pulled him towards me. "Please. Sit with me." I turned off the light so the cabin was dim, hoping it would help him rest.

To my surprise, he didn't argue further and sat down. Letting go of my hand, he again rubbed his large palm over his pectoral. Then he leaned his head back and closed his eyes.

Before he could fall asleep, I quietly asked, "How can you share all this with me? I was under the impression that Adriel had petitioned the council I be placed under her guardianship and that it was forbidden to speak with me about such things."

"When the council ruled in Aleece to have you excommunicated, Adriel's petition was no longer valid." Elijah's jaw clenched after speaking and I could feel that he was in pain.

I reached out and stroked his face. His jaw relaxed and he turned his head towards me. He opened his eyes then and burned me with his look. "I thought I lost you. When you showed up at my door and you were consumed by dark energy. I thought you were a Shadow then, lost to me forever. It's hard to believe you've come back."

I wanted to reach out and stroke his face again, but I held back. Instead I asked, "Do you have any idea how I ended up at your cabin?"

He closed his eyes and turned his head, looking up at the ceiling. "I can only guess it was because of our connection. In spite of losing your power and your memories, or more likely because of that, our connection flared to life. I became a sort of homing beacon for you. Though how you made it to my cabin, I don't know."

He closed his eyes and pinched the bridge of his nose. "That storm was violent. And I think you had been out in it for some time. I sensed a dark presence outside the cabin and went to see what it was. That's when I found you collapsed and soaked in the mud wearing a flimsy robe. I don't know how far or for how long you had traveled to get there. I have no idea where you had been before arriving outside the cabin.

"I recognized you immediately but couldn't understand why you reeked of dark energy." He looked at me again. And again, so much regret was there in his eyes. "I could only surmise that the Shadows had gotten another of us. It also made sense that sending you was some ploy to get rid of me as well and possibly infiltrate the Radiant Court."

"But you don't believe that anymore?" I asked.

"No. I don't. Your little boyfriend is too honor bound to the Radiant Court as a whole and too in love with you specifically to be anything less than honest about the details of you leaving. If he says you intended to make an attempt on the Dark One, I believe it. Although why you would even begin to think you could successfully accomplish that is beyond me.

"And how you made it back alive..." He exhaled, shaking his head.

We sat there in the dim light of the cabin while the jet whispered through the night sky. Neither of us spoke again. Elijah's exhaustion was a heavy weight, saturating the air. I reached over and took his hand in mine trying my best to stroke his fingers with a lulling energy. It seemed to work and within moments, he had fallen into a deep sleep.

In spite of all of it, I still didn't trust Elijah completely. There was something...Some forgotten detail that niggled.

I had grown to care for him. I had undeniable feelings for him. I wanted to be with him. But I didn't wholeheartedly trust him.

And yet I had left Aleece and jumped onto a jet with him. Had traveled to London with him. And was blindly following him in the oldest and dirtiest elevator car in existence which was most likely descending into hell.

But before I could contemplate our relationship any further, the elevator jolted to a stop and the door slid open.

CHAPTER 26

I LET OUT A GASP. A posh, opulent club lay before us. Hypnotic music pulsed from wall to wall and bodies swayed on a crowded central dance floor. Several bars were stationed throughout the expansive space as well as cocktail tables, dark booths, and roped off bottle service platforms. Leather, dark hardwood, and steel seemed to have been the interior decorator's materials of choice.

A cocktail waitress carried a tray of drinks as she walked past us totally naked. However, she wasn't exposing herself because a bright green boa constrictor was conveniently draped around her covering everything that mattered.

"How is the snake staying in place?" I blurted. Although it was slithering around the woman, I couldn't see so much as a nip slip.

"Snake Charmer."

"What?"

"She's a Snake Charmer," Elijah said. "She can command it to do her bidding. Now come on. And stay close to me."

We made our way through the crowded club to an empty high-top table. Elijah pulled out his wallet. "Sit here." He tossed a hundred-dollar bill on the table. "Order one drink and one drink only. Do not go anywhere. Do not tell anyone who you are, what you are, who you know, or what has happened to you. Just don't talk to anyone. And do not look at anyone. Trust me it's all the invitation most of the beings in this place need."

"Where are you going?"

"I'm going to go talk to someone about helping you."

"Then I should come with you."

"No."

"Is it the oracle?"

"No."

"Elijah—"

"Why do you have to be so difficult when I'm trying to help you?" Elijah opened my hand and placed the bill in my palm. "The individual I need to see has a private room here. You won't be allowed in. So," his jaw flexed, and he took a deep breath, "*please*, wait here for me." He glanced around the club. "Believe me, I loathe the idea of having you out of my sight, but I think you should be safe here. If anyone tries to talk to you, stab them."

I put my hand on his arm before he could leave. "Elijah—"

He cupped the nape of my neck, his gaze flaring with those golden sparks. "I will come right back for you. You're mine now. Fight it or accept it, I don't care. We're bound beyond any capacity you can imagine."

And then he turned and stalked off.

I watched Elijah bulldoze his way through the club goers to a roped off curtain along the back wall. A giant of a man with molasses skin, who must have been eight feet tall, stood guarding the curtain. After a perfunctory nod, the gargantuan bouncer unhooked the velvet rope to let Elijah pass.

The man caught me staring at him and bared his teeth in what, I guessed, was supposed to be a smile. Rows of razor sharp teeth glinted in the light. I imagined it was like having a shark smile at you right before he had you for dinner.

I quickly turned away and decided a drink was just what I needed at the moment. Making my way over to one of the large central bars, I spied an open seat and removed my coat.

A group of women, each dressed in tight black leather from head to toe, each stunningly gorgeous in her own way, milled about the seats to my right. Two average looking guys were discussing something over a couple of beers to my left. I didn't have to wait long before the bartender was asking me what I'd like.

I stared at the wall of bottles behind him uncertain what to order.

"She'll have a Jamieson. Neat," someone said to my right. The bartender nodded and walked away before I could respond.

I turned and found myself staring into the loveliest hazel eyes framed by incredibly long, thick lashes. Her light blond hair was styled into two voluminous pigtails, at the nape of her neck, giving her a sexy baby doll look.

"Don't worry, you'll like it," she said popping a maraschino cherry into her mouth. She reached up and began stroking my hair. "Wow, you've got great hair. It's so soft and shiny. I'd kill to have hair like yours."

"Thanks," I told her with an uncomfortable smile. "I haven't washed it today."

I didn't know if I should lean away from her or bat her hand down, or what. Luckily, she withdrew her delicate caress with a pained smile. But after what seemed like an inward shake, she sat down on the bar stool next to me with a little hop and began twirling a pigtail while unnerving me with her seductive gaze.

The bartender dropped off my drink, but when I went to hand him the cash Elijah had given me, the sexpot closed her hand over mine.

"Put it on my tab, Mick."

"Sure thing, Lilly," he said as he walked away.

Instead of releasing my hand, Lilly began caressing the back of it with her thumb. "Your hair is beautiful, but what's really stunning about you are your eyes," she murmured. Then she let go of my hand to pick up her own drink and empty it in one fluid toss.

After watching her, I did the same and began coughing and spluttering as the burn of the alcohol choked me. Lilly gave me a look. It was almost as if she was annoyed with me. But then she patted my back and pouted.

"You poor thing." The patting turned into rubbing.

After I could finally breathe again, I turned to face her. "Look, you're really nice and I appreciate the drink, but I'm not interested."

Her eyes went wide, and she blinked her feathery lashes at me. "What do you mean?"

"Are you...are you coming onto me?" I figured being direct was the best approach.

She leaned into me pressing her lips against my ear and whispered, "So what if I was?"

I stood up and gave her a tight smile. "Thanks for the drink, but I have to get going."

She let out an upward breath sending the wisps of hair framing her face to lift for a moment and turned back to the bar grumbling.

The woman sitting next to her began laughing as the other girls from the group threw money down on the bar in front of her.

"Pay up ladies! I knew she wouldn't close."

A petite friend with dark brown hair in a long pixie cut patted Lilly on the shoulder. "Don't worry Lills. It's just a dry spell. You'll bounce back. She looked like she had a stick up her ass anyway."

"I'm still standing right here," I said to the pixie.

She shrugged. "So you are."

"Look, I don't mean to be rude, but—"

"Yes, you do," she fired at me.

"Unbelievable," I muttered with exasperation as I turned to walk away.

"Instead of whispering things behind my back, why don't you say what you have to say to my face," she challenged.

I whipped back around unable to keep the anger from my stare.

She closed the distance between us so that we were nose to nose. Actually, since she was so short it was more like nose to chin.

"You don't know who you're messing with, little girl," she challenged.

I laughed without humor. "If you only knew. And really? You're calling me *little girl*, Tinkerbell?"

Her diminutive fist came flying at my face. The little brat took a swing at me!

I grabbed her wrist with both of my hands, leaned into her, and flipped her over my back. To her credit, she landed on her five-inch-high heeled boots. It threw me off a bit to see her standing as I pivoted around.

She had a look of shock on her face as well, but it was quickly replaced with fury. "I'm going to make you my bitch, Sasquatch!" she screamed at me.

"Not if I make you mine first," I told her.

She launched herself at me and we went down in a tangle of limbs. Her friends just circled around us to watch and bet on the outcome, throwing money down on the bar again.

My kidney and jaw took brutal hits, but she ended up kissing the floor with me sprawled out on top of her. I had my arms locked around her throat and thigh. "I'll let you up if you apologize, Tink."

She squirmed and bucked under me. "Never!"

The bookie of the group had a waterfall of straight, shiny black hair down to her lower back. She laughed tucking a few strands behind her ear and squatted down next to the pixie.

"Come on, Gem. She got you fair and square. Do you want to lie on that filthy floor all night or do you want a little medicine?" She held a shot glass out at Tinkerbell's eye level and wiggled it back and forth."

At the sight of the shot, the pixie caved.

"I'm sorry, okay? Now get your fat ass off me! I can't breathe. You must weigh two hundred pounds. Maybe you should make nice with a treadmill."

"As far as apologies go, I've heard better," I sighed as I disentangled myself from Gem and stood up, rearranging my clothes. I reached up the back of my shirt.

"Did you unhook my bra?"

Lilly cleared her throat and eyed the toe of her boot. "Ah, that was me."

The bookie with the long dark hair shoved a shot glass in my face. "Damn, you can move girl! You have no idea how much money you've made me tonight. Drink up."

I hesitated for just a moment before I thought, *fuck it*, and downed the shot. I slammed the little glass down on the counter and the group of women cheered.

***

Lilly handed me another Jamieson with an apologetic smile. "I'm sorry about all that. They bet that I couldn't seduce the next person to sit down here. And that happened to be you." She clinked her glass against mine and downed the whiskey before sinking onto the bar stool with her head in her hands.

The bookie grabbed one of Lilly's pigtails and gave it a light yank. "Don't worry, little chickie. It was a stupid bet. You'll get your groove back. You need to stop stressing about it."

The dark-haired beauty turned to me. I noticed she had a slight accent, and I would come to find out that she was Brazilian.

"I'm Bianca, by the way, and you are?"

"Violet," I told her.

With a knowing look, she asked, "Is this your first time at the *Den of Inequity*, Violet?"

"Yes." I looked around. "Well, I think so anyway."

"What are you?" Bianca asked, eyeing me up and down. "You're not a mortal."

"What do you mean?" I asked.

She raised her voice and spoke slowly, as if talking to an idiot. "What kind of immortal are you?" She squinted at me. "You some kind of fae?"

"Oh, no. I'm a…" I hesitated. Did I identify myself as a Radiant? Elijah had warned me not to talk to anyone. It probably was best to stay as vague as possible. Especially seeing as I had some evil being currently trying to hunt me down.

"Ahh," Bianca's eyebrows lifted. "You got something to hide. It's ok, chickie. I get it. Ha! *Believe me*, I get it." She put her arm around my shoulders before continuing. "But listen, Violet—and it's none of my business, I know—but that guy you came in here with? He's bad news."

"What do you mean?" I asked.

"I've seen that golden boy in here plenty and he's always hanging around shady characters."

There was a loud clatter on the bar and Mick, the bartender, made an announcement as he lined up shot glass after shot glass off of a large tray.

"Ladies, ladies, may I have your attention please." He pulled a bottle containing a green glowing liquid and began filling each shot glass with it. "A round of *The Green Fairy* has been ordered for the lovely Fallen Angels, compliments of the Brevis."

A cheer erupted from the clique as they all turned to wave, blow kisses, and bat eyelashes at a few small men in business suits across the bar. The three men, who were all under five feet tall, raised their glasses and each gave a solemn nod towards the ladies.

Bianca handed me one of the small glowing glasses. "Drink up," she commanded.

"But I'm not interested in any of them." I told her.

"You can't be serious. You're going to turn down *The Green Fairy?*"

The incredulity in her voice made me curious and I took a look at the shot glass I held. The glowing green liquid seemed to swirl and sparkle.

"What is it?"

"It's alcohol infused with a drop of blood from a Green Fairy." She spoke like I was an imbecile for not knowing. "Trust me, if anyone can afford a thousand dollars a shot, it's the Brevis. They're alchemists."

She downed the shot before turning back to me. "Look. I'm not going to force you to do something you don't want to do, but you're insulting them by declining their generous offer, you know."

I eyed the shot again. The previous drinks I had were beginning to take effect. Although I thought the *Green Fairy* sounded disgusting, I was also a little curious. My inhibitions were beginning to shed, so I tipped the tiny glass against my lips.

I was instantly euphoric. Suddenly all my cares and worries were gone and being in the club with Lilly, Bianca, Gem, and the rest of the leather clad women was the only place in the world I wanted to be.

"Wow," I sighed on an exhale.

Bianca put her arm around my shoulders again. "I know, right? It's going to be a great night." Then she pulled away and slapped her hands together before reaching for my pants. "Alright. Let's get you out of these clothes."

CHAPTER 27

ONTRIBUTIONS HAD BEEN MADE HERE AND THERE from the Fallen Angels. Someone had donated a black scarf, which Bianca had tied around my waist thereby creating the tightest shortest sarong ever to be donned. Then she unceremoniously stripped my pants from me. I was wearing a freakin' scarf as a mini skirt.

Someone else named Cammy, bequeathed her black stretchy sweater. Well, she called it a sweater. It *was* stretchy knit, and it *did* have long sleeves, but it was skin tight and low cut and stopped just past my boobs where it tied around my ribcage. She said she had brought it along in case she got cold but didn't need it. How this teeny tiny little scrap of fabric would help warm a person, I couldn't comprehend.

Bianca and Lilly stripped me of my top and stuffed me into the little wrap right there in the middle of the club. Under normal circumstances I would have objected, but with the high I had incurred from the Green Fairy, I just went with it.

Another one of the hot chicks gave me her shiny-leather-skintight-five-inches-high-spikey-heeled boots. When I offered her my more demure heels in return, she gave them a disapproving look before informing me with a lot of stammering and pausing that she required shoes with a special kind of arch support. Then she whipped out her cell and requested a new pair be delivered—to the bar.

After being dressed up like their own personal doll, Bianca and Lilly pushed me onto a barstool and did things to my hair and face.

"She could be so hot if she just made an effort," Lilly said in earnest to Bianca.

"I can hear you, you know."

"Oh yeah," Bianca replied right over me, "It's always so sad when the young ones completely give up on themselves."

"Wow. Rude." I muttered.

"Well I'm done with her hair," Bianca continued as if I hadn't said anything. "What about face, Lills?"

Lilly let out a heavy exhale looking down at the makeup in her hands that had been collected from various clutches and back pockets. "I did what I could with these limited resources."

Bianca inspected my face. "Lills, you're a magician. She actually looks presentable now."

I slowly waved my hands in front of them convinced I was somehow invisible to them.

"Give it a rest, new girl," Bianca said batting my hands down. "We see you. We're just charmingly candid."

She pulled me off the bar stool and turned me towards the large mirror behind the bar that shelved all the alcohol bottles. "What do you think?"

I inhaled sharply at the half naked hooker staring back at me. "Oh. My. God." My eyes bugged at my reflection. "I can't believe you did this to me. I look...*fucking amazing*!"

Lilly nodded in agreement.

Bianca snorted, "I think that might be the Green Fairy talking. But you do." She gave my reflection an assessing look. "Damn, you could be one of us. Eh, Lills? She looks like she could be one of us, yeah?"

But Lilly, along with the rest of the Fallen Angels, fell silent as a group of seven men walked by. I turned to see what everyone was looking at.

The males were all bare chested, wearing nothing but low-slung jeans. Even their feet were bare as they padded over the floor in arrogant, confident strides. People hushed as they passed and quickly moved out of their way. Each one was tall, broad, and perfectly sculpted, showcasing flexing pecs and abs with every step. I could feel the temperature in the air warm as the males neared.

"Who are they?" I whispered to Lilly.

"The dragon pack," she whispered back.

"You don't mean..."

She gave a solemn nod. "Yes. Actual dragons. That's why they're practically naked. They run hot."

Then she was stifling a drunken giggle. "Literally and figuratively."

It was true. Each and every one of the seven in the pack were panty droppers.

Somewhere I heard a wistful feminine voice murmur, "They can gang bang me anytime."

As they neared, one locked eyes with Gem. His pupils contracted and elongated into black slits while his irises expanded, glowing a vivid teal as he stared at her. Not once did he blink or look away. Chills ran down my spine at his stare, and I wasn't even the one to whom it was directed.

Gem seemed to accept his stare with a sad pain before breaking the connection they shared and ripping her gaze away. The male continued to rake his gaze across her until one of his pack mates purposefully stepped into stride next to him, blocking Gem from his view.

I let out a breath I hadn't even realized I was holding. The music and noise of the club seemed to rush back towards me and the spell of the moment was broken. I turned to Lilly. "What was that!?'"

Lilly shook her head. "The dragon is Bannan. He thinks Gem is his mate."

When she paused, I supplied, "And Gem disagrees?"

"She tries to convince us all that she isn't into him. She even tries to convince herself. But no one buys it."

"So, where's the problem, then?"

"Oh, you know—"

Out of nowhere a huge golden lion that must have been seven feet tall leapt onto a table and let out an earth-shattering roar, its shaggy mane bristling in hostility.

The club patrons stopped their dancing, drinking, and chatting to stare at the commotion. But no one seemed to be alarmed by the lion.

However, the reverberating roar was answered with an ear-splitting screech. And the dim lights from above were eclipsed as one of the members from the dragon pack shifted into animal form. An electric green and black winged beast the size of a jet was suddenly facing down the lion.

With one swipe of a paw, Gemma was snatched up by the towering dragon. Well, actually the dragon was kind of stooping since it was taller than the ceiling of the club.

Gemma immediately started pounding her fists against the hold which imprisoned her, but it was as effective as a butterfly batting its wings at an elephant.

With another brain melting screech, the dragon sprung straight up from its haunches, crashing through the club's ceiling and then through floor after floor of the structure creating a large hole in the roof high above whereupon it began to beat its massive wings and took off into the night sky.

Two more members of the dragon pack shifted into animal form, directing threatening screeches at the growling lion.

Bianca raised a shaking fist to the sky now visible high above us and shouted, "Bannan, you fucking asshole!" Then she turned a pointed finger on the two hunching dragons. "We'll be coming for her," she warned.

One of the dragons, a midnight blue one, turned his head towards her, bared its teeth and made a hissing sound deep in the back of its throat.

But suddenly none of that mattered. Over the cacophony of sounds in the club, a single pure note sung by a soprano filled the air. The beautiful haunted note was gentle and yet it somehow overpowered all other sounds. It silenced everyone and everything. Voices hushed. Music stopped. Motions froze.

Whether the solo soprano voice sang in words or only musical notes, I couldn't tell. All I knew was that it was the loveliest thing I had ever heard. The song called to something so deep within my bones that I was frozen in place. Even time itself was forced to slow at the depth lacing each clear note.

I realized with an awed reverence that the song was not a melody for the ears. It was music that could only be heard by one's soul. And my soul had no choice but to still and listen— enraptured.

I was dimly aware that I was staring at a woman. She stood on the edge of the now exposed roof high above us all. Her long red hair swirled around her lovely elven face as her long emerald gown swirled around her slim body. Although a few paltry stars were visible in the night sky surrounding her, they were nothing compared to the infinite galaxies which whorled in her eyes.

She stood motionless, a perfect statue. And while her lips did not move, I knew she was the one who sang the song.

The song opened portals I did not know existed. There were things I had always been blind to. Things so obvious and yet oblivious. But realization, self-actualization, was suddenly revealed with perfect clarity.

I was a galaxy unto myself. Every particle that contributed to my structure spun, rotated, orbited.

But just as suddenly as that small fraction of time slowed and expanded, it abruptly ended. I was painfully plunged back into the present. Back into my flesh and bones. Ejected from the swirling cosmos and no longer able to access the galaxies within. I was simply myself once again.

I blinked, adjusting to the jarring sensation of suddenly slamming back into myself, and when I looked up at the exposed roof, the lovely woman was gone. I wasn't entirely sure she had even been there to begin with.

But before I could ask if anyone else had seen her, a deep groaning sounded from the surrounding walls.

The bartender, Mick, leapt onto the bar and shouted, "It's going to collapse! Everybody out!"

And that was when the pandemonium started. Complete chaos overtook the club with all manner of supernatural beings trying to flee at once. The only one not rushing for the exit was Mick. He knelt on one knee still atop the bar and sliced his palm with a pocket knife. He seemed to be drawing symbols on the bar top with his blood and chanting to himself.

I turned to glance at the roped off curtain which Elijah had passed through hoping to spy him. But the area was empty. The gargantuan bouncer was no longer there, and no one was exiting through the curtain. I tried to search for Elijah's energy, to frantically tug on the chord that connected us in a kind of warning. But I couldn't feel him. I hoped that meant he was already out of the club.

Bianca pushed me forward shouting, "Follow Lilly!"

"But Elijah," I protested over the creaking and shouting.

"He has to fend for himself!" She countered. "We have to get out of here. Follow Lilly!"

"She's going the wrong way!" I threw over my shoulder.

"It's a back exit," Bianca countered. With another hard shove she yelled, "Move!"

Beams began crashing to the floor around us. I could see Lilly's platinum blond pigtails bouncing as she jostled her way forward, and I tried to catch up to her.

I reasoned that if Elijah was in the club and in trouble, I would feel it through our connection. Since I didn't sense he was in immediate danger, I decided the best thing to do was get out myself.

Lilly passed through sleek black swinging doors and held them open for me. I turned to hold them open for Bianca, but she was no longer behind me. She had stopped a couple yards back to help another from their group who had been pushed down in the melee.

When she saw us waiting at the doors she shouted, "Go. We're coming."

"Come on," Lilly said grabbing my arm, and we ran down a back hallway which seemed to be lined with offices. More awful crashing sounded out in the club.

"Shouldn't we help them?" I asked running right behind her.

"They'll be fine. We need to worry about ourselves."

"Where are we going?"

"There's a back exit down here. I fooled around with a guy one night and we snuck out this way."

A loud crash sounded behind us and I glanced over my shoulder as we ran. The double doors we had just passed through had collapsed and the ceiling and hallway walls were giving way in a domino effect heading straight towards us. We were about to be buried in rubble.

"Oh shit. Better pick it up a notch, Lilly!"

"It's here!" She exclaimed in response before shoving open the door.

We burst through the door just as it collapsed behind us. We were in a small dark alley and the anterior bricks of the building began to crumble into the tight space.

"Keep going!" I shouted to Lilly.

"On it!" She responded as she bounded down the cobblestone towards the intersecting street.

But as we ran, my spine began to tingle. I could sense something out on the main street. Something *kindred*.

I needed to stop. To turn back. But if I did that, I would be buried by the falling building. I had no choice but to meet what was out there, head on.

I tried to warn Lilly but by the time I had opened my mouth to tell her to be on guard, we were already street side.

The instant I turned the corner, we made eye contact. He had felt me just as I had felt him, and he looked shocked to see me.

I grabbed Lilly's hand and yanked her in the opposite direction. "Run!"

And bless her heart she didn't ask any questions and didn't object. She simply followed the directive.

But they were too close. The man was with others.

"It's her. Get them!" He ordered.

"Run, Lilly!" I swung around to face them. I knew it was me they wanted. Lilly didn't have to go down with me.

In addition to the one giving orders, there were four more of them. Two of the large men flew past me to chase Lilly. The other two stayed to face me.

I went into autopilot.

One swung at me and I ducked while sweeping out my leg. I made contact with his ankles and he went tumbling. When the other launched a kick at my spine from behind, I reached around in time to catch his leg while leaning just out of the strike zone. Then continuing with the force of his own momentum, I jerked to a standing position while pulling his leg up with me which caused him to land on the pavement on his back.

That silky black beast I had been keeping locked up deep inside, roared and I let it free. I could instantly feel dark power flood my veins. I knew my irises were branching with black channels.

I slowly turned to the leader and smiled. "Hello, *brother.*"

He possessed the same dark energy. I could feel it. But I could also feel that mine was older. Stronger. He was a very powerful Shadow. But not as powerful as I was.

However, instead of showing any fear, he shook his head in disapproval and tsked, while his two goons returned to his side.

His accent was cultured British. "You are so naive, young one."

Then he spoke a harsh word that I did not understand, but I felt the dark beast I housed caged once again. Invisible bonds banded around my arms and I fell to my knees.

I fought to stand, but it was impossible. I tried to release the dark energy again, but it was bound just as I was.

At the same time the two men that had run after Lilly returned. She was unconscious and draped over the shoulder of one of them.

The leader looked at Lilly's limp form and smiled before looking back at me. "Regrettably, you are not to be touched. But this one is an unexpected treat."

Then he spoke another harsh, unintelligible word and everything went black.

CHAPTER 28

I KICKED AT THE CHAIN connected to Lilly's shackles. "Wake up," I yelled at her only as loud as I thought was wise, which wasn't very loud. "Lilly! I need you to wake up."

Her head began to loll on her shoulders.

"That's it. Good girl. Wake up for me, okay?"

She started to blink her eyes.

"Lilly, over here. Look at me."

"Violet? What...what happened?" she asked, clearly drowsy.

"Some disgusting thugs jumped us and locked us in a freakin dungeon," I told her none too gently.

She looked around taking in the subterranean room. The stone floor was littered with patches of filthy straw and the stone walls were adorned with various blood-stained shackles and pulleys. We both sat on the floor with our wrists and ankles bound. The bindings were connected to a chain running along the wall.

"Oh."

"Oh? *Oh*?! I tell you we're shackled in a dungeon and all you have to say is 'Oh'?!"

She began rubbing her eyes. "Alright, calm down. It's not the end of the world. Worse things have happened."

"Are you serious?" I asked her in disbelief.

She straightened where she sat and gave me a reassuring look. "It's okay, Violet. I can handle some street thugs."

"Street thugs is an understatement."

"But you said—"

"I know what I said, Lilly," I snapped at her. I lowered my voice and leaned as close to her as possible. "They're bad, Lilly. Not just evil, but sinister. They're powerful. I might be able to take them on if I could get out of these chains, but I can't."

Lilly plastered a patronizing smile on her face and reached her bound hands towards my boots in an attempt to pat my foot. "Aww, that's really sweet, cutie, and I know you tackled Gem earlier, but you should know that her heart wasn't in the fight. Maybe you should let me take care of things."

I let out a huff of irritation. "And what, exactly, are you going to do?"

She opened her mouth to respond, but no words came out. Then her face fell, and she looked down at her hands. "Nothing. At least not now. Not while—"

Then she picked her head back up, her eyes sharpening. "Who are they anyway? And why did they come after us? It was almost like you knew they were there waiting for us."

"God, Lilly, I'm so sorry. This is all my fault. It's because of me that you're here."

She looked at me expectantly. "Well then the least you can do is explain."

"Right," I agreed. I had no idea how long we would be left alone in the dingy dungeon, and I didn't waste time.

"The Prince of Shadows is hunting me. It must be why these Shadows took us and locked us up here."

"Fuck me!" Lilly whisper shouted. "Oh we are so fucked. I've heard some serious shit about that guy lately. Like messed up shit." She began tugging on her chains. "Are you sure it's *The* Prince of Shadows that's after you?"

I lifted my bound hands to my face and pinched the bridge of my nose. "Yes."

"And you couldn't have told me this sooner? Everyone's been gossiping about his sudden claim of the Shadow throne, but no one thought it was serious. If he's half as bad as the stories, we're in deep shit!"

"I'm sorry you got caught up in this." An apology felt pathetically insubstantial, but I didn't know what else I could do.

"Why is he after you?" Her voice had shifted an octave higher and she sounded like a squeaky mouse.

I winced. "I might have made an attempt on his life. It's all a little unclear at this point."

"Let me get this straight. You knew something truly evil was after you and instead of keeping a low profile, you decided that you just had to get your club on?!"

"No!" I countered, "I've been searching for an oracle. I need her help. The man that I've been traveling with has been trying to help me find her, and the latest information we had indicated that she was at that club."

"Okay. Okay," Lilly began repeating to herself while closing her eyes and taking deep breaths. "Okay. Yup. I can do this. I am a fucking badass. I *can* do this."

"Lilly, I—"

"Shh! Just give me a moment. I need a minute."

Then she went quiet. It seemed as though she was composing herself. I began trying to look around for something we could use to pick the locks on the chains.

I had tried accessing the dark energy I had, but it was somehow caged, and I couldn't release it. I was about to try again, but then I could feel Lilly's eyes on me. I was confused when I saw that they no longer held a hint of fear or panic and instead smoldered with sensuality.

Her head tilted to the side. Her shoulder came forward in a seductive posture and she licked her lips.

"Violet," she sighed my name, "I want you. Tell me you want me too."

I did want her. I wanted her right next to me so I could slap some sense into her. "What is wrong with you?! Did you hear anything I just said? Are you serious right now? Is this a joke? Are you trying to lighten the mood or something? Because let me tell you—it is not funny."

A wild desperation replaced the seductive look she gave me, and then she burst into tears.

I looked around the room for some clue as to what was going on, but there were no answers to be found.

"Lilly, I'm sorry. I shouldn't have responded the way I did. I do think you are very pretty and…fun…and I'm sure you're a great person…and any woman would be very lucky to have you. Maybe we can talk more about this when we're in a better situation.

"You don't understand," she sniffled.

"Maybe you can help me," I offered.

She lifted her bound hands to wipe the tears from her cheeks. "I'm not a Fallen Angel. None of us you met tonight are." She took a deep breath and straightened her spine before pinning me with a solemn stare.

"We're Femme Fatales. Do you know what that is?"

I shook my head. "No, but—"

"Good," she said. Then she continued with an unwavering gaze. "We have a seductive power over men. Actually, women too. People are unable to resist us. We use the sexual desire they feel towards us to get close to them and assassinate them.

"Our anonymity is crucial not only to our mission but to our survival. We cannot get close to our targets if they know what we are and are already on the defensive against us. More importantly, though, if our secret was uncovered we would be hunted down by those in powerful positions and eradicated."

She closed her eyes and her voice became haunted. "It happened once before. We were discovered for what we truly are. Many were killed. A scant few of us were able to flee and go into hiding."

She opened her eyes and looked at me, almost pleading. "I could seduce whoever walks in through that doorway. I could get him, or her, to free me. And I could kill him while he's lost in desire for me. I could get us out of this. It would be so easy." She paused leaning her head back against the wall behind her and gazing up to the ceiling. "But there's something wrong with me. I haven't been able to access my power for a few weeks now."

Her explanation made me recall the way we had met, the way she had tried to hit on me and how disappointed she had been when she failed to get a reaction from me.

"So normally you would have had me drooling all over you back at the club?"

She sighed. "Yeah. Normally."

"Do you know what happened? Why you aren't able to—"

She cut me off. "No. I don't."

I tried yanking my chains apart. "Is there anything I can do to help you regain your power? I really think it could be used against the guy who took us. He made some disgusting comment about you."

Lilly's eyes flashed and she looked to be contemplating something. Then she squared her shoulders and set her lips in a grim line. "Stop trying to break the chains. For some reason, yours reek of dark magic. You won't be able to get out of them. Conserve your energy for when we need it. Now tell me exactly what happened and what was said when we were taken."

I slumped against the wall letting the chains rest. Now that Lilly had said something, I did feel a type of malevolent vibration seeping off the shackles.

I thought back to the alley where we were attacked. "Nothing very significant happened," I told Lilly. "The two men who had chased you came back with one of them carrying you. You were unconscious. The man in charge leered at you and said that I wasn't to be touched but that you were an unexpected treat. Or something like that. Then he spoke in a language I didn't understand, and I fell unconscious too."

I shrugged not knowing what else to say about the matter.

"Do you know if they were in the club at any point?" She asked.

I shook my head. "I don't think so. I didn't feel them inside, and the leader looked surprised to see me when we ran into them on the street."

Lilly nodded as though she had come to some sort of decision. And then we both froze as footsteps sounded outside the dungeon door.

"What do we do?" I frantically whispered to her.

In a clear, unwavering voice she said, "Oh honey, you're on your own. Did you really think you were anything more than a meal ticket to me?"

Then the door swung open and the man from the alley walked through. When he saw us, a perverse smile spread across his lips.

"How nice," he purred in a silky voice. "You're both awake."

"So we are," Lilly replied arching her back in a mock stretch and sending her chest jutting out in front of her. The swell of her breasts strained against the fabric of her low-cut top.

The male's dark eyes were glued to her movement, and he reached up to rub his jaw. He would have been attractive in an affluent sort of way if not for the psychotic gleam in his eye.

He removed the tailored suit jacket he wore and laid it over the back of a chair with care, all the while keeping his eyes on Lilly's body. Then he undid his tie placing it over the jacket, and rolled up his sleeves, all with a deliberate languidness which I knew was meant to intimidate. He looked down at the tie resting on the chair and then back at Lilly. He seemed to change his mind about leaving the black silk on the chair and picked it up letting the fabric run through his fingers.

"What are you going to do with that?" Lilly asked, all breathy sexiness.

I didn't know what her plan was, and I didn't know if it was now every woman for herself or if I should be doing something to help out the team.

The male raised an eyebrow. "I think it will look good wrapped around your neck while I choke and fuck you at the same time."

I let out a gasp of horror, but Lilly let out a moan and rubbed her leather clad thighs together.

The male's lust filled gaze turned suspicious and his upper-class accent turned sharp. "What are you doing?" He demanded.

"I'm trying not to soak my panties," Lilly told him, "but I'm failing pretty miserably."

"Listen to me you little bitch, if you think pretending to want me is going to save you, you're fucking stupid."

Lilly let out a throaty laugh. "Pretending to want you? You have no idea how happy I am to see you." She tilted her head in my direction without looking at me. "When all hell broke loose I grabbed this little thing desperate not to leave without a meal for the night. She would have been a boring lay and I doubt she would have done much for my appetite. But you...You're going to make my teeth rattle, aren't you? Umm..."

She gave him a thorough perusal from head to toe. "I bet I wouldn't need to feed again for weeks after the likes of you."

The man sneered at her. "You are a stupid bitch. Do you really think I would just offer myself up to a Succubus?"

Lilly gave another throaty laugh. "Come on, tiger. You know that Succubae are all tall and dark. Look at me. I'm the complete opposite of that. I'm just a simple little Coitus Nymph."

The man didn't respond right away. Instead he stood there assessing Lilly, taking her measure and probably trying to decide whether or not to believe her.

"What's your name?" Lilly asked biting her own shoulder.

"Why the fuck do you care?" he shot back at her.

"Because I want to know what to scream as I come."

I wanted to throw up.

That perverse smile spread across the creep's face. "Marax."

Lilly pouted and rose to her knees. "I'm so sick of talking, Marax. I *need* you. The instant you walked in here I got so hot and wet. I'm aching. I don't want you to save me. I want you to wrap that tie around my pretty little neck and fuck me over and over again."

I cringed not wanting to hear any more.

"Do you know what happens to a Coitus Nymph?" Lilly continued. "We shrivel up and turn into old hags without sex. And I'm getting dangerously hungry, Marax. So if you want me, we need to do this *now*."

Marax took a step towards Lilly.

"I just need you to unchain my ankles."

Anger flashed over Marax's face.

Before he could respond, Lilly continued, "You can leave my wrists bound, though. In fact, I want to keep my wrists bound, but I need my feet free so I can spread my legs wide. I can see," she raked her gaze below his waist, "that I'm going to need my legs as wide as I can get them just to fit you."

293

I probably threw up a little in my mouth at that point. Lilly was pouring it on so thick, there was no way Marax could be buying what she was selling.

Marax stood there for a moment studying Lilly. Lilly was playing a dangerous game and I was afraid for her. There was nothing from stopping Marax if he decided to keep Lilly chained as she was. Even if he did agree to unchain her ankles, though, she would still be weaponless and chained by the wrists which connected to the wall. It was difficult for me to believe that she could get free while so handicapped.

Lilly reached her bound wrists up to her face. She stuck her pink tipped index finger into her mouth, sucking hard, before slowly drawing it out all the while staring at Marax with utter worship and need. He made his way to her taking slow steps while running the tie through his palm. He stood looming over her for a moment and my fear spiked. This was a terrible idea.

He removed a key from his pants pocket and unlocked the shackles around her ankles with a click. I expected Lilly to spring upon him immediately and incapacitate him. The intro to the Soho Dolls' *Stripper* began to play in my head.

Okay. Here we go. Any moment now. Only, nothing happened. There was no explosive tackle. No powerful kick to his balls. She just sat there staring at him like a starving woman.

Marax began to unbuckle his belt. "Get on your hands and knees, pet." Although his voice was cold and quiet, his eyes gleamed with an eager excitement.

Lilly licked her lips and did as he commanded. I couldn't believe she was obeying him. I was afraid that she had lost sight of her original goal. Maybe Femme Fatales had some condition that made them agreeable to sex with anyone? Even someone who wanted to harm them? Or maybe Marax had the power to illicit desire from his victims?

I let out a strangled cry as he undid his zipper. Freeing himself from his suit pants, they sagged around his thighs. He got down on his knees behind Lilly and spread his hands over the snug leather that hugged the curves of her ass. He gave her a bruising squeeze with both hands before grasping the leather and ripping her pants apart at the seam exposing a black lacy thong covering her sex.

Lilly let out a moan, panting, "Hurry," while leaning her backside closer to him.

I wanted to scream at her to snap out of it. To remind her that we were supposed to be trying to escape. But I didn't know what was going on in her head. We hadn't covered what to do in the event she completely lost her mind! Was she really going to let him have sex with her? And was I supposed to just sit here and watch them!? I could feel panic begin to rise.

With one hand Marax grasped himself. With the other, he reached to shove Lilly's panties aside.

Then Lilly drove the stiletto heel of her boot right into his crotch, impaling him. He let out a scream as he doubled over. Just as lightning fast, she withdrew her heel, rolling over onto her butt. With incredible speed, she swung the toe of her boot square into his temple. Marax came flying into me and collapsed.

"Oh, gross, Lilly! His bloody junk is on me," I screeched. "Get him off of me!"

"Okay, calm down," she said in such a blasé manner that I wanted to punch her. Instead I tried to buck Marax off of me. He moaned at the motion.

"He's rousing," I told Lilly in alarm.

She was working on using her booted foot to try and scrape the key from the floor where Marax had put it down. It slid close enough for her bound hands to reach it. Without any difficulty, she unlocked the manacles as if she had done so many times before. By the time Marax let out a second moan, Lilly was dragging him by his ankles to the space she had occupied. His eyes began to blink open as soon as she had him chained.

"Pig," Lilly said with disgust just before she cocked her arm and let a solid punch connect with his nose. A crunch of bone was his only response as he passed out.

A dark familiar power caressed my back from the base of my spine up to my neck. Need speared through me. I had to go to the source of the power. It beckoned me like nothing else could. He was near. He was coming for me.

I began to pull at my chains with desperation. "Lilly, hurry! He's coming for me!"

Lilly sighed. "Violet, really, calm down. He's chained and unconscious. He can't get you." She bent down to unlock my manacles.

"Not him," I told her, stilling so she could unchain me. "The Prince of Shadows. I can feel him. He's coming for me."

"Oh, shit," Lilly breathed.

"Exactly," I agreed.

Lilly shook her head, silky blond pigtails bouncing, "No. I mean, this key isn't working. Your chains require a different one."

296

I looked around the dungeon, gaze frantic. "Try his pockets."

Lilly was already reaching her hands into his pants before I finished my sentence. She checked his suit jacket as well but came up empty handed. Then she hefted an axe that was practically as large as she was from the wall and made her way back over to me.

"Do you trust me?" She asked.

"I—"

Before I could answer Lilly swung the axe and an ear-splitting clang reverberated through the dungeon. The vibrations from the clash of metal on metal rattled my teeth together and the heavy chain connecting my shackles to the wall came crashing down on me.

I didn't even care. I just wanted to be free before it was too late. I knew if the Shadow Prince reached me, there would be no escape. I had felt the overpowering possession radiating off of him at our encounter in the threshold. And I was certain I would not escape a second meeting.

"Ha! Got it in one swing," Lilly said with pride. "Don't move," she warned, and when I looked up at her the axe was arcing down towards me. I had to fight the instinct to pull my feet back and curl up in a ball. A second bone clattering clang and the chain connected to my ankles was broken.

Lilly hefted the axe. "I kind of like this thing." She reached her hand down to help me up and I grasped it between my own.

Although I was no longer chained to the wall, my wrists and ankles were still in manacles that connected to each other. There was enough chain length between the wrist and ankles that I could stand upright, but I took one waddling shuffle step and stopped.

"This isn't going to work," I told her. "How am I supposed to run, much less walk out of here. You need to cut the chains binding my ankles too."

"I can't," she countered. "There is heavy magic on those and I guarantee an axe won't break them."

With a sigh, I tried to shuffle forward.

The last thing I saw was Lilly rolling her eyes before my stomach was introduced to her shoulder.

"I have to do all the work," she grumbled as she marched us out of there carrying me like a useless sack of potatoes.

I was about to hiss at her to put me down, but really what sense would that make. She was clearly capable of hauling me off and if I tried to shuffle along on my own, I'd only slow our pace.

"Um, thanks, Lilly," I said awkwardly.

"You can thank me when we make it out of here alive." She was jogging up a stairwell after exiting the dungeon and reached old fashioned wood doors. With a solid kick of her boot, the door burst open into a deserted cobblestone street. Without pausing Lilly jogged for the busy intersecting street just ahead. The cool night air poured over us and it was a refreshing reprieve from the festering dungeon.

But along with the evening's caress came a pulse of power. It was a kind of recognition. Of like sensing like. The energy was so strong my back bowed and my torso jacked off Lilly's shoulder for a moment.

"Holy shit," Lilly breathed. "What was that?"

"*Him.* He's here for me. So close. He'll take me."

The dark energy I housed was still bound. The beast was rattling its cage, baying to get free and answer the pull of energy saturating the night air. I had a feeling the chains I wore were what was keeping my inner beast caged.

Lilly let out a piercing whistle and I heard wheels screech on pavement. I flushed with embarrassment when I realized what she had done. While I was clad in *fuck me* attire and chained up, Lilly had dumped me into the backseat of…*a cab*.

CHAPTER 29

Violet's Playlist:
LeDisko, Shiny Toy Guns
Ooh La La, Goldfrap

A VERY STARTLED CAB DRIVER was turned in his seat staring at us with eyes as wide as saucers.

"The Boltons," Lilly directed.

The driver showed no indication of hearing her. He just kept staring at us.

"We're really into BDSM," Lilly told him.

Still no response.

Lilly snapped her fingers twice. "There's five hundred pounds in it for you if you get us there in fifteen minutes."

The driver finally roused and nodded. Turning back around he stammered, "Where to?"

"The *Boltons*," Lilly repeated.

The driver was staring at us in the rearview mirror as he pulled out onto the road. Another vehicle swerved to avoid a collision and blared its horn.

"Eyes on the road, mate! There's no money in it for you if you kill us!"

Lilly put her arms around me and placed her mouth at my ear. "The Fatale house is nearby. We'll be safe there. Luckily that asswipe didn't take us far from the club."

"Lilly, I can't put you in any more danger. *He'll* come for me."

"The house is protected. He won't be able to get to you."

"What about Marax? Should we have left him alive?"

"It would have been better to take his head, but that can be dangerous when you don't know who or what you're dealing with."

More break screeching and horn honking sounded as the cab swerved. "You just lost yourself a hundred pounds! Now eyes on the road!" Lilly shouted at the driver.

"What about everyone at the club?" I asked her.

"One thing at a time, chickie. One thing at a time. They're big girls. They can take care of themselves until we get to them. We're no good to them chained up in a dungeon."

"You're right. Thank the light you were able to access your power. I thought we were screwed."

Lilly shook her head. "I wasn't able to. My mom always said, 'Fake it till you make it.' So that's what I did."

"You really are a badass," I told her with all sincerity. "I owe you."

She shrugged, and I knew that in spite of her amazing performance, she was disappointed to be lacking her power.

We got to the house in six minutes. Lilly pulled a wad of cash out of her bra and handed the driver five bills. "Since you got us here so fast, you earned your hundred back." Then she grabbed his face and kissed him full on the mouth with a loud smack.

I shimmied my way across the back seat and hopped out of the cab. Row after row of beautiful white brick mansions lined the street.

"It's this one here," Lilly said and I shuffled along behind her through the street front gate.

An incredible array of cars was parked out front. They were mostly six figure vehicles with a couple of seven figure ones. We ascended a set of stairs to enter the mansion. While the exterior of the house was classically beautiful, the interior was trendy and modern, but a bizarre mess.

Women's lacy panties and bras littered the entryway light fixture as well as what looked to be like quite a few pairs of men's tiny briefs. I had to shuffle around a pizza box and several empty vodka jugs as we crossed through the living room and into the kitchen.

Men were cleaning throughout the house. The odd thing was that they were all huge and packed with muscles, incredibly attractive and practically naked. They wore tiny black sport shorts with black work boots. They each had a black band around their necks and wrists.

"Your maid service?" I asked Lilly while raising my brows towards one of the males.

"Kind of," she shrugged. "They're paying off a debt."

"Hey, Juan Carlos," she called in greeting to one particularly handsome man servant.

He looked up from the stack of dishes he was cleaning at the kitchen sink and glared at her, baring his teeth in a frightening snarl.

"Yeah, don't get too close to any of them, 'kay?" she mumbled under her breath.

As we made our way to the back of the house I could hear loud music blaring. We passed through French doors which had been flung open into a spacious backyard that had a large swimming pool, two hot tubs, outdoor showers, an oversized television, and several blazing patio heaters. A few cabanas surrounded the pool complete with plush couches, lounges and fluffy faux fur rugs. Blue lights illuminated the grounds. On the muted large screen T.V. a blonde buxom Jane Fonda was flying through the air in the arms of some golden-haired man with massive wings.

Most of the Fatales that had been at the bar with Lilly were scattered around in the hot tubs and cabanas. Two of them danced—in a way that would make any hardworking stripper envious—on top of the outdoor bar in teeny tiny barely there bikinis while Goldfrap's *Ooh La La* played on the speakers.

Bianca, I noticed, was relaxing in one of the hot tubs with a glass of champagne in hand. One of the man servants was kneeling along the edge of the hot tub as he refilled her glass with each sip she took. His sculpted, bare arms and pectorals flexed with his movements, and his chest sheened with humidity from the rising steam of the hot water.

At the opening lines of the next track to play over the sound system all the Fatales stopped any conversations they were having to sing along. Even Lilly paused to shout the lyrics. The sound system monitor read: *Le Disko, Shiny Toy Guns.* The song seemed to be a sort of anthem for them as they stressed certain lines.

Lilly turned down the music. There was a boo, a couple hisses, and one platformed high heel chucked at her face. She ignored the hisses and caught the shoe without the bat of an eye, as if flying heels were an everyday occurrence.

"How did you guys get out of the club?" She asked the group.

"Bannan's mates flew us out. I had to agree we wouldn't go after Gem," Bianca answered. "Everyone else is still holed up in there. Mick is preventing the club from completely collapsing, but who knows how long he can keep that up." Bianca shrugged, unconcerned. Then she scowled. "I am so sick of those Banshee bitches. If I hear another of their screeching death songs one more time, I am going to shut them down—for good. She ruined a perfectly good night."

I realized she was referring to the beautiful woman who appeared on the roof of the club. It seemed that Bianca blamed her for the club collapse, but if someone had asked me, I would have thought it was the twenty-foot-tall dragon that bulldozed through the structure.

"Hey, nice access hole, Lills!" someone called from behind her.

Lilly simply bent forward at the waist, stuck her ass out, and wiggled it back and forth a few times showcasing the gaping hole Marax had ripped in her pants.

"Oi! Give us a look over here," Bianca demanded.

Lilly turned around and did the same shameless little butt wiggle.

Bianca's face lit with appreciation. "Lills. You got a little something tonight?" She sat up and shooed the chiseled man servant away with a dismissive gesture. As he exited into the house through the large French doors, one of the Fatales who was long and lean with blonde hair down to her back—the one who had lent me her sweater—started to leave in a quiet hurry.

"Cammy! Where are you going? I've got a serious tale to tell," Lilly scolded.

Cammy stopped in her tracks and turned back as if busted with her hand in the cookie jar. Her eyes were feverish, and pink flushed her cheeks. "I have to go to the bathroom," she said in a rush.

"What's wrong with the ones out here?" Lilly asked, gesturing to one of the cabanas.

"I…um…" Cammy cast a quick but longing look into the house. "I have really bad diarrhea. Don't want to ruin the atmosphere for everyone else. You know?" She darted into the house before anyone else could comment.

"That was weird," Lilly mumbled before she perked back up, "Anyway!

"What's with the new chick's jewelry?" One of the Fatales asked. "A little chunky, isn't it?"

"Yeah, about those. B, I think we're going to have to call Eva," Lilly said to Bianca.

"Absolutely not," Bianca scoffed. "She costs a small fortune."

From the shadows of one of the cabanas, a striking woman stepped forward. She was tall and toned. Her snug leather pants and jacket emphasized her strong frame, and the spiky high heeled boots she wore only added to her already tall stature. She hadn't been at the club earlier. I would have noticed if she had. Her dark hair was pulled back into a long braid which highlighted her sharp bone structure, and her jade eyes almost glowed. Her piercing gaze was fixed on me and I felt stripped bare beneath her stare.

With a cool commanding voice, she said, "We will aid this one." She gave me a knowing look and I had a feeling she knew things about me, I had yet to discover myself. "She will be indebted to us."

It was clear this woman was some kind of leader figure for the group. But before anyone had a chance to respond, the doorbell rang inside the house. The Fatales exchanged questioning glances with each other. It seemed that a guest was not expected.

A moment later one of the men from the house escorted a woman into the pool area. She too was tall, but her clothes draped over her frame in bright flowing fabrics. She wore purple lipstick, and her dark hair was swept up in a sleek chignon.

With a coy smile directed at the Fatale leader she said in a Haitian accent, "I saw that you would be needing me."

From her place across the pool, the Fatale leader replied, "You spend too much time looking in your crystal ball, Eva. Careful you don't go blind."

Eva threw back her head and laughed. Then she shook a finger. "You should come take a look sometime for yourself. You might be intrigued by what you find, Evelyn."

"Never," was Evelyn's immediate response.

Eva simply shrugged.

Evelyn seemed to be running short on patience and demanded, "Can you help here or not?"

Eva pursed her lips. "I can feel the dark magics on the chain. A sacrifice to dark spirits would have been required. A greater offering must now be made. My price will be steep.

"Your price will be paid," Evelyn said, her words coated with frost.

Bringing her hands together in a prayer gesture and bowing her head, Eva declared, "Then it is settled."

Without another word, Evelyn slinked off into the grounds behind the pool area. Eva simply sighed at the dismissal and shook her head, then she walked up to me and, grabbing my chin in her hand, she began to inspect my eyes.

I gave a start and jerked back in reflex as Eva's own eyes became coated with a milky white film. However, the grip she had on my chin was unbreaking and I remained face to face with her.

Lilly took a few retreating steps away from us and my gaze flew to her in panic. She held each of her forefingers out making a cross with them and directing it at Eva.

Eva gave a soft chuckle. "I make them a bit nervous." She raised an eyebrow as she stared into my eyes. "Oh, my, my. What have we here?" She tilted my head to the left and then the right, seeming to look deep down inside of me. "Powerful. Dark and Hungry. You better hold on to those spirits, girl. Do you understand? I will remove the binds, but you must not release the spirits. Otherwise I will have no choice but to send them back to the grave and they will drag you there with them." She released my chin and her eyes returned to their normal amber. "Do we have an agreement?"

"I don't know if I can control it—them," I told her in all honesty.

She gave an unaffected shrug. "Then the chains stay." She turned to leave calling over her shoulder to no one in particular, "Tell Evelyn I will send her a bill for the house call."

"Please, wait!" I called after her taking a shuffling step forward.

Eva paused and turned, the fabrics from her dress flowing around her.

"I'll contain them," I told her with a confidence I did not feel.

She smiled. "Then let us begin."

She removed a pinch of black ash from a locket which hung around her neck. She tossed the ash into the pool and the water at the center began to churn and turn black. Two of the Fatales had been lounging in the pool, leaning against the side and observing everything. As soon as the water began to blacken and bubble they scrambled out and scurried for safety.

The black waters of the pool rose in certain areas and began to take the shape of hunched, gnarled figures that swayed and rippled. Dark, aqueous ghosts.

Eva got down on her hands and knees at the edge of the pool, her head hanging between her shoulders. She began to chant in Haitian Creole. Her voice rose and fell, increasing in tempo as she spoke. Her body began shaking, slightly at first and then violently.

I looked around the pool at the Fatales. None of them seemed to be concerned about Eva. They were watching as if this was a standard occurrence.

Without warning Eva sat up on her knees and released a keening cry. Tracks of blood were running down her cheeks from her eyes. As the blood dripped from her chin into the black churning waters, the red drops transformed into a glowing crimson orb. As the orb pulsed in the water, scarlet veins branched through the dark aqueous figures.

The figures exploded in a burst of water, shooting straight up into the night air. Then all the water thundered back down into the pool, settling into complete stillness with a smooth tranquil surface. Although the water was no longer black, there were streaks of crimson floating throughout.

For an uncertain moment, no one moved or spoke.

Then one of the Fatales grumbled, "Great—now where are we supposed to swim."

Eva collapsed back to the ground. In response, Bianca grabbed a lounge chair and brought it over to the pool edge. She helped Eva into the chair chiding, "Always with the dramatics, Eva."

In a reedy voice Eva responded, "Why are you always getting tangled up with the darkest of magics?" Without turning back to me she told Bianca, "You can free the girl now."

Bianca looked to Lilly and jerked her head in my direction.

Lilly grabbed the manacles around my wrists in each hand and squeezed. They popped open under the pressure. She did the same to the ones around my ankles and I was blessedly free from the chains.

A man dressed in a black suit appeared from the side of the house. He walked up to Eva without sparing a glance at any of the scantily clad Fatales and picked her up in his arms. He said something to Eva in Haitian Creole and she responded in like. Without a glance or a word of parting, the man simply carried Eva away.

"The hot tub still works," someone shouted and then Shiny Toy Guns' *Le Disko* was cued up on the sound system again. The backyard party resumed as if never interrupted.

With a pat on my hand, Lilly said, "Come on, let's get cleaned up."

CHAPTER 30

LILLY'S BEDROOM WAS POSH, modern and feminine. A glass vanity table sat near the entry with an oversized crystal framed mirror hanging above it. Elegant vases of perfect pink roses were subtly placed throughout the space. The black bedroom walls and shiny black bed frame were offset with snowy white bedding. And a fluffy black cat slept curled up in a massive white wingback chair.

Lilly crossed to a pile of shopping bags on the floor and reached into a small pink one which had Agent Provocateur in black script printed on the side. From the bag, she handed me a tiny black thong and matching black quarter cup bra. "Here. My gift to you."

Then she pulled an article of clothing from the closet and tossed it to me. "Something comfy to wear," she commented as she headed into the connecting bathroom. She reemerged almost immediately with a couple soft pink towels. "Cammy has the room next door. She won't mind if you use her shower. Follow me, I'll show you."

The diarrhea bathroom? I thought. But I knew I was in no place to complain. I was just grateful for the chance to wash the dungeon off me.

I paused out in the hallway. "Lilly. I can never thank you enough for everything you've done for me tonight. I don't know what I can do to repay you."

Lilly simply shrugged. "No sweat." Then a mischievous smile lit her face. "It turned out to be a pretty fun night."

I was surprised when she didn't knock on the closed bedroom door and instead simply barged in.

Cammy whipped around, clearly startled by the open door and clamped her hands over her bare breasts. Her long blond hair swished over her naked skin, and even in the dim lighting of the room, I could see a pink tinge to her cheeks. She stood in just her bikini bottoms with her mouth agape.

What made me uncomfortable was not the fact that we had walked in on Cammy half naked. It was the fact that a man was in the room with her.

It looked like he had been sitting on the bed, but the moment we entered he turned to start tucking in the comforter. He was wearing those small black shorts, and he had the bands around his wrists and neck that all the man servants of the house wore. I realized he was the one Bianca had dismissed earlier.

"Lilly! I was just…just…" Cammy stammered.

But Lilly didn't seem to notice Cammy's flustered state. Instead she flipped the lights up from their dim setting saying, "Geesh, Cammy. It's okay. I think we can afford a little extra electricity.

You don't need to take Evelyn's latest spending lecture so seriously." And without sparing so much as a glance to the awkward scenario, she went straight into the bathroom turning on the lights and starting the shower.

With my eyes averted to the floor, I mumbled, "Sorry. Excuse me," and followed into the bathroom. I shut the door and turned to Lilly. "That was so embarrassing. I feel so bad for intruding."

"What are you talking about?" Lilly asked.

"Well, you know. Obviously, something was going on between them."

Lilly laughed. "No. That's not possible."

"Lilly, they're both practically naked out there."

Sweeping her arms open wide, Lilly said, "Welcome to the Femme Fatale House, where almost everyone is almost always practically naked. And I reassure you that none of us would hook-up with the indebted. Evelyn would never allow it. And trust me, you do not cross her. Besides, the bands on their wrists and necks prevent them from being able to touch any of us. Without those bindings, I'm sure they would have killed us all in our sleep by now. I'm pretty sure every single one of them hates us. It's not like they're here by choice. I mean they are demi-gods, after all. Cam probably just needed her room tidied up and happened to be changing out of her swim suit."

"You're holding them here against their will?" I asked, aghast.

"No. I mean, yes in a way. But no, not really. They needed a favor. We helped. Now this is their payment. A hundred years of service to the Fatale House. They hate us for it, but really, they're the ones who accepted the favor." Lilly pursed her lips. "Pretty ungrateful, if you ask me."

315

She turned for the door. "Go ahead and get washed up. I'm having some food made for us. I'll see you downstairs."

Alone in the bathroom, I thought about Evelyn's comment down by the pool when agreeing to help me.

She will be indebted to us.

I suddenly wasn't so certain I should have accepted the help. Was I going to find myself serving the Fatales for a hundred years?

I needed to find Elijah. I was fairly certain he had escaped the club before the collapse since I hadn't felt his presence when we were evacuating, but even if he hadn't, it seemed that the interior was being supported temporarily. I would take a shower, get dressed in more borrowed clothes, and start looking for him. He would know what to do. I hoped he had been able to find some information that would lead us to The Oracle. I was determined to focus on my main objective: reclaiming my memories.

***

I stood in the modern dining room of the Fatale House tugging on the hem of the dress I wore. Lilly's idea of comfortable was not even in the same ballpark as mine. The black stretchy knit dress was made from soft fabric and it did have long sleeves, but it was skin tight and barely covered my butt. I couldn't complain, though. I was clean, chain free, and I had ditched the borrowed boots I had been wearing, opting to go barefoot.

Lilly had clearly showered and changed as well. She wore a fresh pair of leather pants that did not have an "access hole." And paired with the leathers was a tight pink baseball tee that stopped just past her breasts. I now knew just how capable she was. But looking at her bouncy platinum pigtails and baby doll face combined with the pink bubble gum tee—well, I doubted anyone would believe that she had single handedly saved us from certain death.

Platters of fluffy waffles with berries and whipped cream had been set out on the large dining table. Most of the Fatales from the pool area now sat around the table enjoying the decadent food and sipping Bellini's.

Bianca pointed a finger at me. "You, sit down and eat." Then she pointed at Lilly. "You, start talking."

But before I could take a seat, goosebumps broke out over my skin and the air charged with electricity. Slews of lightning erupted around the mansion. The entire structure shook as I heard my name bellowed outside.

Lilly scrambled out of her chair, knocking it over. "Oh, shit. He found us."

"No," I breathed. I knew she thought it was the Dark Prince, coming to finish what he had started when we escaped him earlier. But I also knew she was wrong.

I could feel Elijah's presence. As well as his frenzy. He was desperate to get to me. And I couldn't fight the answering response which flared within my chest. I ran headlong for the front door and flung it open.

His towering frame was coiled with tension as he stood, hulking in the middle of the street. Flashes of lightning struck and sizzled around him. Wild eyes that blazed with light locked on mine. "Come here," he grated.

317

I ran for him, down the stairs, and leapt into his arms. A violent boom of thunder reverberated through the night as he caught me, and electricity sparked on the asphalt under our feet.

His hold on me was unbreakable, and his mouth came slanting down over my own in utter possession. My lips would be red and swollen when he was finished with the kiss, and their bruising would be a brand. His brand. A sign to others that I was his.

And light help me, I reveled in it.

There might have been some wildly inappropriate calls from the front door of the Fatale house, but if there were I didn't hear them. The charge between Elijah and I had ignited, demanding all my attention.

I gave myself up to his claiming kiss, lost in it. When I moved my lips over his strong jaw and down his throat, he began to stride forward.

"I can walk. Put me down," I panted.

"Never," he swore.

Before I could argue any further, my back was shoved up against a brick wall. Elijah had taken us around the house down a dark deserted alley. His voice was strained. Rough, deep gravel. "I can't wait, Violet. Light help you, you better want me, because I don't think I can stop myself right now."

He still held me with my legs wrapped around his waist. His fingers dug into my ass where he cupped me. His jaw was clenched so hard the muscles on the side of his face popped.

In spite of his words, he was holding back, waiting. He wouldn't really take me against my will. I didn't doubt that he was at a razor's edge, but he was still fighting for control.

I didn't say anything in response. Instead I reached down between us and stroked him over his pants. He let out an aching groan. Then he slanted his mouth over mine.

He began to lower me. I slid down the length of his hard-muscled torso until my feet touched the ground. My head fell back in surrender. My senses were heightened. I could feel the rough cold brick against my back. The heat and clean fresh scent of Elijah's tanned skin overwhelmed me, ratcheting up my arousal.

Elijah's large rough hand slid up the dress I wore to shove my panties to the side. Then he was freeing himself from his pants.

It was all so right. I couldn't wait to be connected with him. To feel him sliding, in and out, over and over again. I needed to be that close to him. I needed for him to give me everything he had. All that he was. Because I was going to give him all of me. Somehow, I was falling for him. In spite of the ways things had begun between us, I had come to see him for what he was: a strong determined man. It was that simple and that basic.

Why I had ever tried to fight the bond—the Vinculum—was beyond my comprehension at the moment. What we felt for each other was so raw and pure and base. It was foolish to think it could be ignored.

The night we had spent together in Aleece had made that clear. Elijah was for me. There could be no other. He consumed every part of me.

No. That wasn't true. Not every part of me. There was still the darkness buried deep inside. And that darkness was not a part of my union with Elijah. That part remained, still prowling the cage in which it was kept. Longing for its master.

But I had mastered caging it. And that was all that mattered. I didn't even allow the Shadow's Kiss to be a thought in my mind. I looked up at Elijah's angular jaw, rough with sandy colored stubble, his blazing eyes, the jagged ring of golden light burning through the brown. His rugged features were tight with absolute need, and his large towering frame tense.

But there was also something else in the way he looked at me. There was a determination. An unspoken promise. I knew that Elijah was claiming me in all ways this night. And there was no going back.

He grabbed one of my legs and slung it over his hip. Then with one large hand under my ass he picked me up against the wall, lining up my throbbing wet core to where he palmed his shaft. The broad head of his cock rubbed against my entrance.

I let out a moan. It was so right. All that mattered was him being inside me, pumping deep and hard until we both found release. And I would make him do it over and over again right here against this wall until neither of us could stand any longer.

His voice was savage raw sex when he said, "You are mine."

CHAPTER 31

AN UNHOLY ROAR FILLED THE NIGHT. The air around us plummeted into freezing temperature. Cold malevolence slammed into me, and a sinister lust rose within my chest.

Before I could process what was happening, Elijah spun around pinning me between the brick wall and his back while zipping up his pants. I yanked my panties and dress into place.

Elijah let out his own answering bellow. I knew it was borne of frustrated rage.

At the other end of the alley the menacing form of the Prince of Shadows lurked. Those shadows cloaked and swirled around him spewing cold and darkness, whispering with the sound of faraway screams.

"Run," Elijah commanded without turning back around.

I grasped the back of his arm, fear and adrenaline spiking through my veins. "I don't want to leave you."

His voice was hard and unyielding, "Obey me in this. Go now. I'll be right behind you."

I wanted to stay with him, but I didn't argue. I turned and ran.

I couldn't make my way back to the entrance of the Fatale house since the Shadow Prince was blocking that side of the alley. Even if I could have, I wouldn't. I didn't know if their mansion really could keep him out as Lilly had claimed, and I didn't want to put others in danger.

The alley was long and narrow. I was afraid it would be a dead end, but as I neared the back, I saw that it led into a large park. It was empty of any people due to the late hour. And for that I was grateful. It meant I would not be endangering innocent bystanders.

The winds picked up and black clouds roiled through the clear night sky. Thunder reverberated through the air and rain began driving down. A storm appeared out of nowhere.

I ran blindly, my bare feet slipping on the wet grass. I kept glancing over my shoulder dreading the sight of a shadowy figure pursuing me. But with the darkness of night, sheets of rain, and my hair lashing into my eyes, I could see nothing.

I turned ahead, determined not to look back any longer, and redoubled my efforts at escaping, but I collided with something big and solid. I landed hard on my ass in the mud.

When I looked up, an immense figure loomed over me. The figure was cloaked in shadows. Menace seethed off of it.

He had found me.

Somehow, he had gotten ahead of me, and he had found me. I lifted myself up on my hands and feet and began to crab walk as fast as I could away from him.

He stalked towards me without haste. We both knew it was over. He had me. With one final step, he lunged down landing on his knees and grabbed my ankle. Then he yanked me to him, letting go of my ankle to wrap his arms around me, pinning me to his chest.

I began to struggle in his grasp but when he raised his head to the sky and howled, I stilled. I knew it was an exclamation of certain triumph. He had me and I wasn't escaping. I tried to look for Elijah, but it was in vain. I could see nothing but the shadows surrounding the Dark Prince. I was enveloped by black inky swirls of darkness.

I might have let out a wail myself then. I'll never really know whether the scream born in my heart ever made it past my lips or not because that was when he pulsed us. We disappeared from that park and my heart broke as I slipped into darkness and further uncertainty.

***

Being teleported had rendered me unconscious. When I came to, I was in a quiet dark space. I waited for my eyes to adjust before making any movements. From what I could tell, I was not bound in any way, and I did not feel physically injured. However, I was incredibly cold, and a dank musty scent permeated the space.

After a few moments, I still could see nothing. The space was just too dark.

I believed I was lying on the floor of an enclosed room. With cautious sweeps, I began to feel the floor around me. The hardwood was warped and split in certain areas. Emboldened, I stretched to reach out even farther.

In some spots, entire planks of the flooring were missing, revealing frigid dirt. And within arm's reach was what felt like a stone wall. Just as the floor was rotting, the stones seemed to be crumbling and loose in certain sections.

I couldn't be certain, but I suspected I was alone. I could hear no breaths being taken in the silent room other than my own.

I began to crawl in an attempt to discover more about the space and how I might get out. I kept one hand along the decrepit wall as I scuttled along. Not too long after taking a corner, I came across what had to be a door. Although it too was made from rotting wood, it was sturdy, and I imagined it must be quite thick. It was wide, as well. I stood to inspect it and found it lacked a door knob, but it did have an antique keyhole.

No light crept in from the bottom, sides, or keyhole of the door. If possible, the darkness seemed to be even thicker in the space beyond the door, and a chill ran down my spine as I felt the residue of a famished malevolence out there.

In spite of my inability to see, I stumbled away from the door in a hurry, desperate to put as much distance as possible between myself and the soul sucking bleakness that lurked beyond. The backs of my legs bumped into a piece of furniture and my butt landed on a bed.

I took in a sharp breath as something warm washed over me. In this wretched room of cold and darkness, there was also light. Just as the space beyond the door held the residue of sinister darkness, the bed was saturated in remnants of radiant energy. In this bed had been something incredible.

There had been light, laughter, and love. Worship and gratitude. Something so profound and altering had occurred here, that the very molecules in the cocoon of the bed had shifted. Whatever had happened, it had been true magic.

Although still unable to see, I ran my hands over the soft sheets trying to soak up as much of the positive energy as I could. How could there have been such beauty and light amid such wretched darkness, I wondered.

I curled up in the bed, determined not to leave it. There was nothing good out there. I would stay where there was hope and avoid the bleakness.

I don't know how long I stayed on that bed soaking in the residual light. Time certainly passed. But eventually I realized...I was no longer alone.

***

A match was struck and a candle lit. In the corner of the room stood a hunched, robed figure. The cowl of the ragged brown robe was drawn, and the person's face was hidden. Gnarled hands held the single candle, and the flickering flame could barely slice through the dense darkness in the room as it sputtered and fought to remain lit.

I sat up with a start and an arthritic finger beckoned me. I automatically shook my head in negation and the finger beckoned again.

A weak, withering voice issued from the figure. "Come."

I shook my head a second time and the stooped figure began to limp towards me. I scrambled off the side of the bed, trying to put as much distance between us as possible. I looked around the room for some kind of weapon. But the only object in the crumbling, dilapidated space was the bed.

The figure was moving very slowly and as if in pain. I could surely overpower it. I took a fighting stance.

The figure stopped and shook its covered head. "Come. Not. Safe. Here." The figure had to pause and take a few deep breaths before continuing. It sounded like the voice of an ancient old woman. "Take you. To. Own room."

Then she turned and shuffled towards the door. From inside the folds of her robe she procured an antique key and unlocked the door. The rotting wood swung open silently. The old woman continued out into the hallway without looking back, taking the candlelight with her.

I quickly assessed my options. I could stay in the miserable dark room or I could leave it and look for an exit.

I also did not know who this old woman was. It seemed she intended to help me. While I knew it would be foolish to implicitly place my trust in her, I was relieved it was not the Dark Prince who had come for me.

So, with an overwhelming sense of unease, I followed.

The clawing hunger of despair hung in the air of the hall. I was overwhelmed by the lingering presence of desolation. I had been mistaken during my initial assessment. Although there was the ingrained presence of malevolent forces, what truly saturated the air was sheer dolor. It hung so heavy and thick in the space that any hope or light I might have held in my heart was lost.

I realized that the only reason this palpable bleakness had not been overwhelmingly present in the barren room, was because the light and beauty once present in that bed had kept it at bay.

It took every ounce of my strength to follow the dying ember of the candlelight. I came close to stopping where I was and giving in to the desolation a few times. But eventually the robed woman reached a set of stairs. She began to ascend with difficulty, and it took quite some time for us to reach the landing at the next level.

I found I could breathe easier, though, and I realized I was no longer drowning in darkness and despair. Thankfully, whatever ghosts haunted that dark and desolate hall remained there.

However, as we had climbed the stairs a faint pounding sound had begun. It gradually became an incessant boom of hammering thunder. And as we passed through the hallway, the walls shook with each violent crash.

Eventually we ascended more flights of stairs and passed through more halls. We did not pass any windows and throughout the entire course, the single candle was the only source of light.

However, my eyesight was keen enough to see that we were in some type of opulent manor. The marble floors, Persian rugs and crown molding were a jarring contrast to the decrepit hall which now lay far below us.

Finally, the hobbling woman stopped in front of large double doors. She opened them to reveal a cozy sitting room with two huge fireplaces, one on each end. And thank the light, a roaring fire burned in each.

I immediately ran over to one, basking in the glow and warmth of the firelight. But the sound of the door shutting startled me. I glanced back and saw that the old woman was gone.

"Wait!" I ran over to the door and tried the handle. Locked. I was locked in. I began banging on the door with my fist. "I am so sick of this shit!" I shouted. "Let me out of here!"

I continued beating the door with my fist for a solid minute, although it was probably impossible to hear my objections over the ceaseless thunder. When I had had enough I gave the door an angry kick—and instantly regretted it. I was still barefoot and had smashed my toes right into the solid wood. I grabbed my foot in my hand hopping up and down in pain.

Feeling defeated, I turned to lean against the locked door and assess the sitting room.

A pristine antique looking settee sat in the middle of the room. It looked quite inviting with fluffy pillows and a cozy throw blanket. An expensive coffee table and two wingback chairs also sat on the sizable Persian rug, which covered the hardwood floors. And two floor to ceiling bookshelves lined a wide archway which led to a beautifully arranged dining room as well as a broad hallway.

I sighed. It was admittedly a preferable prison to the black hole I'd been in.

I looked down at myself—and sighed again. I was filthy. Dried mud caked my feet, legs, hands and arms. Not to mention the borrowed dress I wore.

I didn't bother with caution. I could sense I was the only being in this wing of the manor. And so, I trudged through the hallway and went to explore the other rooms of my prison.

CHAPTER 32

~Violet's Playlist: Closer, Kings of Leon~

THERE WERE THREE BEDROOMS, three bathrooms, the dining room, and the sitting room. A fire burned in the largest of the bedrooms and it was furnished with personal items. The two smaller bedrooms appeared to be unused guest rooms. There was a covered tray of food and another fire burning in the dining room. It was also apparent that there was no electricity, just large fireplaces and candelabras in all the rooms.

Each of the bedrooms had oversized windows, and I immediately drew the curtains shut as I passed by. A torrential downpour of rain beat the glass while that ceaseless thunder boomed. But what made me want to avert my eyes were the streaks of angry red lightning that tore through the sky. There was something demonic in its presence. And I had also started to notice a hellish baying underscoring the bomb blasts of thunder.

As I wrapped my arms around my waist, I exited the last bedroom. Overlooking the storm from hell that was happening outside and the animal howling that was rising from the manor, this wing was quite amenable. I almost began to appreciate being locked away.

For whatever reason, hot water was only available in the bathroom adjoining the largest of the three bedrooms. I had tried to draw a warm bath in each of the guest bathrooms without any luck. I had been hesitant to try the master bath since the room seemed inhabited, but whoever lived in there wasn't here now.

It was a beautiful room, expensively and tastefully furnished.

But it creeped me out.

There was something about it, some energy to it, that made my skin prickle. Something wasn't right. I just didn't know what.

Not wanting to spend any more time than necessary in the space, I turned on the water and stripped. I grabbed a neatly folded towel from a bin and quickly rinsed off all the mud under the running tub faucet in lieu of taking a bath.

I didn't care that the dress Lilly had given me was caked in dried mud. I was going to put it back on, but I hadn't realized that it had ripped in certain areas and was now a tattered rag. I balled it up and threw it in the waste bin.

With incredible unease, I crossed into the connecting closet which was a room unto itself. There was more of that eerie energy in here. It seemed that it was particularly intense in one section of the closet. I avoided going any deeper into the space than just a couple steps inside.

There was a rack of dresses near the entryway and although I would have preferred some practical pants, I grabbed the closest gown on the rack and immediately stepped out.

Back in the bathroom, I put the white dress on. The bodice and long sleeves were lacey with a deep V in the front that went down to the high waist. The bottom half was a simple white silk that hugged my hips while flowing to the floor.

Seeing my reflection in the bathroom mirror, I almost laughed. I was incredibly overdressed as far as prisoners go, and looked more like a bride than an abducted captive, but I was not about to spend any more time than necessary in this space searching for more suitable attire.

My hair had dried in loose wild waves. There were a few hair pins on a vanity tray, and I was going to grab a handful and immediately return to the main room of the wing. But when I began to reach my hand out toward the tray, I noticed a strange vibration in the air.

A silver brush also sat on the tray. It was lovely. It was mesmerizing.

It was...wrong.

The darkness within began to churn—frenzied. That eerie, ominous energy vibrated so strongly from the silver brush, it was tangible.

For some reason I couldn't explain, I had to pick it up. My hand seemed to move on its own accord.

I shouldn't pick it up. I didn't want to pick it up. But I couldn't stop my hand. Try as I might, I couldn't stop the collision that was about to happen. Come what may, the connection had to be made. I had no choice in the matter.

I wrapped my hand around the lovely silver and picked up the brush. Searing heat burned my hand immediately. The thing crackled with intense residual power. Radiant energy. And a flash of light flared between it and my palm.

I instantly dropped it, slowly backing away. In spite of the flash of heat, a chill crept down my spine.

I stared down at where the brush had landed on the floor. On the back of the brush, amidst chased flowers and vines were the initials *V. A. A.*

In that moment, I was transported back to Adriel's cozy little cottage. To sitting on her couch. Unsure and unaware. I could once again hear clear, strong voice.

Your name is Violet Archer.

I ran out of the bathroom into the connecting bedroom and headed straight for the door. But in my haste, I stumbled over a pair of running sneakers that had been left in front of the main bureau. My hand shot out to the dresser in an attempt to keep myself from falling.

Although I righted myself, I sent a small music player flying off the bureau, across the floor, and into the wall. The screen on the small device lit up and music began playing from speakers in the room. I halted for just a moment.

The little music player was just like the one Killian had given me and the song playing on the speakers was one that I had listened to on the device. The Kings of Leon's *Closer*.

A chill should have come over me. Paranoia should have set in. I should have been unable to take a deep breath due to paralyzing panic. But Something shifted in me then.

Enough. I had had enough.

I narrowed my eyes at the small device. I took a deep slow breath and threw my shoulders back.

I took down Giddeon. I took down Marax's two goons. I stabbed the goddamn Dark Prince. Whoever I was…In spite of whatever had happened to me…I was a woman with whom one did not fuck.

And I had had enough.

Whatever juju bullshit was going on in this place, I wasn't buying it. I wasn't scared. And I wasn't panicked. I was fucking angry.

I charged to the main doors of the suite and with one precise move, kicked them open. The thunder crashed and that demonic lightning sent a flash of red through the hall. With the sounds of glass shattering and wood breaking, I marched directly towards those incessant calls of hellish baying.

***

I descended a wide stairway knowing the evil bastard lurked in the grand foyer, waiting for me. I could hear snarls and crashing. I could feel his wrath, but I refused to fear him. As I neared the bottom of the staircase all noise ceased except for his panting breaths. He knew I approached.

The foyer was massive—the size of a ballroom. Broken mirrors lined the walls, some with the glass cracked and others like dust piles on the floor. Blood was smeared all over the glass.

What had once been side tables were now pulverized wood. And large chandeliers littered the floor, now garbage. Scraps of black fabric were strewn across the clutter.

At the other end of the room stood the Dark Prince. He was still surrounded in shadows, but I could see his form. From the bloody scratch marks across his chest, abdominals, and arms it seemed that he had torn his shirt off in pieces. His broad shoulders rose and fell with each panting breath, and his hands at his sides curled into fists over and over again.

Although I couldn't see his face I knew his eyes bored down on me. An icy wind swept through the room chilling me to the core, and I sensed that it had come from the monster before me. I threw my shoulders back and raised my chin. I would not cower before him.

He growled and then began to stalk towards me in a straight path pushing aside whatever debris was in his way and crunching broken wood and glass under his oversized boots. I stood my ground. I would face him head on. He began to slow as he got closer.

"You don't scare me," I said to him.

He paused for a moment and then raised his head. A slow chilling laugh echoed through the room. He raised a hand and beckoned me with the crook of his finger. I shook my head once, refusing to take commands from him like a little pet. The entire manor shook as red lightning struck outside and thunder exploded.

He charged me, brutally grabbing me by the arms and shoving me against the wall. My skin froze where he grasped me, and my entire body was blanketed in the chill that exuded from him.

He had bent his head so that his face was buried in my hair and icy breaths slid down my neck. That was when I realized he probably planned to do worse than simply kill me, and the fear I had been staving off began to creep down my spine.

I gasped at his size. He completely covered me. While he was easily the size of Elijah, the features of his body were distorted and enlarged by the shadows surrounding him. After I regained my composure I raised my hands to his chest to shove him off of me. He didn't budge, but he did lift his head to look down at me.

I saw his face for the first time. His irises were black, blending in with his pupils. Shadows swirled within them. Shadows also crawled across his flawless skin like constantly transforming tattoos. They were everywhere, over his face and down his massive chest and arms. His thick dark hair was in disarray matching the rest of his appearance. A tightly clenched jaw accented the angles of his face.

His features were not overtly masculine like Elijah's. His were more refined, more modelesque. He was beautiful. Terrifyingly beautiful. As a dark prince should be, I realized.

He spoke and the air around us froze. My hectic breaths came out in visible puffs and tiny ice crystals covered the surrounding walls. The few candles that were lit in the one remaining candelabra overhead extinguished and the only illumination was the flashes of lightning that lit the sky every few moments.

His voice was quiet but layered. It seemed as if he spoke with hundreds of dark voices at once. "Every night I would lie awake hearing whispers of your voice calling to me. Torturing me. I conjured a specter of you. She haunted these halls. When I walked down a hallway I would catch a glimpse of her turning a corner, floating, glowing, hair flowing around her face though no breeze stirred.

"Some nights I would see her as I looked out the windows. She would dance in the storm up on that cliff. Rain poured from that black sky and violet lightning scorched the earth and still she danced. I had to shut every shutter on every window because she would tap and sigh upon the glass. Torturing me."

His haunted layered voice was cold and controlled. It terrified me, but the worst part about him was the madness in his eyes. With each strike of lightning I would drown in the insanity I found in those eyes.

"What are you going to do to me," I whispered.

He laughed softly and then in a cold low purr he said, "I'm not going to do anything to you."

"You're not?"

He laughed again. Cruelly. "No. What you should be asking is what are you going to do to me?"

I unintentionally stuttered. "Wh—what do you mean?"

"You tortured me. I suffered. You have driven me to the brink of madness." He gripped the back of my neck and yanked my body into his, thrusting his pelvis into mine. His shaft was hard and bruising. His lips brushed my ear as he spoke, and his cold breath chilled my skin.

"I have stared into the abyss of insanity." I began to hear a faint rhythmic thumping beneath his words. "I have peeled off my skin, ripped out my eyes, and impaled my heart." The thumping began to grow and with each thump a bolt of lightning struck, illuminating the foyer through the windows with an eerie red glow.

"I have had my very soul, my essential essence rendered from me." Louder still, the relentless boom began to echo in my ears creating a reverberating bass to underscore his words. As the pounding grew louder so too did his words. "I was gobbled up by the abyss. I was chewed by razor fangs into torn pieces of flesh and bone. And as I sat in its belly all I felt was searing agony and pain. All because of you."

He grabbed a handful of my hair at the base of my neck. "You sentenced me to this madness. You were half of my essential essence. And you thought to deny me of that. Of sanity. You thought to simply transfer your energy to me. You were my tether to this world. I thought you were dead."

With his last word, he punched the wall next to my head. Ice cracked and tinkled to the floor. He pulled his head back to look down at me. The pounding was so loud it was echoing all around us in time with the pulsing red glow. As his chest rose and fell in heavy breaths, I realized what I was hearing was his maddened heart.

When I finally found the courage to look up and meet his eyes I had to fight not to shiver. He raised his hand and I stiffened, thinking he was going to strike me, but instead with only a whisper of a touch he trailed the backs of his fingers down my cheek ever so slowly.

His touch was so chilling, it left a thin trail of ice down my cheek. A single tear slipped from my eye running through the line of ice, thawing it.

"I'm so sorry," I choked out. He was mad and rambling incoherently, but he clearly blamed me for causing him untold pain. He was so far gone from reason I knew I couldn't try to talk him out of his insanity. There was no point in trying to reason with him or make him understand that he was confused about who I was.

"I know, sweet." His whisper was full of understanding. "That's why I'm going to let you run. I hope for your sake that you get away in time, because I am now a monster."

He grabbed my forearm without any gentleness and dragged me to the door. He didn't bother with the locks, he simply thrust the massive double doors open with an ear-splitting crack.

Solid wood splintered from the locks and hinges as he tossed the two doors aside. I ducked my head and threw an arm over my face crying out. He grabbed my raised arm and flung me out the now gaping maw of the mansion.

"Run. Run if you value your life."

"Please—"

"RUN," he roared. The candelabra smashed to the floor.

I didn't hesitate a moment longer. I took off through the rain as fast as I could. As I ran down the front lawn, I heard an explosion of glass behind me. I didn't have to turn around to know that every window along the facade of the mansion...had just shattered.

CHAPTER 33

I RAN WHILE SHEETS OF RAIN drenched my hair and clothes. I didn't know where I was going, only that I had to get away. The ground began to incline, and I slipped several times in the mud, falling to my hands and knees. The lightning and thunder continued without mercy. I desperately climbed for what seemed like an eternity until I finally reached level ground.

I realized that I was now on a cliff overlooking the manor grounds. Because of the continuous lightning, I could see that a lone cypress tree, gnarled and twisting, grew in the flat plain until the forest began hundreds of yards away. I knew I might stand a chance of escape if I could reach the cover of the forest.

I accelerated, giving this last dash all the energy I possibly had. But before I could even reach the lone cypress, any hope I had of escape was lost. In one flash of lightning I had seen the forest and began to run for it. Then utter darkness surrounded me in the interim between lightning strikes.

When the next flash struck, I skidded to a stop. There between me and the salvation of the forest was the outline of a huge hulking figure. Of him.

With each flash of lightning he was closer to me. I turned to run, but it was too late. He grabbed my arm and dragged me to the cypress tree, shoving my back against it. A red glow now seethed from the blacks of his eyes, and those menacing swirling black shadows loomed over him in a churning turmoil.

I opened my mouth to scream and he clamped a huge hand over it.

This time when he spoke it was with his voice alone, cold and low. "You do not get to play the victim, wife."

My eyes widened in shock and disbelief. He was clearly insane, completely out of his mind. I couldn't actually be bound to a monster, not just a monster but the enemy. I shook my head under his hand trying to convey to him that he was mistaken.

He ran his free hand down my left arm until he delicately grasped my hand and raised it in front of his face. "Ah, wife," he spat the word like a curse, "it is so good to see that you continue to wear my ring. All the while you act like a whore with another man, yet you do it while wearing my ring. How touching."

As he spoke he rubbed a finger over the onyx stone and it began to glow with a violet light. Something stirred within me and my knees buckled. The monster removed his hand from over my mouth and caught me around my waist keeping me upright.

Holding me caused him to press his body into mine. He reached up to grab my hair and yanked my head up, forcing me to look into his crazed face.

"Do you feel what you've done to me?" he demanded as he ground into me. He was hard and overwhelming. I knew he wanted to punish me, to hurt me, and that if he tried to rape me with how hard and large he was he would succeed in causing me not only emotional pain but physical pain as well.

With each angry thrust red lightning scorched the earth around us. I was dizzy and my eyes fluttered closed. He began to laugh, but it quickly turned into a furious roar. My eyes flew back open.

He looked down on me with what seemed like a brief moment of pity. "You're so much stronger than this, Violet. You foolish little girl."

The way he spoke my name. With such familiarity. There was something about it. Something that resonated. I felt a spark of recognition. It awoke some long slumbering part of me, and I began to shake.

He let go of my hair to caress his hand down my neck and then up to my face, holding my chin in his hand. "I will not let you hide from your guilt. You must face what you've done."

A bolt of his lightning struck the cypress tree, and as he held me in place there against the trunk, the obliterating energy, his energy red and hot, coursed through me. I screamed as my insides seared.

And. I. Remembered. Everything.

Find *Shadow's Touch, Book 2* on Amazon

and

Follow along on Facebook at

TMHartShadowSeries

Or on Instagram at

TMHartAuthor

For book release announcements

Made in the USA
Monee, IL
08 July 2021